the
Woma
46 Heatn
Street

BOOKS BY LESLEY SANDERSON

The Orchid Girls

the Woman at 46 Heath Street

LESLEY SANDERSON

Bookouture

Published by Bookouture in 2019

An imprint of StoryFire Ltd.

Carmelite House
50 Victoria Embankment
London EC4Y 0DZ

www.bookouture.com

ISBN: 978-1-78681-891-1
eBook ISBN: 978-1-78681-890-4

To Nut, Ellie and Izzy with love

PROLOGUE

The answer to my question, of how to carry out the perfect revenge, was to be found in the library. Within the pages of none other than a thick medical textbook, would you believe, in the reference section: *Not To Be Taken Away*. I had no intention of absconding with the book, only with the information inside, which I pored over, squirrelling the contents away in my memory. After many hours of research, I found the perfect answer.

The perfect answer for perfect revenge. Revenge for tainting the house that I once loved. Revenge for robbing me of the best friend I ever had. Such wicked things have taken place within the walls of my home and can never be undone.

Oh yes, it was the perfect answer. I laughed out loud in the middle of the fusty old reading room, causing an inebriated man with tattered clothes and a dubious smell to rouse from his slumber and stare at me with bleary eyes before returning his head to the desk.

The solution had been in front of me all the time. Within view of my kitchen window, in fact, and it required no alteration of my daily routine or behaviour that might arouse suspicion. Everything I needed was out there on Hampstead Heath, that magnificent space that lay behind my house in Heath Street, giving a stunning view that could be seen from any north-facing window. All I needed to do was to go and collect it, and then exact revenge.

CHAPTER ONE
ELLA, 2018

Tap, tap, tap. My pace quickens as it always does when I get to the end of the lane and turn the corner into Heath Street, this winding, terraced street tucked away in front of Hampstead Heath. Trees rustle in the late-autumn breeze. My mood is a muddle of feelings: joy at returning home; sadness at the reminder that Nancy is no longer waiting for me upstairs. Only a year ago I'd turn this corner to see her pale face at the window, watching out for me. Regardless of what the will said, she wanted me to stay here, she told me so, her birdlike hand squeezing mine, surprisingly strong. I steady myself at the gatepost and look at the dove-white front of my house and the sash windows reflecting the autumn sunlight. Arriving home is the best part of any trip away. The door gives its familiar creak and I breathe a sigh of relief as I press my back against its cold wood, my heart pulsing in time with the kitchen clock, the only sound in the still room. I'm home.

Light fills the hall and I pause for a moment to reorientate myself. Sun trickles through the stained-glass windows surrounding the front door, catching the warm red of the rich carpet which covers the hall and sweeps up the spiral staircase. I mouth 'hello' to the painting of Nancy which hangs in the hallway in a gilded wooden frame, as I always do, and slip off my coat.

I was right to come back early. The strain of being away for the past couple of days evaporates and I relish the knowledge that Chris will be at work for a good few hours yet, giving me much-needed time to settle.

I pick up the post from the mat and drop it onto the large wooden table, the centrepiece of the old-fashioned country-style kitchen, which has pots and pans hanging above the kitchen sink, before running around the house and opening the windows, letting fresh air blow away the closed-up atmosphere. The flowers I always have on the kitchen table in Nancy's favourite vase are no longer fresh. Again I feel a pang of guilt, but I've only been gone two days and the spa weekend was a treat from Chris, so I couldn't say no, could I? I'd smiled and hugged him, but really, I'm happiest in this house. *Our house.* It still feels unreal that I finally have somewhere to call home. Chris didn't reply to any of my messages yesterday and I've heard nothing from him today. *He must be busy.* Once he gets engrossed in his woodwork he forgets everything and time gets lost. I push away thoughts of how strange his mood has been lately, his reluctance to talk. '*It's work,*' is his constant refrain. He's forever telling me how he can never take the success of his business for granted.

I pause outside Nancy's room – *the nursery*, I correct myself. Yet Nancy lived and died in that room and I can't just forget she was ever there. Time, apparently, is what I need, but I don't want to wish my life away. I unpack my bag, impressed by how tidy Chris has been in my absence. His boxers are neatly folded under the duvet and the cushions are plumped up on the bed.

Downstairs the laundry room door is closed and a smell of lavender mingles with the warm air of the tiny room as I open it up. The enclosed space needs air.

The kitchen is still: no signs of use. Milk festers in the fridge; I wrinkle my nose at the smell and stick the kettle on, which brings life into the room. Chris hasn't left one of his funny little notes for me today; he doesn't know I've kept every one of them. My favourite lives in my purse: *Look in the fridge.* That note referred to a bottle of champagne nestling in the fridge door; there was another note on the bottle: *To celebrate meeting you*. My phone stays silent in my pocket. I wonder if he's spent any time at home at all aside from sleeping. Knowing Chris, he'll have eaten out, spent all day in his office and come home late into the night. He doesn't like being alone. He told me that when he was a bachelor he'd often spend the evening at his office, until the inky darkness outside alerted him to the time and sent him home in search of sleep.

The kitchen is warm, so I open the back door to let in some fresh air. A sheet hangs on the washing line and I frown; Chris never does any washing, but it explains the smell of lavender in the laundry room. The sheet is almost dry and I smile to myself: Chris must be trying to impress me.

Apart from the small rectangular area directly outside the house where I've managed to squeeze in a table and two chairs, the garden is a wilderness of weeds. The wind ripples through the unkempt greenery and I curse Chris as I do every time I step out here, wishing he'd let me do something about it. Apart from anything else, it's so embarrassing. *What must the neighbours think?*

I hear a miaow and follow the sound; Lady sits in front of the shed, looking out to the heath, eyes fixed ahead, tail flicking up towards the cloudy sky. I follow her gaze and see a magpie staring back with its beady eyes. It opens its beak and lets out a rattling screech before flying away over the heath.

I'll never tire of the view, glimpses of the pond amid an army of trees, their leaves protecting the trails across the heath beneath them, but Lady is winding between my legs, mewing for food. Chris doesn't pay attention to her like I do; I'll never replace Nancy in Lady's affection, but I try.

I text Chris to let him know I've got food for this evening and then unpack my shopping. I keep an eye on my phone but the screen stays blank. He hasn't been in touch the whole time I've been away. A slither of worry enters my mind. *What if something's happened to him?* I reassure myself I'm being stupid as I take a box of Earl Grey teabags from the cupboard. I haven't had any calls from the emergency services. *But what if he's fallen in his office, how would anybody know?*

A green light glows on the kettle and I pour water into a china mug with a leaf design – it's from the first range I sold in my shop. I poke the teabag with a spoon and imagine Nancy's reaction. She always understood why I react the way I do. She would have told me to '*get on as normal*', so I take my cup of tea to the table and open the post. That's a normal thing to do. Pizza leaflets go on the recycling pile and I put aside a credit card bill for Chris. The last letter in the stack piques my interest as there's no stamp. Swirly handwriting in black, a woman's I'd guess, and my heart stops at the thought it might be *her*. But it won't be, it's been at least a year since she told me she didn't want me in her life. It looks like an invitation. A wedding would be nice. It's a medium-sized envelope and only lightly sealed. Addressed to 46 Heath Street, but no name. I hesitate for a second before carefully prising it open, pulling out a sheet – I recognise the luxury cream writing paper I stock in my shop. I stiffen when I read the handwritten message. Neat block capitals.

YOUR HUSBAND IS HAVING AN AFFAIR.

I stare, incredulous. My hands tremble, the paper slides to the floor. I lash out, the mug shattering, hot liquid splattering my feet. Thoughts crash against one another, but overriding them all is disbelief. *It isn't true, Chris and I are solid, he works too much but we're good together, everybody says so. Chris is mine and we have made a home together.* At the thought of the house I jump to my feet, knocking the stool to the floor with a clatter. *Has she been here, in my precious space, the home I've so lovingly put together? He wouldn't, would he?* In our bed with its pure white bed linen, scarlet cushions lovingly placed just so? I'm sure Chris has a good explanation. *Is this why he's been silent, because he's been with her?* Doubts creep in, nights working late, that old cliché. *Has he been with her, was I wrong to be so trusting?* Up until an hour ago I would have trusted him with my life. A flash of white catches my eye as the sheet billows in the wind. I fall to my knees and pick up the piece of paper. Drops of tea have blurred the words and I wipe it on my sleeve, crying now. My heart is pounding and my head feels light. I concentrate on my breathing, in and out, deep, calming breaths. *But how can I feel calm with this fear inside me?* That old sick feeling which used to be as familiar to me as breathing is back. One sentence, that's all it took. I want to rush upstairs to Nancy, to let it all out, her warm words giving me the comfort her ailing body never could. Grief merges with the fear and tears choke out of me once again and I give up trying to breathe myself calm and let it all out. Nancy was a great believer in letting go. *If only she knew.*

After God knows how long my tears are spent and I'm calm. Chris will have an explanation, he'll be furious; he's been set up. But no matter what stories I tell myself, my gut tells me it's true. *Where is Chris? We have to talk.* As if by telepathy my phone plays its tune and Chris's name flashes on the screen: *my husband, my Chris.* He says he'll be home in an hour.

His credit card bill lies on the table. I rip the envelope open, not allowing myself a moment to change my mind. There are four pages filled with transactions. He's maxed this card out – it's a huge amount and I wonder what other secrets there are to discover about this man I thought I knew. Restaurants, drinks, more drinks, Selfridges. Heat rises in my body and I think I might explode when I see he's been using the designer florist from the village. I can't remember the last time he bought me flowers. I knew he had this card, but why hasn't he been paying it off? He's normally so sensible with money; he doesn't have fancy tastes. I leave the credit card bill on the table. *Let him see it.*

I run upstairs and get changed, sinking into the rocking chair placed strategically at the end of the bed, and gaze out at Hampstead Heath. The view over the pond never fails to move me and I see how the leaves on the sturdy, ancient trees are losing their green, signifying the season change. I breathe deeply and rock in the chair until my pulse stops racing. I listen to the natural rhythm of the house, the familiar creaks which lull me to sleep each night, until I am ready to face him.

CHAPTER TWO

ELLA

I'm up in the bedroom when Chris gets home. By the time his key turns in the lock everything appears normal and I'm feeling more in control. There has to be some explanation for this – I can't believe my husband would do this to me. I've opened a bottle of wine and the soft tones of a saxophone are playing on the radio. The note is back in the envelope, which is sitting on the table next to a flickering scented candle. The radiator gurgles warmth into the room but despite a thick jumper, my body feels like ice. I hear his keys jangle as he hangs them up in the hall; his shoes clatter as he takes them off and he whistles, puts the kettle on. Such familiar movements now accentuated with a different meaning. *Is he thinking about her?* He can't know what she's done, surely not. That jaunty whistle would be cruel if he did, and Chris isn't cruel. That much I know.

'Ella?' he calls in his deep voice, one of the first things I noticed about him. A confident voice. *Will he be confident when he's seen the note? How will he feel about her, once he knows how careless she's been? He'll hate her once he sees it. It's a trap, it must be, he'll be innocent of this, he will.* I run my hands through my hair and give myself a quick appraisal in the mirror before I go downstairs, not wanting to face the moment when everything in my life could change.

I pause mid-staircase to look at him, wishing this wasn't happening. Standing there in his old chinos with a checked shirt accentuating his broad swimmer's shoulders and tortoiseshell glasses sliding down his slightly prominent nose, he's my Chris, unchanged from the man I first fell in love with. He's scrolling through his phone, hasn't noticed the white square of the envelope on the table, hasn't recognised the writing. *Does he even know her handwriting?* I don't want her to be real. I watch him, twisting my hair in the way I know annoys him, but what he thinks doesn't matter. Not today. He senses me watching him, looks up, a quizzical look, before crossing the small gap between us and aiming a kiss at my lips, but I turn and his frown deepens. To think that only a few hours ago I'd thought I was pregnant, cutting my afternoon short to drive back and surprise him, until the familiar dull ache in my stomach dashed my hopes for yet another month. I look into his eyes, wanting answers.

'You're being weird,' he says and I push him, pick up the card and thrust it into his hands. His light tan fades to a sickly beige in front of me. He shuffles from one foot to the other, a man caught in headlights, staring at the card. I wait for him to look at me, but he won't. It's begun. His eyes shift, flicker around, and I notice him spotting his open credit card bill on the table.

'Why have you been going through my post?'

'It wasn't sealed. And I'm glad I did.' I stick out my chin, faking bravado.

'I can explain,' he says, pulling at his recently acquired beard.

I want him to be right but the sickening twist in my gut and the way his eyes avoid mine suggest the note is the truth.

I pick up the bill, wave it at him. 'I didn't want to believe it, but all these drinks, meals out.' My voice shakes. 'You said we needed to tighten our belts after we took on the new mortgage, but this…' I slap my hand against the page and drop the sheet of paper onto the table. 'Is it true? Have you been spending money we don't have on *her*?' A sob bursts out with the last word.

His hands grip the kitchen counter as if to keep himself upright. 'I never meant for you to find out like this. I've hated deceiving you. I've been wanting to tell you for a while, but this note, she shouldn't have…' He pushes his glasses up his nose. His hand is trembling too.

So it's true.

Bile rises in my throat hearing him say '*she*'. He's acknowledging her for the first time, and he's not denying it. The world I've carefully crafted is collapsing like a house of cards.

'Who is she?'

'Nobody you know.'

'You can't know her well yourself if she's being so careless, or deliberate. I bet you didn't know she was going to do this, did you? How well *do* you even know her?' I stumble over the words as I speak, my heart racing with shock.

He's chewing the inside of his mouth, turning the card over in his hands.

'She isn't like that, she wouldn't have done this, but—'

But you can't deny the evidence.

'Who is she?'

'You don't know her, I promise you don't. I couldn't do that to you.'

'I'm so glad you have good morals.'

His face twists in discomfort. He hates sarcasm.

'Has she been here, in our bed?' My voice cracks on the last word. He pushes his glasses to the top of his nose again and for the first time the gesture irritates me.

'We didn't mean to hurt you.'

So that's a yes. The '*we*' stings like a wasp.

'How long has it been going on for?'

'Six months.'

I feel as if he's thumped me in the chest. It's too long, but it's not that long and hope flutters in my chest. It's swiftly followed by shock, making my whole body tremor. He can't mean what he's saying; she's pushing him into doing something he doesn't want to do.

'Did you know she was going to send the letter?' I clench my hands together, willing him to say no.

He shakes his head.

Hope flickers again. *Married men never leave their wives, everyone knows that.*

'Is she married?' It hurts to hear the answers to these questions but I want to keep him talking, force him to see he's made a terrible mistake.

He nods. 'I am sorry to hurt you like this, it's the last thing I wanted.'

He looks distraught and I can't help the familiar ache at seeing the man I love in distress. 'Can't you see she's trying to trap you, to force the issue out into the open?'

He sighs and collapses onto a chair, rubbing his eyes, adjusting his glasses.

'Who is she?' *I have to know.*

'I met her through work, she's married, it's a mess. I knew she liked me and I resisted for ages, but what with Mum dying and you being so distraught, I needed comfort you couldn't give me.' He sees the agonised expression on my face, holds his hands up. 'I know, I know, it was the shittiest thing to do, but you kept pushing me away when I tried to comfort you. I didn't want you worrying about me on top of everything else.'

This is Chris, my Chris, and I can see how much this is hurting him. Again my feelings for him surface. I kneel down beside him.

'We can get through this, I know we can. Let me…'

'No.' He jumps to his feet as if he's scared of letting me in. *He still has feelings for me.*

'I'm so sorry, Ella, but I can't fight this, we've fallen for each other hard. We want to be together.'

'But…' I can't express the agony that's tearing me apart; Chris's last words are like poison darts. With one conversation he's destroying everything, our marriage, our life together, the nursery upstairs, our home. My legs weaken at the thought of losing him, of losing this life, our future family, and I drop onto the sofa. Hope surfaces when I see the flicker of compassion crossing his face. *He still cares about me despite these false words he's coming out with. I know he does.* She's making him do this, and I have to stop her.

'You must have noticed something's up. I've hated lying to you.'

But I hadn't noticed. My grief for Nancy wrapped me up in its cloak and I was oblivious to what was going on around me. I lost myself for a while. But I'm better now, he knows that.

'Chris, stop and think about this. We're happy, aren't we, our life here, our home? I know Nancy dying has gutted us and things haven't been the same since she passed away, but grief is natural. You can talk to me about anything. Or I thought you could.' I bite into my lip to stop myself from crying.

'I've made up my mind. This isn't easy, don't think for a minute it is. I'm so sorry – you're the last person I want to hurt. But it isn't working any more, Ella.'

'How can you say that? I didn't even realise we had a problem. You've been out working a lot so we haven't been spending as much time together. Well, obviously you weren't really working.' My voice almost breaks. 'But this house, our home, it's my home, the only home I've ever known. You know that.'

'It's too much pressure on me, can't you see that? I can't be everything to you. It was OK while Mum was around, you spent so much time with her. But now she's gone—'

'So Nancy died and you started seeing someone else, like that would make it better? That doesn't make sense.'

'It wasn't like that. I needed someone to talk to, she was there—'

'Why did you need someone to talk to? Why, when you have me?'

But as I speak a memory surfaces, Chris texting me from work one day saying he needed to talk. Me, preoccupied with helping Nancy shower when he got home, too exhausted for conversation. *How many times did I push him away, focusing all my energy on Nancy?*

His eyes slide away from mine as his phone pings. *I bet it's her.* I push his hand away from his phone as he goes to pick it up, my nail catches his skin and he flinches. I hate that she's got his attention. A bead of blood appears on his hand and he sucks at the tiny cut, glaring at me.

'I realise this is a shock. You need some time to get used to the idea. I'll give you some space.' He gets up and goes into the hall. I hear the cupboard door open and a clattering sound. He bashes around while I remain stunned, as if I've been hit around the head. *Surely this can't be happening. Nancy would…* The thought of his mother causes my breath to catch in my throat and I cough, tears springing to my eyes. I can't lose both of them.

Chris appears at the door with his overnight bag. The sight of him fidgeting in the doorway almost hurts more than the bag, his awkwardness at being with me. *What happened to my best friend?*

'Chris, you can't do this to me.' Something breaks inside me and I rush over to him, bursting into tears. I grab his arms, inhaling the familiar tweedy smell of his jacket. 'Please, stay, we'll talk, talk as much as you want. We can sort this out, I know we can. Please don't leave me. I hate being alone, you know I do.' I drop my hands, my energy suddenly depleted.

'We need some space. It's for the best, you'll see when you've had time to think about it.'

'Where are you going? Are you going to her? Have you got some sordid love nest somewhere?' The idea of Chris sharing a home with another woman strikes me and I dig my nails into my palms, pressing hard. I won't cry again.

He takes his jacket from the peg.

'Please Chris, don't go, let's talk some more.' The neediness in my tone makes me grimace.

'I'm sorry, Ella, I really am.' His voice sounds strained. 'This must be a terrible shock for you, I do understand. I'm in the wrong and I'll try and be as fair to you as possible. You need time to take this in, I understand that.'

He's right. I'm in no fit state to talk to him at the moment. And he'll see sense; he can't be in his right mind. A little time apart may do us good. He'll realise what he's throwing away. I'll give him time to see what he's missing. Time to come back to me.

He shrugs the holdall over his shoulder and walks to the door.

'And don't worry, I'm not going to ask you to move straight away, I'll give you some time to sort something out.'

'Move?' The word scratches my throat.

'You can stay here for a month, say six weeks, max. That should give you plenty of time to find somewhere else.'

'Chris, no…'

The sound of the door closing rings in my ears. My legs give way beneath me and I sink to the floor. If Nancy were here she'd sort him out. But she isn't and I'm on my own. Chris grew up in this house and I wouldn't want to take that away from him, but it's become my home, too. *Our* home. Tears run down my face and I wail into the empty house. Memories flood my mind: sobbing my guts out as a child, wondering why my mother had given me away, leaving me alone, unloved. I love Chris so much, I won't be alone again. I won't. I can't.

I hug my knees to my chest and talk to Nancy in my head. Nancy will know what to do. She always does.

CHAPTER THREE

ELLA

After a while I put the chain on the door, go round the house and make sure every window is shut. Every room except the nursery, that is; I can't face going in there. The weekend's disappointment is too fresh.

Chris didn't even try to deny the affair. He's left the credit card bill on the table and I run through the items listed, each one causing anger to spiral within me. Countless expensive restaurants; Bertrand's, where he took me to celebrate our engagement, features more than once last month. Heat rushes to my head and the familiar pulse of a headache beats behind my eye. I reach out to the wall to steady myself. The last time we went out to eat was months ago. Little clues that I've missed – why haven't I noticed? *How could I be so stupid?*

I pour myself a glass of white wine. It's only five o'clock, but today doesn't call for rules. It was only two days ago on this very spot that Chris hugged me before I got in my car and drove off to a country spa. Over his shoulder I'd caught sight of the tree we planted where Nancy's ashes were scattered and I'd thought that if my period really was late, the two of us might become three again. Not that Nancy could ever be replaced. Her tree became symbolic to me, nurturing it to life as if that could stop her memory fading away. A sob lodges in my throat as the reality of my situation hits me. Here I am in a position I swore never to be in again. *Alone.*

I sink into the softness of the sofa and sip my wine. It won't help my headache but I'm past caring.

The sky is darkening and I switch the spotlights on, illuminating the soft green of the recently painted walls. Chris was impressed with what a good job I'd done. My last foster-parents had run a decorating business and I'd discovered that stroking paint onto walls was therapeutic, helping me to get my thoughts in order. Decorating eased my grief over Nancy.

A sharp pain causes me to gasp aloud. *I can't lose Chris too.*

I check my phone but there's no word from him and I wonder where he's gone. *Has she held on to her house, too, kicked the husband out and taken mine in his place? Is she dolled up for him, all cleavage and crimson lips?* I get up and look at myself in the mirror, surveying my pale blue chinos and white designer T-shirt. My blonde hair will never be thick and luxurious; my eyes are dishwater grey. Chris professed to like my 'simple elegance'. I think about our relationship, and as much as I want to deny it, we have drifted apart lately, ever since Nancy's death. The heath was hidden beneath a blanket of white snow when she died and now a new winter is approaching with a blast of icy wind. Her death hit me harder than it did Chris; he even accused me of liking her more than him. I didn't understand why they were forever sniping at each other. Maybe I didn't know either of them as well as I thought I did. *Surely he can't have been jealous, jealous of the time I devoted to her?* He knew she was like a mother to me, the mother I've been looking for all my life. My father was a blank on my birth certificate, but somehow that never got to me in the same way.

It's been ten months since Nancy died, but whenever I'm troubled her voice echoes in my head: '*do something normal*'. Eat, that's what she was always encouraging me to do, despite her own minimal appetite. I stick a slice of bread on the grill before going into Nancy's room. *The nursery*, I tell myself. For a month after her death I dusted and hoovered it daily, keeping it nice. Her dresses hung pristinely in the wardrobe, a mix of colours and patterns. Her wicker sewing basket sat at the end of the bed; the never-to-be-finished cushion cover she was working on propped next to a pile of books she'd lamented no longer being able to concentrate on. She'd wanted to die at home, and it was pneumonia that got her in the end. *That terrible day.* I'd known somehow, as I hurried home through the snow-dusted heath. A persistent wind tore at my limbs as if chasing me back to the house. The house had been still, too still, its normal creaks and wheezes suspended, as if in mourning. My heart pounded in my head as I climbed the stairs slowly; fear gripped hold of me and I knew. She lay on her back, eyes closed, hands crossed over her chest. I knelt down beside her and put my hands over hers. That was how Chris found us. Grief gutted me. It still does.

Chris took Nancy's clothes to the charity shop after only six months, despite my protestations; if it had been left to me I'd have kept her room as it was, honouring her memory. Her books had always been on shelves in the box room and he put some of her possessions in there, stuck everything else in the cellar and encouraged me to decorate the whole house. He said it might help me accept that she was gone. I resisted at first, but it gave me something to focus on and helped me pull myself back together. The rest of the house is finished; this is the last room to tackle – I didn't want to forget Nancy, erase her from this place. Now it's stripped bare, tins of pale yellow paint piled in the corner. I thought turning the room into a nursery would help turn her death into something positive. The disappointment that I'm not pregnant tugs at my heartstrings; I'd been so convinced it would happen this month.

I stare out of the large window overlooking the jungle garden. Chris promised to hire a gardener, but he's been so busy lately and he practically bit my head off when I offered to sort it myself. His moods make sense now; he was obviously feeling guilty about *her.*

A burning smell hits me when I go downstairs. *The toast.* I don't think my pulse can beat any faster as I race down to the kitchen where the forgotten bread is blackening, smoke filling the kitchen. My hand wobbles as I slide the tarry mess out and whack my hand on the shelf, dropping the tray as pain sears through me. I let myself cry as I run my hand under the cold tap.

I open the back door and I'm greeted by an eerie rustling noise from the wild garden. A small thought filters into my head. *Silly, really.* Chris can't stop me taming the jungle outside. It doesn't matter what he thinks now. *Stop it! He'll come back, he will.*

The street light from the alleyway running along the back of the garden is on, casting a dingy yellow glow over the bushes. Something clatters and my heart stops as Lady comes bounding towards me. Her fur tickles the goosebumps on my legs: I shiver and she springs inside with me as I slam the back door shut.

I leave the hall light on when I go upstairs to bed. It's not yet nine but I've had enough of today. My overnight case stands forgotten by the bed. The spa feels like a lifetime ago. The face masks, the pedicure, the massage – what difference did it make? He only sent me so he could secretly spend more time with *her.* The sheets are cold and I pull the duvet up under my chin, soothed by the slither of light sliding in from the open door. The bedroom feels less comforting at night, here on my own. I roll onto my front, sob out loud and let the pillow swallow my tears. Nobody will hear me, after all. The memory of hundreds of nights like this from the time before Chris – *BC* as I've always thought of it – engulf me and I give in to self-pity.

I must have fallen asleep, because I wake with a start to the jangling of the telephone screaming into the night. My heart thuds as I run downstairs. *What time is it?* It's still dark.

'Hello.' My voice sounds loud in the empty hall, the moon's rays lighting up the kitchen, my bare feet cold on the floor tiles.

'Is Chris there?' The husky female voice sounds alert, not at all as if she's ringing in the middle of the night. Maybe I've only been asleep for an hour or so, but a glance at the kitchen clock tells me it's half past three. *Her?* I shiver.

'Who is this?'

'Is he there?'

Laughter trickles into my ear and something touches my leg. I drop the phone and it clatters to the floor. Lady jumps away from my legs. When I pick up the receiver with my wobbly hands the dialling tone purrs and I scream into the receiver, sending Lady bolting into the kitchen.

DIARY

1 JULY 1976

A new diary for a new house!

46 HEATH STREET

Doesn't it sound grand? Edward picked me up in his van. Having his own transport is one of the advantages of dating an older man. Thank goodness my parents have finally accepted him.

He wouldn't say where we were going. It was early morning and the day was already hot. We drove towards Hampstead Heath and turned down a tree-lined little lane off the main road. It felt as though we were travelling through a forest. A row of houses, huddled and hidden: one house standing out. I crossed my fingers and looked at Edward. He was grinning and I knew this was it, the secret he'd been holding. I could have burst when he walked towards the house that grabbed my attention. He led me down the path, picked me up from the waist and swung me over the threshold. The full skirt of my dress swung in an arc, made me feel like a ballerina. When he set me down my head was spinning like a top. Dizzy with glee, that was me. Standing in the hallway of my very own house, looking up at the twisty staircase leading to rooms waiting to be explored. I flung my arms around Edward and wouldn't let go. I'd fallen in love all over again.

EVENING

Today was a flurry of excitement. I was too distracted by everything to continue writing earlier. I ran around the house looking at every room, opening the windows to let in the summer heat. Our bedroom is huge; it's where I am now, writing at a table I've moved in front of the window so I can look down at the pretty garden. It's not pretty yet, but in my imagination it's beautiful.

Oh, the garden! It's a long rectangle of grass bordered by flower beds. I've planted them in my head already. I want purple and white crocuses peeping up in spring followed by red roses, sunny marigolds, pale pink snapdragons and a huge cluster of white hollyhocks. I can't wait to get started. There's a shed for Edward, and a little fence which separates our garden from a pond. Gazing out from the bedroom window, I can see Hampstead Heath stretching out beyond the pond; the grass is scorched by this splendid summer and the leafy treetops look golden in the sunlight.

And I've already made a friend! A lady named Doris who lives at number 48. She came into the garden and said hello over the fence. Her house is to the right of ours when you're facing the heath. She moved in a year ago with her husband Fred and I didn't like to ask but she looked about the same age as me. She's got ginger hair, which some people don't like, but it's ever so pretty, chunky curls bouncing on her shoulders. She was wearing a long yellow dress, revealing freckly arms, and dainty white shoes. And what a smile she has! Her smile splits her face and opens up the prettiest dimples. I just know we're going to be great friends. We chatted and chatted and could have gone on all day but there was so much to do, and she laughed at my excitement. She's invited me round for tea next Wednesday. I can't wait, but I want every minute to last. I'll have had a week here then: seven whole days in Heath Street.

7 JULY

Wednesday has finally arrived. We spent today sitting in Doris's garden drinking lemonade under the scorching sun. We talked about the never-ending summer and the neighbours and, well, everything really. Doris's husband owns a bakery in the village and he'd made us some currant buns that we ate after we'd finished our lemonade and she'd shown me round her garden. Noises from the heath punctuated our conversation – dogs barking, children squealing and peals of laughter. A huge splash from the pond made Doris jump to her feet. 'Somebody's fallen in,' she shouted, making me laugh. She's ever so funny. She talked about her husband and how she felt about him without a care in the world. Some of the things she said made me blush and she laughed. Nothing gets past Doris.

The sun was low in the sky when I let myself back into *my house* – how I love writing those words! Edward was in the kitchen, standing looking out at the garden. I laughed and asked if he was imagining flowers popping with colours and maybe a cherry tree; I do so love cherries. But he was holding himself stiff, like a post, and his face wasn't lighting up with laughter like mine.

'What's wrong?' I asked. The room felt chilly, as if a gale was blowing, wiping the smiles off our faces, but the windows were closed. The trees looked ominous in the half-light.

'You're late,' he said.

'But—'

'You weren't in. I want you to be here when I get home from work, waiting for me.'

'I was only next door.' I laughed again, but with a little uncertainty; this wasn't my usual loving Edward. Muscles twitched in his neck, as if he were grinding his teeth. I've heard him doing it in the night when I'm woken by the swishing of the trees out on the heath. 'I was with Doris. Remember, I told you she'd invited me over on Wednesday.'

'Make sure you're back by six next time,' he said, and went upstairs to change out of his work clothes.

I set about making our tea; I made sure I cooked his potatoes just the way he liked them. It was only a small thing, but as I mashed butter into the steaming vegetables and watched it melt away into nothing, I couldn't help wondering about Edward's reaction.

CHAPTER FOUR

ELLA

Her.

The voice down the telephone line was husky, resonant of smoked cigarettes, late nights and illicit fun. I imagine her throwing her head back in laughter and exposing her pale neck; a neck men want to stroke, *my* man, specifically; a neck I could put my hands round and squeeze.

I sit bolt upright in bed, scared by my own thoughts. Even with the curtains left slightly open to let in a slice of moonlight, my heartbeat sounds loud in the vastness of the bedroom – it feels double the size without Chris lying beside me. It's at night that I become aware of how old this house is. Wind rattles the windows in their crumbling frames and the walls creak as if sighing with age. On the landing outside the bedroom, the airing cupboard never rests as water gurgles through ancient pipes and the immersion heater hisses threats into the silence. I switch on the lamp by my bedside; it's pointless trying to sleep with Nancy's voice whispering along with the noises of the house.

Chris has left a thick sweater hanging over Nancy's rocking chair and I inhale his smell as I pull the jumper over my head, a hint of pine from his aftershave, my birthday present to him earlier this year. He'd opened it in bed, ripping through the paper I'd so carefully wrapped, barely acknowledging the breakfast tray or touching the chocolate croissant I'd slipped out specially to surprise him with. He'd kissed me on the head, already checking his phone as he walked out of the bedroom, and left his mug of tea half drunk. Now I see clues everywhere: flashing warning signs that I failed to notice. A trail of crumbs for me to follow. I go downstairs, switching lights on as I go. He's bound to have left evidence somewhere, something that will lead me to *her*.

I go through the pockets of his coat and jackets, which hang by the front door. Plenty of chewing gum, empty sweet wrappers, some loose change and a scrunched-up parking ticket. I smooth it out and check the date; it's over a month old, issued in Oxford. *Was he there for work, or...?* I begin to question everything. *Did he think that by shoving the ticket in his pocket it would disappear?*

Despite having the lights on the house feels surreal at night. Outside, the street is shrouded in darkness but the odd light from other dwellings twinkles in the distance. A couple pass by, their loud and intimate laughter ringing through the silent street as I go back upstairs, stopping outside the box room. Listening to them transports me back to the first time Chris brought me here. We'd been for a meal in Hampstead Village and lingered in the restaurant, Chris drinking an Irish coffee, me sipping a mint tea. A candle flickered on the table between us, the light catching the tortoiseshell rim of his glasses, framing his brown eyes. He'd told me a story of an early trip to the optician's as a kid, his sister forced to tag along, giggling at his inability to read the large letters on the visual chart. Chris described the National Health glasses he refused to wear at school through fear of being picked on. He laughed as he told me this story, but I could see the vulnerable little boy behind the polished exterior. It was the first time he'd mentioned his sister, but he shrugged and said they'd lost touch and switched the focus to me. Watching the dancing orange flame of the candle I told him my lonely experience of growing up in care, searching fruitlessly for my mother with only a few shadowy memories of her. He took my hand in his, the skin rough from years of working with wood, and asked me if I'd like to come home with him.

I'd never been to Heath Street before. I was renting in Kentish Town at the time, a tiny bedsit with a shared bathroom. Turning off the main road, it was like leaving the city behind as dense bushes and towering trees bordered the street on both sides. Only foliage swishing in the breeze disturbed the silence. Chris took my hand as we followed the winding road around a corner to reveal a long row of houses. 'That's us,' he said, 'number 46.' The white-fronted house loomed up at us from the darkness, semi-detached, resplendent in a row backing on to Hampstead Heath, separated from the park by a pond. I shivered to think of that deep expanse of heathland stretching behind the house, dark and silent.

*

I move across to the window in the box room, the spare bedroom where I store my craft materials, Nancy's books and some of her personal belongings. I wouldn't let Chris take them to the charity shop; they meant so much to her – and now, to me. The books are on a shelving unit in an alcove, all of Nancy's paperbacks: mainly romance novels and historical fiction. The light from the landing is enough to illuminate the room and I stand and look at the heath, past the tangled garden of number 46 and across the sleeping pond which shimmers as moonlight picks trails across the water. But the heath itself is still, meadows hidden in darkness, resting from the endless stream of dog walkers, runners and tourists that tramp through, marvelling at such greenery in London.

I sit on the bed and take a book down from a shelf. The novel I'm drawn to is *Rebecca*, Nancy's favourite book. Set in a large brooding house by the sea, a mysterious former wife is haunted by the woman who went before her. *Maybe reading it will help me feel Nancy's presence again.* I grip the book between my hands, looking at the cracked spine, staring at the sea on the cover, the coastline which sweeps across to meet a turbulent sky. For the first time I wish I was there, anywhere but alone in this house. I turn to the front page where my attention is drawn to an inscription: '*To Nancy with love, your dearest friend.*' I frown; she never mentioned any close friends. As I shift on the bed something flutters from the book and lands on the rug. A yellowing sheet of paper, folded. I pick it up and unfold the thin, torn paper which is covered with writing in different shades of ink, much of it faded. It's a school report, dated March 1996, but the top part is torn off and there's no name. Chris's? Each subject is handwritten and initialled by a different teacher, but the student referred to is a 'her' and most of the writing is too faded to read. I can't help feeling a jolt of envy; I don't remember ever seeing a report. I doubt I stayed long enough at one particular school to warrant one. This student's grades are Cs and Ds and the comments I can read describe her as '*not paying attention*', '*easily distracted*' and '*needs to apply herself*'. There's a comment at the bottom beside the number of days absent, which is thirty. '*She needs to improve on her attendance*'. Chris's sister, maybe? Maybe she truanted, wasn't academic. Nancy never mentioned her either. Not once. I'd tried to ask her and she'd pursed her lips and turned away. She must have had her reasons. My birth mother gave me up when I was six. I knew about pain and I understood Nancy's reluctance to go there, not wanting to push her.

My eyes feel gritty and a wave of exhaustion washes over me. This can't be happening again. After Nancy's death I spent most nights roaming the house, haunted by sleeplessness, until Chris took action, forced me to go to the doctor, nursed my broken heart. *But who is there to pick me up now?*

CHAPTER FIVE

ELLA

When I wake and see the unruffled sheets beside me, for a blissful second I think Chris has gone to work. Then I remember and I sit up, heart racing. I don't want it to be true. My eyes land on the photograph of Nancy beside my bed. It's the only one I have: her pale blue eyes clear against her silver crop. Roaming about last night and reading the old report feels like a dream, trivial compared to the cloak of sadness I can't shake off this morning. Opening the blind, I look out at a sea of slate-grey sky stretching over Hampstead Heath. Down in the garden a solitary blackbird pecks at a worm hidden in the long grass. So many times Chris has promised to fix the lawnmower, to sort out the grass; no wonder he didn't have time, I realise now. He's neglected the outside while I've lovingly restored the inside.

I look around at the pale grey walls and the dark blue contrast wall where Nancy's mirror hangs. The gilt frame is old-fashioned yet beautiful. I study my face in the glass. My small, delicate features look pinched; my ashen skin matches the walls. Chris used to kiss me on my button nose, teasing me about how small it was. The sad grey eyes looking back at me from the mirror fill with tears.

Our bedroom was the first room I decorated, contrasting the light grey walls with the rose-coloured rug on which I now stand. It's soft under my bare feet but it cannot cushion the sting in my heart. I wince as something sharp digs into my foot; I pick up the offending cufflink and hop over cold floorboards to the bed, clutching my toe. The pain is mild but tears spill out of my eyes as the reality of my situation hits me. *Chris has left me.*

The piercing sound of my alarm bursts into the room and I curse the harsh noise I chose specifically to make sure I wake up. It sets my nerves on edge and I breathe deeply in and out, try to compose myself. I'm due at work in an hour, but I can't face it today. Not for the first time I thank God, who I'm not sure I believe in, for sending Jamie into my life – my perfect employee, assistant and friend. The beauty of running my own business means I work hours that suit me, and I'm confident Jamie will cover for me at short notice. I know I'd do the same for him.

As his mobile rings I go over what I'll say in my mind. There's no need to tell him about Chris. I keep the conversation brief, but as soon as I start to tell him I'm not coming in he interrupts me.

'What's wrong, Ella? Your voice sounds all funny.'

'That's because I'm trying not to cry, you idiot. I didn't want to do this.'

'This is me you're talking to, remember. No secrets from Jamie. Tell me, come on, what's that husband of yours done now?'

There's a light tone to his voice but despite his young age Jamie's got a wise head on him. He's given me a lot of sensible advice during the last two years since I opened my boutique gift shop and he came wandering in with his CV and set about making himself indispensable. He has a gift for helping me find a solution to things I worry endlessly about. His art degree means he's got a good eye for display, part-time hours give him enough time to work on his portfolio and he's always happy to cover at a moment's notice. Living at home and doted on by his mother, it's easy for him to be flexible.

'Chris has left me.' Saying the words out loud makes it real and I stifle a sob.

'Oh my God. What's happened?'

The note lies on the floor by my foot and I kick it away, hating her for writing it. Somehow it's easier to hate her, this anonymous woman who's burst unwanted into my life, rather than my own husband. The lump in my throat makes it hard to talk, but this is Jamie and I don't need to explain.

'Look, I'll open up this morning; you don't need to worry about the shop. Shall I come round after work? I'll pick up some food and a bottle of something and you can tell me all about it. And you know where I am if you need me. Sending you lots of love and the best bouquet of virtual flowers.'

I manage a weak smile as I imagine the bouquet, Jamie's answer to everything. When his last boyfriend broke his heart he explained how visualising beautiful flowers bursting with colour helped to shift his dark thoughts. Somehow, I don't think that's going to work for me.

The phone ringing in the hall sounds loud in the empty house. *It's Chris, he wants to talk, he's changed his mind, he's made a terrible mistake.* But the man says his name is Jonathan and that he's from the bank dealing with our mortgage. He takes me through an arduous security process until he is satisfied that I am who I say I am.

'Yes, *Mrs*.' I stress the word, push the hair back from my face and stick my chin out. I am Chris's wife, *Mrs Rutherford*, and nothing is going to change that. Our lives are too entwined.

'I'm sure it's nothing to worry about, but we haven't received the latest payment for your mortgage.'

My hair has flopped forward again and I twist it around my finger. 'You must be mistaken,' my voice sounds high, 'there's a direct debit from my husband's account.' We've always had this arrangement in place; Chris pays the mortgage directly and I pay my half to him. The mortgage is in both our names.

'It could be because of the two-month payment break you've just had.'

'Hang on, sorry, can you repeat that please? A payment break?'

'Yes, it's one of the benefits of our range of mortgages, why they are so popular. We understand that our customers sometimes find things a bit tough from time to time, Christmas, extra expenses, a house extension, it could be for any number of reasons. Your husband took advantage of this in the spring. He's probably forgotten it needed to be paid again this month. Is he there now? Do you want to check with him?'

'No, he isn't here.'

'I could call you back?'

'Yes, I'll speak to him, but…' As I speak, I realise I have no idea where Chris is or what he has been up to. I'm forced to tell Jonathan that circumstances are somewhat challenging at the moment and that it's probably an oversight on my husband's part – he's had a lot on at work. Jonathan sounds sympathetic and gives me a couple of weeks to sort the situation out, suggesting that a three-month payment break is not in the terms of this particular mortgage but can be arranged for a fee. He sounds reassured when he hangs up but my nerves are wire-tight.

I can't understand why Chris hasn't told me about this. Money isn't the issue here, but what has he done with my money? The credit card bill, of course. *Why did Chris need a payment break? Surely he wouldn't want to risk losing this place?* The thought of our home being jeopardised sends an icy chill through me. I spent my childhood being shifted from house to house, and in thirty years this is the only place I've dared to call home. The first bedroom I had in foster care was the only one I attempted to make my own, sticking posters of pop stars on the walls only to be moved on six weeks later. I didn't make that mistake again.

I wander into the living room and switch the lamp on; it casts a pattern on the pale floorboards. Despite painting the room in the latest Farrow & Ball shades, the dark brown sofa, the imposing grandfather clock and the old piano add a historical feel to the room. I look out through the patio doors at the darkening sky and the jungly weeds swaying in the breeze. Expense was another reason Chris gave for not tackling the garden. Then I remember the credit card bill and how *he's been spending his money on her.* Anger tingles my nerves. '*You can stay here for a month.*' His words sting more each time I remember them. The breathless female voice, '*Is he there?*' I grab my phone, hand shaking, and dial the number of a local locksmith.

The job takes no time at all. The locksmith gives me two sets of keys and I tuck the spare set under a pile of T-shirts in my bedroom drawer. Chris is going to go mental. *Good.* I'm about to turn the light off when I catch sight of Chris's maroon towelling dressing gown hanging on the back of the door. He'd been wearing the dressing gown the first time I'd woken up in this room; he was pushing through the door with a breakfast tray for us to share in bed, a rose from the garden lying next to the cafetière, a smile brightening his face. The memory floors me and I sink onto the bed and sob. Then my anger dissolves. He has to be in trouble, he needs me. *There's no way Chris would intentionally put our home at risk. Would he?*

CHAPTER SIX

ELLA

I pace up and down the kitchen as I wait for Chris to answer his phone. I go over what I want to say, hoping he hasn't already left for swimming club. If he's still going, that is. Nothing is certain any more.

It rings over and over again, and the sentences I've prepared fly out of my mind as it switches to voicemail. I can't bear to stutter out a message, let him hear me fall apart. I text instead, asking him to contact me urgently. Walking through to the living room, I sink down onto the leather sofa. I focus my gaze on the painting of the back of number 46 done by one of Nancy's friends many years ago, the view across the pond highlighted by a bright blue sky. Seen through the large windows, the sky over the pond today is a murky grey, the weather uncertain. A row of bamboo canes in the garden blocks the light and I switch on the table lamp and start lighting the fire. The central heating is due to come on soon, but the old radiators do little to warm these high-ceilinged rooms with draughty old windows. I draw the curtains against the brooding sky and pray Jamie will arrive soon.

Jamie wheels his bike round the side of the house and leaves it outside the back door.

'You need a strapping young lad to sort out this garden for you,' he says, looking out at the jungle. He places a bottle of white wine and a pizza box on the counter and squeezes me into a tight hug. 'Obviously I'll hold the interviews for you, check out their physique, make sure you get the right man for the job. Listen to me, going on as usual.' He shrugs his shiny bomber jacket off, hangs it behind the door. 'Sexist, too – you might not want a man. I wouldn't blame you in the circumstances. How are you doing? Tell me everything.'

He waves me away when I go to open the wine and he's soon poured two glasses and we're sat on the sofa, bottle on the table, pizzas warming in the oven. I show him the card and recount the events of the night before.

'And you had absolutely no idea? Not been keeping any tiny suspicions to yourself?'

'Nothing. I've been hoping to get pregnant, decorating the nursery: that's how clueless I was. You know how he treated me to a spa weekend? I can't believe I didn't see he just wanted me out of the way. He was relieved I knew, I could see that. That's how I know this is real.' My lip wobbles and I swallow a large mouthful of wine. 'The worst thing is, he's told me he wants me out of the house. You know how much I love it here, what it means to me.' I swipe a tear which trickles out of my eye and I swallow hard, scared that if I start crying I won't be able to stop.

'He can't kick you out, you've got a joint mortgage.'

'But it's his family home. He grew up here.'

'Doesn't matter.' Jamie refills our glasses. 'Even if you weren't on the mortgage, you'd still have rights. This is your main residence, your only residence. Trust me, I know what I'm talking about. It happened to my Aunt Muriel. My uncle tried to kick her out after thirty-five years of marriage when he had a full-blown midlife crisis and wanted to move his twenty-one-year-old secretary in. They ended up having to sell, but she was able to buy her own place. Muriel is happier than she's ever been in her cosy cottage.'

'But I couldn't do that to him. I wouldn't want to sell, either. I love this house.' I don't need to explain to Jamie that this is the only home I've ever known. My longest stay with foster-parents lasted eighteen months, after moving from house to house my whole childhood. And there I was, just one of many needy kids.

'Chris hasn't been straight with me about that, either.' I recount the conversation with the bank. 'And you know the stress we went through to get the mortgage, when we thought we'd finally solved the problem of the inheritance tax. He was thrilled when I offered to help with the mortgage. It's all such a mess. Last night I was so angry I had the locks changed. It was a spur-of-the-moment thing. Chris will go mad. I can't believe I did that.'

Jamie's eyebrows shoot up. 'Wow. You don't waste time, do you? Good on you. Serves him right.'

'I don't know, Jamie, it was a stupid impulse. I just want him back.'

The smell of burned cheese drifts into the room and Jamie jumps to his feet. We sit at the kitchen table and Jamie eats most of the pizza while I nibble on the burned crust, before we take our wine back to the sofa. Darkness has fallen outside and the sound of the wind rustling through the grass makes me shiver. I draw the heavy red-and-gold curtains, wishing Jamie didn't have to leave.

'Cold?'

'It's not that. You'll think me stupid, but I've never been at ease staying here on my own. Growing up in care you're never on your own. Bordering the heath is fabulous, obviously, but late at night it does things to your imagination. Especially with our jungle garden. I imagine all sorts of horrors lurking out there.'

'Look. I know you're hurt and there's tons to sort out, but you will get through this. You could get someone to move in temporarily. Ask a friend to stay, or take a lodger. Rents are all short contracts these days. You could get someone for three months, say. Whatever you and Chris decide, it's going to take that long at least. And I'd get yourself a solicitor, check your rights.'

I nod, trying to appear braver than I feel. *I can't let this happen.*

The glass of brandy I swallow down before bed, squinting my eyes shut and wincing in the hope that it will knock me out into a deep sleep, serves only to give me a slight headache as thoughts batter one another inside my head. A couple of times I begin to drift off when the thought of the missed mortgage payment catches me and I sit up, sweat pooling down my back. *Is he in trouble?* My body radiates heat and I open the window. I stay there for a while, peering out into the black night. I need to raise money – and fast – as there's no way I can cover the whole mortgage payment on my own. In the darkness, alone, Jamie's suggestion to ask someone to stay feels like a good one.

The text Jamie sends me the following morning gives me a possible solution. I'm clutching a cup of tea – black, as I'm out of milk – and staring out into the garden. Last night's wine is pummelling my head and the pizza feels as if it's lodged in my stomach. Lady pads across the lawn and waits, her unblinking eyes focused on me as I interpret her desire to be let inside. If only Chris's intentions could be read as easily. He's still not been in touch. The ping of a text on my phone makes my hands shake and thick drops of liquid plop onto the table. It's from Jamie. I don't bother to fetch a cloth. Chris likes the house to be kept spotless, but Chris isn't here any more and my slovenliness feels like a small, if pathetic, rebellion.

What about Alice?

Alice, *of course.*

Alice would be perfect as a lodger. Jamie hasn't even met her but I've told him all about her. *Good old Jamie*. My mood subtly flickers into life at the thought of her: the friend I met at my yoga class a few months back, who was living with her parents again and looking for a place to stay. Alice, so poised and exotic, with her tanned skin and long dark hair, fringe feathering over her eyes. She was late, the first time; strolled in and slapped a mat down onto the floor beside me, ignoring the glare the teacher threw her way. If someone were to look at me like that, my cheeks would glow red and I'd try to make myself as invisible as possible. Not the newcomer. Lying on the floor, arms stretched out, I compared my thin white arms to her glowing, sun-kissed skin, defined muscles and elegant posture. She obviously wasn't new to yoga – neither was I, but years of practice hadn't resulted in much of an improvement for me. I still found most positions unattainable, but this gazelle-like creature laid down next to me looked at ease, and I wished she'd dropped her mat down somewhere else.

I soon changed my mind. Our regular teacher, a gentle, willowy woman, was on a spiritual retreat, and her replacement was of a different breed. Once the instructor began barking commands, the facial expressions of the new arrival as she caught my eye and raised one shapely eyebrow made me want to giggle like a naughty schoolgirl. In fact, the whole class was rather like one of those hundreds of lessons I'd endured over the years at countless different schools, always the new girl, the one who got stared at. But for the first time someone appeared willing to engage with me, and I embraced it. Never mind the shopping and getting home to cook Chris's dinner. He was rarely turning up on time back then.

'Jeez,' the sun-kissed newcomer said as we placed our mats up on the racks in the corner, 'I thought yoga was meant to be relaxing.'

We fell into step as we made our way downstairs to the changing rooms.

'It's supposed to be dynamic but that was something else. Heidi – that's our regular teacher – is away at the moment. It's usually very chilled out. It's your first time, isn't it?'

She nodded. 'I've just moved to London, thought I'd check out the local classes. If I'd wanted a boot camp I'd have popped over to Hampstead Heath. But if you say it's not normally like that, I'll give it another go.'

'Heidi's back next week, thank goodness. My ears are still ringing.'

'Do you fancy a coffee? You can tell me which other classes are best avoided.'

Alice turned up at yoga again the following week and it became a regular thing to go for a coffee or a juice after class. She told me how she'd been living in Spain for the past year and was back staying with her parents until she found something more permanent. Alice had worked with a friend who was a landscape gardener and she planned to set up an urban gardening business in London. She was warm and friendly, and when Nancy passed away I discovered what a good listener she was.

Alice would be the perfect lodger.

DIARY

1 JANUARY 1977

HAPPY NEW YEAR

So much has happened. I planned to write every day. I was so happy then. How quickly things have changed.

The Wednesday before Christmas should have been another of my weekly afternoons with Doris. It was her turn to come here. I was so looking forward to it. I got up early, walked down to the village and bought some mince pies from Fred's. He made a joke about me not baking them myself, and I joked back that I couldn't compete with him. I was putting the pies in my shopping bag when I heard Fred say 'hello Edward'. That was a surprise – Edward was doing a cake run for the lads he was on a decorating job with. We chatted to Fred for a little while, then Edward went back to work and I didn't think anything of it.

I was in a good mood, and I made a detour to sit by the pond and feed the ducks for a bit. When I got home I finished tidying and had some soup and crackers before Doris came. I was humming along to the radio and I jumped out of my skin when Edward walked into the kitchen. I hadn't heard him over the music, and besides, he never came home for lunch.

I knew something was wrong as soon as I looked at him. His jaw was clenched, his body stiff. I was afraid just looking at him. He threw his bag on the floor and before I could speak he'd grabbed my arms and was shaking me hard.

'Edward, Edward, stop it,' I shouted over and over, but his eyes were glazed and it was only when I screamed that he stopped. He pushed me back into the chair, knocking the table and causing the soup to spill over the floor.

'I caught you,' he said, 'I knew it. Laughing and flirting with that baker from next door.'

I couldn't believe what I was hearing. Edward went on about Doris and her 'fancy ways'. He said she was a bad influence and that he felt he wasn't good enough for me. I told him he'd got me so wrong. I'd never looked twice at Fred, he belonged to Doris and she was my friend. Couldn't Edward see how much I loved him? He grew quiet after that. He kept saying sorry, he went back to work and I was left feeling as if a whirlwind had burst through the kitchen. I cried as I mopped up the tomato soup from all over the floor.

By the time Doris came at three the kitchen was all spick and span as if Edward's outburst had never happened. But Doris saw my hands shaking when I poured her tea and the cup clattering in the saucer gave me away. She made me tell her what had happened, and I told her we'd had a row but I didn't mention Edward's jealousy about Fred because I didn't want her to get that idea in her head in case it spoilt our friendship. I felt better after I'd spoken to her. I always do, which is why I won't risk our friendship with that nonsense about Fred. We agreed that Edward must have had a bad morning at work and left it at that. She joked about him being older than me, more responsible.

But that evening, instead of cuddling up on the sofa to watch *The Generation Game* like we always did, Edward put his coat on and said he was going for a drink. I tried not to mind but he knew I didn't like being alone in the evenings with the expanse of the heath out there. The sound of the wind whipping up the trees and the house groaning and protesting unsettles me. I couldn't relax and I kept looking at the hand on the grandfather clock, which ticked loudly but never seemed to move. Nine o'clock came and then ten, and eventually I gave up and went to bed. But I couldn't sleep with the howling gale making the trees sound as if they were whispering horrible words to me.

I laid awake feeling scared and it was gone midnight when Edward came home and stumbled about downstairs. The worst thing was I wasn't just frightened of what was out there, I was also frightened of Edward and what he might do. He's different now and I don't know why. *What have I done?*

CHAPTER SEVEN

ALICE

The phone call was unexpected, but welcome. Ella Rutherford, my gym friend asking if I'd care to stay in her house for a bit. I'd told her the story of needing a place to live but I hadn't expected this. Her husband was going away for a bit, apparently, she didn't go into detail. There was a catch in her voice; she was upset, I could tell. There would be plenty of time for a heart-to-heart once I'd moved in. Ella and I had lots in common, I'd made sure of that, and besides, we were already friends. I'd taken a quick look around the room I'd be renting and gave an emphatic 'yes'.

After Ella rang to give me the good news I turned up an hour later with a bottle of wine. She hugged me when she saw me. I couldn't wait to see the house. She'd never once invited me round to number 46 Heath Street, even though she talked about it all the time. I couldn't wait to move in.

I took a step backwards when Ella opened the door. Her sleek and straightened hair was pulled up into a messy knot and her eyes were blotchy and red. When she'd told me that her husband was away, it wasn't strictly true.

'He's left me.' Tears poured down her face and she folded into my arms. 'I didn't want to tell you on the phone.' She still wore the thick, diamond-encrusted platinum band on her wedding finger and I was dying to ask more details, but there was going to be plenty of time for that. As soon as I saw the house I knew I had to live there.

Ella pulled the dining room door closed en route to the kitchen. On the earlier tour of the house she'd told me it was her favourite room. It was where she did all her craft work, where she created the cards she sold in her shop. It was a lovely room painted in pale green; the trestle table in the centre was covered with bits of material, paints, paper and card. The window faced Heath Street and the room felt more modern than the rest of the house; everything in it looked new, apart from the old sewing machine passed down from her mother-in-law. I visualised the needle biting down into cloth and looked at the view across Heath Street instead, where a cluster of trees and bushes made it feel like living in a forest.

We sat in the kitchen on high stools, lights turned down low. The stools felt slightly out of place with the rest of the old-fashioned furniture, especially the grandfather clock that still chimed on the hour. The owner of the Wine Cellars shop in town had rubbed his hands at my request for a recommendation, asking the inevitable 'red or white' question; I'd had to make an educated guess. Somehow Ella with her well-cut clothes and dainty ways struck me as more of a chilled white wine kind of girl. The wine merchant wrapped his choice – 'a New Zealand white with fresh gooseberry and intense citrus flavours' – in brown paper, and I hoped Ella would appreciate my offering. The concentration on her face as she sipped it and the way she ran her tongue over her lips followed by a long sigh suggested I'd made a good choice. Champagne would have been over the top, in the circumstances.

'I needed that,' she said. With her pale face and ash-blonde hair she cut an ethereal figure against the backdrop of heavy, country-style kitchen furniture.

'Talk to me. What's happened?' I said.

Her husband had left her. 'Temporarily,' Ella explained and her lip wobbled as she took another long sip of wine. I barely touched mine. Perhaps I'd miscalculated the situation. Maybe it wasn't help with the mortgage she needed from me, but company.

'It's complicated,' she said, and burst into tears again.

By the time I'd squeezed her shoulder, topped up her glass and pulled a flower-embossed tissue from a box in the living room, she'd obviously made up her mind to confide in me.

'I've just found out he's having an affair.' Ella blew her nose, which by now was quite pink, giving her an air of vulnerability.

That old cliché. 'Oh God, I'm sorry,' I said.

'I don't know who she is. She sent me an anonymous note. I couldn't believe it. I couldn't have kept it from him – it would have eaten me up. I'm used to sharing everything with Chris. He admitted it straight away.' Ella's lip was still wobbling and she bit down into it, sniffed. 'I just can't believe it. And he won't tell me who it is – a client, or so he says. Jamie…' She drained her glass and emptied the bottle – it was a good job I'm not much of a drinker – 'you know, from work, said that it didn't surprise him. I had a bit of a go at him and then I realised I was defending Chris when Jamie's only ever been a good friend to me. But I am his boss and I need to remember that. I know I could have talked to you, but I was worried you wouldn't want to move in with an emotional wreck.' She stopped and took a long breath. I've got used to the breathless way she talks.

'Don't be silly. You can tell me anything. I need somewhere to live and I like the house. And you, of course,' I added, because she probably needs to know that. And I want her to tell me everything.

Ella chattered on and it became evident she was obsessed with this other woman. At this point she was too blinded to understand it wasn't going to help, and I was happy for her to offload.

'I bet she sent the card just so I would find it. She's insecure – he obviously didn't want me to know. The man never actually leaves his wife in these situations, everyone knows that. He says he will, of course, makes all sorts of promises when he's getting what he wants, but it never happens.'

Ella opened another bottle of wine – it tasted better than the New Zealand gooseberry in my opinion. I was only on my second glass of the evening – two glasses is always my limit. Ella, on the other hand, was looking a little wild around the eyes. I got the impression that she wasn't usually much of a drinker either.

'I'll pour,' I said as she rather clumsily went to grab the bottle, which could have ended up catapulting off the table and spilling over the shiny, new-looking white floor tiles. The house appeared to have been recently decorated. Only the furniture seemed like it could tell a story, from the rocking chair upstairs to the grandfather clock standing creepily like a sentry behind Ella.

'I feel for you, I really do. Don't be hard on yourself. What a shit he is, doing this so soon after your mother-in-law's death. I'll move in straight away, if it helps. My parents will be glad to see the back of me.'

Ella swallowed. 'I'd like that. I hate being on my own in the house.' She collapsed into sobs and I thrust more tissues at her. She almost knocked her glass over again.

'How about I make us some tea? I might as well start working out where everything is in this kitchen.'

The cupboards were crammed with food and everything was neat and labelled. I found some Earl Grey teabags and colourful Orla Kiely mugs. She went off to the bathroom and looked better when she came back. She cradled the mug in her hands and blew on the steaming tea.

'That's better,' she said. 'I'm more of a tea girl, normally. Please don't think I'm going to be sobbing into my cups every night, because that isn't going to happen. It's the shock, you see, the thought of losing my husband, and our home.'

'So who owns the house?'

'We own it jointly. It's a complicated situation. Heath Street has been in the Rutherford family for a long time and when Nancy died Chris assumed the house would be left to him.'

'Please don't tell me she left it all to Battersea Dogs Home.'

Ella sipped at her tea and managed a smile, 'No, but Chris had a sister, who left home years ago and they lost touch. Nancy left the house to her and Chris was gutted, but Nancy stipulated that if her daughter couldn't be found then it should go to Chris. So it took a while, and after that was sorted out we had to remortgage because the inheritance tax was so high. My business was doing well so I offered to take on my half of the mortgage. I'm so glad I did now.' Ella's voice faltered, 'He wants me out – but please don't worry, if there's no way we can get back together then I intend to fight this. He knows how much I love this house. Number 46 is the first proper home I've ever had, and I can't tell you how much it means to me. I haven't told Chris about you moving in, by the way. I'm scared he wants to move *her* in.' Ella's green eyes flashed, determined. 'I'll do whatever it takes, hire a solicitor, there's no way I'm letting that happen.'

'I'm not taking his side,' I had to say it, 'but if it's his family home, wouldn't you feel bad staying here?'

'I'll feel terrible,' she said and her face crumpled.

'But not as terrible as he should for cheating on you. Men are bastards, as far as I'm concerned. And remember this – this other woman will be feeling threatened by you too. Anyway, you've got me to look out for you now.'

Ella's face lit up and she asked me if I'd ever been through a difficult break-up, but I'm not ready to share that with anyone yet. No matter how sweet she is. Verbally we agree on a three-month stay. Three months should be long enough for what I need to do.

CHAPTER EIGHT

ELLA

All I can think about is *her*. I pull on a sweatshirt and my old, faded jeans and make a strong brew of tea in Nancy's red china teapot. While the tea settles I open my laptop and drum my fingers on the table. *The Other Woman. Do I know her? Think, Ella.*

He met her through work. I open the website for Rutherford Carpentry, shaking my head at the screen at the ridiculousness of my quest. Chris's blue eyes staring out from the home page catch me unawares, and I look up at those same eyes in the photo of ten-year-old Chris which sits on the mantelpiece – he's grinning widely as he holds up the runner-up certificate for 'Best Young Carpenter'. He told me that as the photographer packed his camera away his father muttered in Chris's ear that he should have won first place. That stopped him smiling. He'd never forgotten that comment, despite his success.

Rutherfords is a tiny company with many clients and a good profile locally, and the award Chris won for 'Best Start-up Business' is proudly displayed below his photograph on the home page. I felt like I'd burst with pride when he got the news; we'd ended up spending a passionate afternoon in bed, unable to keep our hands off each other. The photo of Chris accepting the award alongside his PA Jessica Taylor-Scott offers me the first candidate, but for Jessica to be the other woman would be too easy. My stomach swoops as I look at her friendly smile and auburn bob; she's wholesome-looking and has always been incredibly friendly to me. I can't bear the thought that it could be her, I just can't see it. She's been with her boyfriend Rob since her university days and is currently planning her wedding. According to Chris, she's been in bridezilla mode for the past year. The sympathy card she sent me when Nancy died lies in my bedside drawer.

Next is Sara, the admin assistant with short, spiky hair. She's married to Daisy, blissfully happy living in a warehouse near east London's Victoria Park. There's no way it could be her. I pick at the skin around my nails as the face of the only other female employee opens. Tanya joined the company as receptionist a month ago and I've never met her. I look at her photo on the website. Long, blonde, professionally highlighted hair falls down past her shoulders and her thick painted eyebrows give her a permanent air of surprise. She's twenty-five at most. Chris hasn't mentioned her much. Haughty, is how I'd describe her expression, the fussy frills of her cream blouse not to my taste. My stomach lurches as I acknowledge her as a possibility.

By now the tea has been brewing for a while and I hope a strong cup will zap my headache away. My stomach growls and I realise I haven't eaten since yesterday morning. Part of me wants to crawl back into bed and bury myself under the duvet, but I won't give in.

Dust has collected on the surfaces in my absence over the weekend and I occupy myself by cleaning the house. Most of the people on this street have cleaners, but I wouldn't let another person look after my house. Chris laughed at me when I first moved in, said I was like a kid in a sweetshop, but he would never understand what growing up in care was like. I was brimming with pride the first time I put my key in my very own front door. Keeping the house clean is my way of looking after it, of loving it. The hoover whines as I work up a sweat running it up and down the parquet wooden floors. But sucking up the dust doesn't delete the other woman from my thoughts. She's become a temptress with bouffant blonde hair, red lips, a pencil skirt and stilettos, digging her long, sharp, painted fake nails into his flesh. There's no way I am letting her get her hands on this house. *Not our home.*

I shower and dress before walking across town to his office. It's early afternoon but the sky is dark and the pavements glisten with the rain that fell throughout the night. I lay awake listening to it pouring interminably, battering against the windows. A car swishes by and a spatter of rain hits my tights. I swear under my breath, watching the car drive off, oblivious.

There's no sign of Chris's car yet, but the café opposite is open. I order a large cappuccino and on a whim select a pain au chocolat, remembering a magazine article I read reminding me to look after myself in times of stress. Nothing could be more stressful than this. I sit on a high stool at the counter that runs along the window and focus my gaze on the building opposite. The barista has carefully crafted a heart on the top of my coffee and I dash my spoon through it until it disappears.

The building is fairly new; there's a small Waitrose on the ground level and office space above. Chris hired an interior designer when he moved in and the first time I visited I was still living in my bedsit. I squeezed Chris's arm tight, checking this new life of mine was real. He'd kissed me passionately and we'd ended up making love on the sofa in his office. The memory tastes sour as I look up at the building. His office is in the corner on the first floor and from where I'm sitting I can see his desk. The lights are off and there's no sign of life. I sip at my coffee and try to forget the feel of his stubble grazing my skin as I break off a little of the pastry, nibbling at it. Café sounds fill the space behind me, whooshes of steam from the coffee machines, the whirring of the fridges, the clinking of spoons against mugs. A steady stream of people go in and out, and each time the door opens a gust of air blows my way.

I lick pastry flakes from my fingers, eyes focused on the building. I've been here an hour now and there's still no movement across the road. I stir the dregs of my coffee. I could drink another, but I don't want to leave my spot.

A pink Fiat 500 pulls up outside the office and two elegant legs appear from the driver's door, a polished exit like something from a movie. The woman lifts her curtain of sleek, long blonde hair and rearranges it down her back. In her neat suit and stilettos she looks like she's going for a job interview. Her hair swings as she checks up and down the street, then crosses the road to the café, heading straight towards me. It's Tanya.

I pretend to look for something in my bag so that she doesn't see my face. Although we've not met, if she's the other woman then she's probably got a good idea of what I look like. A waft of musky perfume tickles my nose and her heels clip across the tiled floor. I risk a glance now she's got her back to me at the counter and she's ordering a takeout coffee. She emits a throaty chuckle at something the barista says. I try to check if I recognise her voice from the phone call, but I can't make out the conversation. Her heels clip away again and she pauses outside, holding two cups in a cardboard tray. *Is one of those for my husband?* Her eyes flicker over me, not seeing me. As she walks across to the office I take out my phone and snap a photo of her buzzing into the building. *Evidence, just in case.* Then I wait.

Ten minutes pass before the lights go on. I reason with myself that she wouldn't be taking coffee in if she was planning a passionate encounter, but the little voice whispering doubts in my head doesn't fall for that. A waitress is wiping the table down next to me and she looks at the half-eaten pain au chocolate on my plate. I smile apologetically and push it towards her; the churning in my stomach has made me lose my appetite. Next time I look up at the window I spot Chris seated at his desk, his back to me, coffee in one hand. *How did I miss seeing him go in?* He doesn't move for the next half hour. I look around. I'm the only person left in the café and I stand up abruptly, realising I'm being ridiculous.

Back home I go straight to my laptop and look up Tanya Redmond. I find her on Facebook. I learn that she's '*in a relationship*' but not with whom. She likes posing for the camera and posting cute pictures of dogs. Chris and I prefer cats. As if she can read my thoughts, Lady jumps onto my lap, purring loudly, blocking the screen. Her warm body soothes the thoughts sending a shiver down my spine.

I spend the afternoon finishing cleaning the house, getting it ready for Alice to move in. Chris won't throw anything away and his paperwork going back years is stashed in boxes piled in the corner of the dining room where I do my crafts. I've wanted to shift them for ages. For the first time in a while I go down to the cellar, lugging boxes as there's nowhere else to store them. Chris doesn't like me coming down here: everything that belongs to his parents is stashed away in this chilly space, waiting for him to sort out. Another thing he never gets around to doing. It smells damp and it's so cold goosebumps appear on my arms. I can't wait to get back upstairs.

I'm just putting the keys back on the hook by the front door when a piercing sound screeches into the air and I drop the keys on the floor. I stand rigid and it takes a couple of seconds for me to recognise my car alarm. I grab my car keys and rush out into the street. The road looks deserted save for the black cat from the house on the corner who stands rigid, fur on end, staring at me. I turn and look at the car. A window opens across the street and a topless man leans out.

'Turn that fucking racket off, will you!'

His words break the spell and I zap my fob at the car. Silence descends but the ringing continues in my ears. The cat miaows and I realise what I'm looking at. The side of the car has been scratched. I stare at the jagged lines where five letters have been gouged into the side of my car: L E A V E. I look up and down the street, but it's deserted. My head is pounding with disbelief. Chris wants me out of the house, but surely he wouldn't have done this? A voice whispers in my head, the silky voice on the phone asking for Chris. *The Other Woman – this has to be her doing.*

CHAPTER NINE

ELLA

The scratch on the car looks worse in the morning light. I could report it to the police, but what's the point? Such a trivial crime in a city like London. My niggling suspicion won't go away. *It has to be her, Chris's other woman. Jealous of me, lashing out. What if this is just the beginning?* I lock the front door with shaking hands, dropping the keys twice and grazing my finger on the gravel before finally locking the door.

Ordinarily I enjoy my walk to work but today everything feels as if it hides a threat. Shadows lurk behind parked cars, and when a man steps out from behind a tree I cry out loud and his eyebrows shoot up in surprise. I stop at a café and order a strong tea, adding extra sugar – it's good for shock, which is what I feel at the way my life has changed overnight.

After leaving the café, my shop on the corner is a burst of colour and I pause to admire Jamie's latest display. Vibrant orange paper flowers dominate the window, and my mood dips a little when I spot that the centrepiece is a tiny wooden chair Chris made specially for my shop window. I cross the road but the sharp stench of urine outside the door makes me bury my nose in my sleeve; I'm furious that someone has used my doorway as a urinal. I unlock the door and go to deactivate the alarm. But it isn't set. It's unlike Jamie to make such an error; he's usually meticulous. I hover on the doorstep clutching my nose to block out the smell and my heart beats in my throat. *What if somebody's inside?*

The door squeaks as I push it open and my pulse knocks even faster. The only sound is muffled traffic; the shop is silent, waiting. I take a long, deep breath and step into the room. Sunlight streams in through the windows and illuminates a bucket of pink roses.

I text Jamie to ask if there was a reason he didn't set the alarm, then I roam around the shop switching the lights on. The safe is locked and the till undisturbed. Cards and gifts are artfully arranged. Displays immaculate as ever. Ten o'clock registers on the clock and I'm spurred into action. *Time to open.* I turn the sign on the door and switch some music on. Classical piano notes tinkle into the air and render everything back to normal – or almost. I can't quite rid myself of a sense of unease.

A bell rings and I jump. A young woman wheels a pushchair into the shop and the baby facing me gurgles. My stomach cramps as if in direct response. The weekend's disappointment feels like a lifetime ago – Chris's revelation had almost eclipsed it from my mind. I was driving home early to surprise him when the tell-tale pain had forced me to turn off into a service station, flying to the bathroom, already knowing my hopes had been dashed. I wasn't pregnant – the cramps in my stomach were evidence of that. *How could I have forgotten the crushing blow I'd felt?* I've wanted to start a family ever since I can remember. Once again the fact that Chris has left me slams like a right hook to my face. *He can't mean it. He can't.*

'Are you OK?' the woman whose existence I had forgotten asks. Her child coos again and I force myself to look down at the chubby baby wrapped up like a parcel.

'I'm fine, a moment of dizziness, that's all, nothing to worry about. How can I help you and this gorgeous little fellow?'

She smiles and shows me the stationery set she wants personalised for a present. Getting into conversation helps me switch into professional mode, and I immerse myself in work for the rest of the morning.

But the chubby-faced baby has unsettled me, reminding me that I am not pregnant. Tears spring to my eyes. Chris's words from that night echo in my mind, '*You can stay here for a month, say six weeks max.*' After everything I've done for his mother.

Nancy had just been diagnosed with stage four breast cancer when I first moved in. She was a tiny woman with a steely silver crop and piercing blue eyes. Her warm handshake and smile – identical to her only son's – endeared me to her immediately.

Soon I was accompanying her to the hospital for her treatments, chatting about anything and everything to take her mind off the gruelling chemotherapy, which zapped her of energy and eventually led to her spending more and more time in her room. Those moments when I was supporting Nancy's thin frame as I helped her back into bed, running a cold flannel over the papery skin of her forehead, made up for some of those thousands of other moments in foster care, when I'd longed for a mother, a *real* mother, who needed me as much as I needed her. Caring for Nancy made me feel worthwhile at last.

One evening when Nancy had been consumed by pain for what seemed like hours, and it had taken all my strength to calm her down without crying, I'd gone downstairs and poured myself a large slug of gin. Chris was late again and I was sitting on the sofa wishing he didn't have to work so hard when he finally came home. He threw his corduroy jacket on the table and picked up the gin bottle, a look of surprise on his tired face.

'Mother's ruin,' he'd said. 'But I'll join you.'

I'd curled into him on the sofa, burying my face into his jumper, which smelt of wood shavings and pine aftershave. He didn't need to ask what was wrong, and I let him think it was just Nancy's pain. How could he possibly know his words were a trigger?

Mother's ruin. Mother's day. Parents' evening.

How I hated those innocent expressions. At one school I attended for six months, the popular girl who made everyone laugh when she pointed out I was wearing a jumper the school office had provided, asked in a loud voice which of my parents would be coming to parents' evening. Laughter echoed around the room and I hated those girls with their mothers they took for granted. Most of all I hated the mother who had abandoned me at the age of six. Despite her advanced illness, Nancy took me into her heart; she filled a void in me and I let her mother me. I knew I could never replace her own absent daughter, but I like to think Nancy needed me, too.

The sun has vanished and I switch the lamp on as the sky darkens outside. There's a thank you email from a customer regarding some wedding stationery I'd designed, complete with photographs of the place cards and menus we'd provided. The shots are beautiful and I save them for publicity purposes, trying to ignore the thoughts bombarding me about the contrasting state of my own marriage. A noise makes me look up. Rain is pouring down outside, the wind blowing it towards the windows where it streaks down the glass as condensation steams up the insides. A flash of lightning blasts across the street outside and I stand, taking deep breaths in and out, too late to stop the images flashing into my head, the blurry memory catching me unawares as it always does. Me screaming as a woman straps me into the car, rain pelting on the window, my small hand wiping fruitlessly against the steamy glass as her face becomes a blur and I can no longer see her features. Features I have long since forgotten, despite doing everything I can to remember them. But the emotion I felt at the time has never left me. Like a knife digging out my innards, twisting and scraping at the injustice of it all.

The sound of my phone ringing jolts me back into the room. It's Jamie returning my call.

'I one hundred per cent know I set the alarm because I talked Sam through the procedure to make sure she knows what to do. I know she won't normally be setting it herself, but just in case, you know?'

With everything that's been happening I'd forgotten about our new shop assistant.

'Yes, I'd have done the same. But it definitely wasn't set.'

'Is everything OK, no signs of a break-in?'

Jamie obviously got distracted when he was showing Sam the procedure.

'Everything looks fine to me. How was last Saturday?'

'Your latest range of cards are selling super-fast. Mrs Donovan called in to thank us for the wedding stationery and left us a huge box of chocolates. I'm afraid I just had to open the box, and honestly, they are so delicious I had to stop myself gorging the lot. They're in the fridge. Very complimentary about the shop she was, too. *My* display, obviously.'

I smile, my pulse returning to normal. We have a running competition over who can create the best window arrangement. So far, Jamie's winning.

'And was Sam OK?'

'Sam was great, you picked a good one there. And she's got the most divine shoes. But more importantly, how are you feeling?'

'Oh, you know. A bit shaken up, to be honest. What with everything that's been going on at home—'

'Maybe you need to take more time off.'

'No, I'll be OK. Being in the house is a constant reminder that Chris isn't there. And the good news is that Alice is moving in.'

'Fab, that's great news.'

'There is one thing, though.' I hesitate; it's petty, but even so. 'The window display is great, honestly it is, but would you mind moving Chris's chair out and redoing the display without it? I'm not sure I can face it every time I come to work at the moment.'

'His chair?'

'Yes, you know, the one he made—'

'Of course I know which chair, but I'm not that thoughtless. I didn't put it in the window display.'

Then who did?

DIARY

3 MARCH 1996

What have I done?

Those were the last words written in my diary, some twenty years ago. A journal suddenly cut short. I couldn't face ruining the fairy tale that I'd begun with the ugly tale my life became. Edward changed, and I couldn't bear to record that change. But now I fear I must.

The changing of Edward. Writing it down helps, because this low pain in my stomach makes me uneasy. I stand here in our bedroom of twenty years, looking down over the garden at the man who once made my heart swoop every time I saw him, and I see a man I don't recognise. His age shows now; he carries too much weight and his hair has grown thin. But I wouldn't undo anything, because Edward and I created our beautiful children and I would fight to the death to protect them.

As much as I don't want it to be true, my hands tremble as I write this down because then it becomes a fact. Edward doesn't encourage original thought. Especially from his wife. '*Women should know their place.*' No, what I fear – and I must write it down – is that Edward may do something to harm me. There, it's done now, recorded for posterity. I've said it, outed my fear. I write this for my children so that if the day comes when they wonder why their father would do such a thing, they will know that I, their mother, loved them more than anything else. And I no longer love my husband: that love died a long time ago. There. I've said that too. I—

Another unfinished sentence, he almost caught me again. I have to be more careful.

One thing that hasn't changed over the years is my Wednesdays with Doris. I look forward to our time together all week. We've been meeting every Wednesday for years now. Doris was a slip of a thing when I started writing my diary, wearing her old flower-print sundress and platform shoes, thick eyeliner rimming her eyes. Edward would have had a heart attack if I wore a dress that length, but Fred chuckled and said hadn't his girl got a lovely pair of pins? I stopped mentioning Fred after that incident in the baker's. That was the start of everything.

Originally we'd taken it in turns to go to one another's houses, but soon after that incident Edward stopped working Wednesday afternoons and it was never the same. We couldn't share confidences in the same way when he was around. We've been going to hers ever since. Fred is usually at work but if he were there he wouldn't insist on listening in like Edward does. Edward always wants to know what I'm doing; I've told him I don't tell Doris any of our current troubles with Melissa, but I do. My daughter is becoming secretive. Normal teenage behaviour? I'm not convinced. Sharing my worries with Doris keeps me sane. Most of my worries, that is. My worries about Edward are written down; I'm too scared to say the words out loud. But Doris knows all about this journal and where it's hidden. One day, should the time come, she'll know where to find it. I'll make sure of that.

4 MARCH 1996

Edward was tidying his shed, muttering to himself as he removed gardening implements: an old bicycle I'd forgotten he owned; rolls of wallpaper from years ago – relics of his long-forgotten decorating project, born from the enthusiasm of the energetic young man who moved into his first home. A man who no longer exists. He's changed, as have I, no longer the pretty young thing he scooped into his arms and carried over the threshold of 46 Heath Street, the house I'd not been allowed to see until he got the keys. He likes surprises, does Edward. Unfortunately his surprises are not so nice these days; they have a nastier feel about them. Like creeping upstairs to spy on what I am doing. That's one of his favourite tricks. I have to remind myself of how hard my heart hammers in my chest when I hear his footsteps on the stairs. I fear my hiding place isn't good enough. I fear for my life.

CHAPTER TEN

ELLA

I press the bell, say 'Rutherford Carpentry' when prompted and walk up the stairs, my legs heavy, my stomach clenching. Chris isn't replying to my calls or messages and I'm not leaving until I get an answer. My nerves aren't eased when I push through the office doors and come face-to-face with Tanya behind the shiny reception desk. She's partially hidden behind a large pink orchid, but stands when she sees me.

'Good morning, oh, it's Ella, isn't it? Hello, how are you?'

If she is the other woman then she's a good actress.

'I'm good thanks, how are you?'

'I'm fine. Chris is in with a client at the moment. Is he expecting you?'

'No, I was passing by, thought I'd drop in.'

'Take a seat, he shouldn't be too long. Can I get you a coffee?'

'Yes please.'

Tanya emerges from behind the desk, elegant in her pencil skirt, silk blouse and high-heeled red shoes. She makes me feel mousy, with my thin frame and pale hair. She pushes through double doors, where I catch a glimpse of the open-plan working space.

'I've told Chris you're here,' she says as she comes back into reception with a small tray holding an individual cafetière, a cup and sachets of milk and sugar, placing it down between us. The phone rings behind the desk and she pats down her glossy hair with her red nails as she answers. 'Yes, that's what I said.' She flashes a glance at me and lowers her voice. 'Later, OK.'

Her carefully made-up cheeks are flushed as she avoids looking at me and taps at her keyboard. *It's her. It has to be her.* The office door opens and a man in a suit emerges, signs out and leaves, followed by Chris. He appears in the doorway, looks over his glasses at me and beckons me through. He isn't smiling and my thoughts are all over the place. I leave the untouched tray on the coffee table and follow him. The desk is covered in paper, which strikes me as odd given Chris's OCD tendencies, and his swimming bag is in the corner of the room, unzipped, water bottle sticking out. He closes the door behind us.

'What are you doing here, Ella? I wouldn't come to your shop looking for an argument. It's so unprofessional.' Chris pushes his glasses up, which he always does when he's nervous, and leans against the desk. I sit on a chair, flustered at the thought that Tanya could be the other woman. I flick my unhelpful thoughts out of my mind and focus on why I'm here.

'You don't answer my calls. How else can I get to speak to you? The bank rang, and said you haven't been paying the mortgage. The man on the phone mentioned a payment break. Why don't I know about this?'

Chris stiffens and I see confusion in his eyes, but he quickly composes himself. 'The bank, of course. What with everything that's been going on I'd forgotten I hadn't told you. I changed the mortgage payments temporarily, that's all. It was after Mum died. You were having a hard time with it and I didn't want to bother you with the intricacies of the mortgage.'

He sinks onto the couch below the window. Our moment of passion on there feels like a lifetime ago.

'The mortgage, Chris. I'm scared. What's going on?'

He runs his hands through his hair; his nails are bitten, sore-looking. *Good.* But he looks lost, vulnerable, and despite everything

I feel a pang of sorrow – even now I hate to see him hurting. His voice is quieter when he next speaks. 'It's nothing to worry about. I took the payment break over the summer because one of my clients hadn't paid on time, but that's been sorted, and this month I forgot to change the standing order. That's all. Nothing to worry about, honestly.'

'But I can't help worrying. We own the house jointly, remember?' I breathe deeply. 'You didn't mean what you said about me having to move out, did you?'

He stares at me for what feels like a long time, shaking his head.

'Are you serious? Of course I meant it. You can't tell me you're expecting to stay? It's my family home, Ella.'

My cheeks burn as the enormity of what he says hits me.

'I thought I was family,' I whisper.

Chris closes his eyes, breathes out loud. 'Can't you see, that's the problem. You want too much from me. You took over Nancy, and now she's gone…'

'Took over?' My whole body feels hot. 'She was sick, Chris, dying, I looked after her. I did what any decent human being would have done. Where were you when she needed you?'

A phone rings from the office outside and Chris gets to his feet, looking behind me. He pushes his glasses back up the bridge of his nose.

'I can't do this, Ella. Not here, it isn't appropriate.' He gets to his feet. 'I've explained the situation to you. I'm sorry, I really am. I never wanted to hurt you. Let's wait a little to get used to the situation, then we can talk, I promise. It will give you time to work out what you want to do. But you must understand, it's my house. Plus, there are so many memories there for you, of Mum dying. Do you really want to stay there?'

He wants to move her in.

Something snaps inside me and I grab my bag from the floor.

'Just so you know, I'm not going anywhere. And we haven't mentioned the scratch on my car. I know it was you – or your fancy woman. There's no way *she* will ever live at 46 Heath Street.' I open the door and pause in the doorway. Slamming the door behind me, I walk on shaking legs back through the office. I maintain my composure as I sweep through reception past Tanya and out to the staircase. Only then do I collapse against the wall.

The next morning I take the car to the garage to get the paintwork fixed. Seeing that word engraved on the side makes me feel all churned up inside.

The garage is conveniently only a few streets away; Ron, the mechanic, is doing a crossword in the office over a cup of tea when I call in.

'I haven't seen you for a while, Ella,' he says. 'Any good at crosswords? I'm stuck on eight across – a type of lizard.'

I smile wryly as Chris springs to mind – I need to find some humour in this situation, but Ron wouldn't get the joke and I wouldn't know where to start explaining. 'Gecko' is the only example I can come up with.

'You're a star,' he says, writing it down. 'All done. Now show me this car of yours. What's the problem?'

I point out the scratch and he walks slowly around the car examining the damage. It looks worse, somehow, under scrutiny: L E A V E.

Ron shakes his head repeatedly. 'Do you know who did this? What does it mean?'

I shrug. 'It was parked in the street and the alarm went off, but of course they were long gone by the time I got out there.'

'What did the police say?'

'I didn't call the police.'

'Why ever not? This is nasty. It's also going to cost you a bit to repair.'

'They wouldn't catch anyone. It's petty crime, it's not worth reporting.'

'They could have done a bit of the old door to door – you never know, some old biddy might have been looking out of her window.'

'I doubt it. Nobody came out to speak to me.' I shrug. 'It's too late now, anyway. I just want it sorted. I need the car.'

'Can't you borrow your husband's? Or has he sold it already?'

'Sold it? He's only had it a few months. He cherishes that thing. Besides, he needs it for work, he drives all over the place. And he hates public transport.'

Ron crinkles his face in concentration. 'That's funny. He rang me to ask whether I could sell it for him. He was meant to be dropping by, but he never did. Must have changed his mind.'

I nod, trying to hide my confusion.

'Tell you what, I'll take some photos before I fix it, in case you change your mind, want to claim on the insurance. I'll have it done in a couple of days.'

I nod again, but my mind is elsewhere, wondering why my husband is thinking about selling his precious car.

How many more secrets has he been keeping from me?

CHAPTER ELEVEN
ALICE

I moved in early on a Thursday. Ella had offered to take the morning off work to be there but I insisted I'd be fine. I wanted some time alone in the house. She told me that she'd planned to turn the room she'd given me into a nursery – it was here that her mother-in-law lived and died. *Nancy*. I've never liked that name.

Standing in the room for the first time made my head spin, but I unpacked the few possessions I'd brought and reminded myself to think positive. The room had a perfect view over the back garden, which pleased me. The quick glance I'd had the other evening had given me the impression that it had been neglected. It was dark, of course, but I thought it would be a nice surprise for Ella if I offered to sort it out. It would be a great project for me too, a way to help me get my new business off the ground. An old man was pottering about in the garden next door but I made sure he didn't see me. I don't like people knowing my business.

That first day I had a good old nosy around the house. Ella's bedroom was a right mess, such a contrast to the immaculate rest of the house: clothes lying all over the place and piles of books on the floor, mostly thrillers, the kind you can pick up from the supermarket. I like a good murder story too, as long as there's nothing about kids in there – I can't be doing with anything like that. Just thinking about it makes me feel sick.

When I opened the back door and stood in the garden for the first time a sense of calm descended on me. The sound of traffic from the nearby road was muffled and the overgrown bushes rustled gently in the wind.

Directly outside the kitchen window there was a table and four chairs set on a square of paving stones, the surrounding borders sporting foot-high bamboo shoots. It was secluded and accessible, the only part of the garden that could be used. I pictured Ella out there reading, the sun dancing over her arms and face, a large hat shading her blonde hair. I played around with this image in my head. Something about Ella captivated me, her vulnerability, her fierce desire to hang onto her home and her husband at whatever cost. I hated him on her behalf. I knew too well the pain of betrayal, and how it can drive a person mad. Unwanted memories rose into my mind and I wandered away from the shed down to the end of the garden.

I recalled the elderly man I'd seen in the garden next door as I wondered if the garden had always been like this. Old people loved talking about earlier, better times, when their memories fooled them into only remembering the good bits, unwanted images censored out. I won't let that ever happen to me. I make sure I remember everything. Speaking to the man was obviously out of the question. I like to keep people at a distance.

My feet trampled through an area which was once a lawn, now completely overgrown. Rustling from the bushes alerted me to what sounded like mice and suddenly a large tabby cat jumped to the top of the fence, fur on edge and tail wavering like a snake about to pounce. I tensed, waiting for her to attack, and she flew down to the grass and hurtled towards the house, her invisible prey attempting a hasty exit. An idea formed in my mind.

A rusty old sign was propped against the shed. The lettering was faded but I could make out *Fred's Bakery*; it was the sort of thing that goes for extortionate prices at antique fairs. The wood on the shed bore a dark rectangular mark where the sign had previously been attached before sliding down into a bed of weeds. A padlock secured the door and dirt covered the windows and obscured the view. A bicycle, some tins of paint and a lawnmower were all I could make out inside. A large wheelbarrow stood in the long grass outside. I thought it might come in useful when I sorted out the shed.

Back in the house, behind the kitchen there was a locked door leading down to the cellar. I looked all around the kitchen but couldn't find a key. Dust gathered in the wooden grooves on the door and it didn't look like anyone went down there much. The garage was empty and there weren't any keys in there, either. The cellar had to wait. Ella's kitchen cupboards were rammed full of ingredients but she hadn't been using them – she wasn't looking after herself, so I decided to make myself useful by taking care of her. I'd promised to cook, so I went off in search of a shop. I walked through a string of pretty streets and it wasn't long before I came across a lovely deli, so I popped in to pick up some fresh vegetables and spices.

I was in the middle of cooking when she got home from work and she seemed really grateful. She looked knackered, so I made her a cup of tea. We chatted about nothing much while I cooked but as soon as we sat down to eat I couldn't ignore the way her hands trembled. I waited until we'd eaten as she looked as if she needed food inside her. I was right to wait because as soon as I asked her if she was OK, her lip wobbled and she crumbled.

'You look like you need a drink,' I said. 'Let's sit in the garden.'

'Are you sure? It's a bit of a mess—'

'You've got a table and chairs. What more do we need? It's not too cold. I'm an outdoors person, I hate being cooped up inside.'

Ella didn't seem to mind me taking over and I poured us two glasses of lemonade and added ice, while she went upstairs to get a jumper. By the time she came back I was sitting outside with a candle on the table. Being out there felt strange. The light was on in the kitchen but the moonlit heath, stretching out beyond the garden, looked like a forest. The bamboo shoots stood like a fence along the path, swaying and swishing in the gentle breeze. Ella switched a light on, illuminating the table. The white cotton jumper she'd put on glowed against the lamplight, making her look otherworldly.

'Oh, that's so nice,' she said, looking at the candle, which flickered when the wind blew, but her expression betrayed her sadness.

'You sure?'

She gave a rueful smile. 'Oh, it's nothing, only that Chris used to do stuff like that when I first moved in.'

I pulled a chair out for her. 'Sit, drink, talk to me. Talking helps.'

'Thank you,' she replied, looking grateful.

'Oh, you won't believe what happened to me,' I said. 'On the day I moved in, the moment I turned into Heath Street, a magpie swooped down. I said that magpie thing before you make a wish.'

Ella looked puzzled.

'And what I wished for was that the marvellous house I saw when I turned the corner into Heath Street would turn out to be number 46. And it was! I was so excited. It's such a gorgeous house.'

She smiled and it lit up her face. 'What's the magpie thing?'

'It's an old wives' tale. If you see a magpie on its own you have to do this.' I stood up, pretended to doff my hat and made a sweeping bow. 'Good morning Mr Magpie, first letter in the post to you.'

Ella laughed again and it reached her grey eyes this time.

'Now I know what you mean. Nancy used to say that.'

A gust of wind swept through the garden and the candle went out. The moment was ruined. I lit another match.

'Forget magpies, I want to hear all about the house. Have you lived here long? Tell me everything.'

And so Ella told me the story of 46 Heath Street. The house had belonged to Chris's parents – the Rutherfords – and had been in the family for some time, but she didn't know how long. Chris's father had died in 2005 and he had a sister who ran away after some kind of teenage trauma. Chris had left home for a few years, but had to come back to live with his mother as he was out of work for a while. *Enter Ella.* From the way she talked it sounded as if she'd fallen in love with both Chris and his mother, who she'd cared for until she died.

'Maybe it is my fault,' Ella explained. 'Chris said something earlier – we had a row – about how I doted on his mother. Maybe I excluded him; I didn't realise.'

'None of this is your fault,' I put on my stern voice, 'don't go there. Never let a man turn you into a victim. Or a woman, for that matter. I can see how you adored Nancy – you talk about her as if she'd been your own mother.'

Ella's eyes filled with tears.

'What have I said?'

It turned out she was adopted, never knew her mother and could remember very little about her early years. I went and fetched her a glass of gin at that point – she looked like she needed one. More stuff came pouring out. How she'd requested her adoption file, tracked down her mother, only to be told she wasn't interested in getting to know her.

'She made it quite clear she didn't want me in her life. Ever. She rejected me twice.' Ella drank some gin and burst into tears, which trickled over her delicate features. 'What must you think of me?' she said, blowing her nose with the tissue I'd fetched from the kitchen. 'I'm supposed to be welcoming you. Going on about myself like this. It's just that Chris means everything to me. Every time I remember he's gone, my heart breaks all over again.'

'Of course you feel like that. And living here in this house must make it harder, being reminded of him and Nancy all the time.'

She shook her head, a fierce expression on her face. 'You don't understand. I've never had a home before, not even as a kid. Foster homes don't count, I was never wanted. Chris only came back here because he had to care for his mother and she refused to sell up. I loved this house from the moment I first saw it, and I helped him to love it again. This is our home, mine and Chris's. And yours, for the moment, of course. What you said earlier, you understand its magic. I want you to love the house as much as I do.'

'Oh, I'm sure I will. It's beautiful.' I didn't mention the garden – not yet. I needed to think about how I was going to approach that. I did ask her about the cellar though.

'I haven't been down there in ages. I thought it would be good as a wine cellar, but it's full of Chris's parents' old junk and he wanted to go through it himself. Another thing he hadn't got round to.' She looked downcast again as a woman's laughter burst through the garden, making us both jump.

'It spooks me that the heath is always open,' I said. 'That great expanse of land, waiting in the darkness.'

Ella looked at her watch. 'We've been out here ages. Sorry for going on about myself for so long… I bet you regret moving in already.'

'Don't be silly,' I said, patting her hand. 'Talk as much as you like, that's what I'm here for.' I had no intention of spilling my guts. The focus needed to be on Ella. And on 46 Heath Street.

DIARY

3 APRIL 1996

Kit told us his news today. He said he's not going back to school; he wants to train to work with his father. Edward smirked: this is his doing. My heart ached, my dreams for my clever boy crashing down around me. I'd hoped Kit would be the first in the family to go to university; Edward used to want the same for him. How he's changed.

We were eating steak and kidney pie. At Edward's insistence, I'd spent the afternoon in the kitchen making it, with the oven on and the early sun beating down on the windows. Edward was in that old shirt he refuses to throw away, asleep in his deckchair, kicking at next door's cat when it dared to rub against his legs. It flew back next door with a yelping sound. Sweat ran down my face and into the pastry. Good. These little acts of revenge satisfy me. But I am careful. The slightest thing sets him off these days.

Melissa said nothing when Kit broke his news. Like me, she's learned to hide her feelings. She chopped her food into tiny pieces and kept her gaze on her plate as she ate. Her thoughts are more important to her these days than interacting with us. I don't want to lose her to him, too. Edward kept asking her to fetch things for him during the meal; up and down she got with an expressionless face. He didn't even try to hide his sneer. His preoccupation with tormenting his daughter meant I was able to exert control in the only way I know. I dropped chunks of my dinner into the pocket on my apron and mashed the potatoes into the gravy. Once Edward had left the table to watch television, I scraped my food into the bin and welcomed the dull pangs of hunger.

I tried to talk to Kit later, when Edward went off on his nightly visit to the pub, but he wouldn't listen to me. His father has changed him already. Rarely do I get a glimpse of the cautious little boy who used to hang onto my skirt whenever another person came in sight. He rudely cut off my pleas to rethink his intention to give up school, and ice cut into my soul when I caught a glimpse of his likeness to his father, his use of the same dismissive hand gesture. Who am I, a mere woman, daring to question him? I know I'm too late.

One blessing I took this evening was that Melissa wasn't in the room to witness Kit's harsh words, his eyes full of scorn. As soon as the meal was over, she went up to her room as she does every night, preferring her own company to that of her family, broken as we are, separate strands struggling to weave together. But Melissa's eyes are furtive and won't meet mine. I know she harbours secrets. The only time I see her old spark, her old enthusiasm, is when she goes off to school in the morning, and I wonder what attraction it holds for her now. For my daughter has always hated school, and this sudden change brings me no relief. Oh, if only I could write some good news here. But that feels impossible.

CHAPTER TWELVE

ELLA

The phone is ringing downstairs in the hall. The red carpet is soft under my bare feet as I run down to get it. It might be the bank.

'Hello, is that Ella?' An unfamiliar male voice, gruff-sounding.

'Ella speaking.'

'Hi Ella, this is Geoff from the swimming club.'

'Oh, hello Geoff. I didn't recognise your voice. Chris isn't here, I'm afraid.'

Geoff sighs. 'He's proving very elusive, your husband.'

'Haven't you seen him at the club?' Chris goes religiously to his swimming club, two evenings a week, plus Saturdays.

'I haven't seen him in weeks.'

I hold the receiver away from my mouth as I catch my breath, letting news of another of Chris's lies sink in.

'He's been very busy at work lately. Is it anything I can help with?'

Geoff's breath sounds in and out down the line, sighing once again.

'It's a bit awkward. Actually, no, it's not. He owes me some money that I lent him weeks ago and I need it back. He's not answering his phone, either. Is he alright?'

I decide I'm done protecting Chris. 'I'm sorry to hear that, Geoff. To be honest, I don't know what he's up to. Things are difficult at the moment, and he's moved out. I don't know where to, and I hadn't realised he'd stopped swimming. That's so unlike him.'

'My thoughts exactly. Look, I'm sorry to bother you.'

'It's fine. I wish I could do more. But I will be speaking to him and I'll ask him to get in touch.'

After the call ends, I sit in the hall for a while looking at Nancy's portrait.

'What's going on with your son, Nancy?' I say out loud. *The mortgage, the car, now this.* I haven't had a chance to ask him about the chair in the window display – he could have had keys cut to the shop. It seems unlikely, but after everything that's come to light, I don't know what to believe any more.

Normally Chris is addicted to exercise; his nights at swimming club were non-negotiable, he'd made that clear when we first started dating. And owing people money was so out of character for him. I think about my visit to his office, Tanya on reception, the way she looked at me and lowered her voice.

I make myself some tea and curl up on the sofa with my laptop. I open Tanya's Facebook page. Her puffy pout is all over her photos. *Is this really the kind of woman Chris would go for?* Based on my stake-out of the office the other day, there was nothing to make me suspicious. *And yet.* I still don't understand where Chris and I have gone wrong. We were dealing with grief, yes, but… round and round my thoughts go as I scroll through Tanya's pictures wondering how I can find out for sure. I hear the front door open and for a second I think it's Chris. Alice appears in the room. She's wearing smart cropped trousers with a high waist and a boxy jacket. She carries herself with a confidence that has always eluded me. I glance at my phone. It's late afternoon. The day has flown by and I've spent most of it thinking about Chris.

'Hi,' she says, placing her leather bag on the table.

'Hi. Good day?'

She nods. 'I've had an interview. Got myself a few hours' work at a garden centre. The money will help while I'm setting up my gardening business.'

'Great.'

'What's up?' she asks, picking up on the tone in my voice. Alice kneels down beside me; she's so close that I inhale the musky smell of her perfume. She looks at the screen. 'Who's she?'

'Her name's Tanya, she works with Chris. I think they might be having an affair.'

'Based on…?'

I shrug. 'The note I found. She works with him. I called in at the office and she was definitely looking at me strangely. I have to know who this other woman is. I'm terrified he wants to move her into the house.'

Alice closes the laptop. 'Stop,' she says. 'You're torturing yourself.'

'But I don't understand. The evening he left I was upset because I'd started my period. We were planning a family. The room you're in was going to be for our baby. It would have helped me get over Nancy's death, converting her room into a nursery. It's what she wanted too, she told me. She even knitted me a baby blanket.' Tears well up as I think about the pale yellow blanket she so carefully crafted for our future baby.

Alice makes us both some camomile tea and we sit together on the sofa. 'I'm doing it again, aren't I? All I've done since you arrived is cry.' I dig my knuckles into my eyes.

'Sometimes it's better to let it all out. Come here.'

She puts her arms around me and I give in to the emotion, loud sobs followed by silent tears, until I'm spent. I rest my pounding head on her chest and close my eyes. For the first time since Chris left I feel a glimmer of hope. At least I have Alice.

*

The next morning I hear the toilet flush, movement downstairs, the front door closing. I pull up my blind and see Alice running down the street, sleek in Lycra, taking long, purposeful strides. Cold air tickles my arms and I grab my white towelling dressing gown and fasten it tightly around my waist. It's so early. The bathroom door is open and an unfamiliar citrus smell hangs in the air. I hesitate on the landing, fighting the urge to look in Nancy's room. *The nursery. No, Alice's room*, I correct myself. A car engine revs outside and roars down the road, too loud at this time of the morning. When it's gone I become aware of a tapping noise. I pull my belt tighter and listen. I'm sure it's coming from Alice's room. The door isn't shut properly and it swings wide when I push it. The window is open and the wooden blind is rapping against the window frame. Half listening out for sounds of Alice returning, knowing I shouldn't be here, I look around the room. Tap, tap, tap: the noise plucks at my nerves. Alice's clothes hang neatly on a rack: dark trouser suits, elegant garments in bursts of deep orange and yellow. Books line the shelves, a thick Spanish dictionary, some Spanish fiction. A whole shelf of books on gardening, flowers and trees. A painting of three tall sunflowers reaching up to a blue sky rests against the wall. The smell of Chanel No 5 hangs in the air. A framed photo by Alice's bed snags my attention: a dark-haired woman, glass in hand, laughing. *Who is she?* Olive-skinned, she has almond-shaped eyes that seem to follow me, making me feel like an intruder. The tapping gets louder. Alice's bed is unmade, her pyjamas are folded on the duvet and a pang of shame hits me. *I shouldn't be in here*. I pull the door closed and go into the bathroom, dousing my face in cold water.

Downstairs, a door bangs and I hear pipes gurgling from the kitchen. For a split second I imagine it's Chris, back from one of his bike rides. Drinking a glass of cold water while he stands at the sink, sweat glistening on his forehead. I twist my gold wedding ring around my finger, remembering his cruel words at the office.

'*We're over, Ella, and the sooner you accept that and move on, the better.*' Disappointment sticks in my throat.

Chris is gone and he wants me out. How quickly my life has changed. Suddenly I have no one. My pale face gazes back at me from the mirror as I scrape my hair back into a band. Feeling sorry for myself is not going to get Chris back.

The coffee machine is a fancy Nespresso one which arrived with Alice. She swears she can't live without it. It's gurgling and the smell wakens my taste buds. Alice is crouching on the floor under the sink, looking into the cupboard.

'Hi,' I say, 'everything OK?'

She pulls her head out from under the sink. 'The cold tap isn't working properly. If I see a problem, I like to fix it.'

I frown. 'I've not had any problems before. Mind you, I'm not great with DIY. Chris took care of all that. Not very feminist of me, I know.'

'It's easy when you know how. I can teach you the basics if you like. You might need to know this kind of stuff now your husband isn't here.'

I clench my hands into fists. *No*, I want to shout. *He won't leave me, he can't.*

'Are you feeling better today?'

I nod, embarrassed at the memory of sobbing on the sofa.

'Where did you run to?' I ask, changing the subject.

'The heath. I hope I didn't wake you. It was so hot in Spain I got used to going out early, otherwise it was impossible.' Alice finishes her glass of water. 'Right, time to get ready for a day at the garden centre. By the way, I'll be out late tonight.' She disappears upstairs.

The idea of being alone all evening makes me want to go back to bed and stick my head under the duvet.

As soon as the front door slams I check the cold tap. It's all very well being determined to stay but not if I can't afford extras like replacing faulty taps. But the water runs out fine. *Alice must have fixed it.* She's making herself indispensable already and my mood drops as I acknowledge how much harder it would be for me if she wasn't here. I wish she wasn't going out tonight. I used to think that about Chris in the early days on a swimming night. I can't believe he's been missing swimming club for *her.*

When I'd been seeing Chris for a few weeks, high on infatuation, I remember how hard it was for me not to see him on his swimming nights. One Wednesday, when I couldn't get him out of my mind, when all I could think about was the way he made me feel, I decided to surprise him. The club met at the leisure centre in Swiss Cottage, and the café there was perfectly placed for watching the swimmers. I put on my new little black dress and waited for him in the foyer. When he'd emerged from the changing room, pink-faced and hair still damp, chatting to one of his swimming friends and wearing a blue sweatshirt instead the checked shirts he wore most days for work, he'd done a double take. Just for a second I saw a look of consternation cross his face, which swiftly turned into a grin. He said goodnight to his friends and took me out for dinner. But lying in bed that night, he told me it had to be a one-off. He loved me but he couldn't let me distract him from swimming. Exercise helped him process his thoughts, it was a necessity. I understood, and I found ways of occupying myself until I moved in and it was no longer an issue. But Geoff's call scared me, because whoever she is, she's obviously more important to him than his precious swimming.

Is he with her now?

I pick up my phone before I can change my mind. When he answers I'm lost for words initially as I'd expected him to ignore my call. Hope flutters. *Stay calm.*

'Hi Chris.'

'Hi.'

'Are you at work?' I can hear chatter in the background.

'Coffee break. I needed to get out for a bit, clear my head.'

'Are you OK to talk for a minute?'

'Yes.' He sounds wary. 'I am sorry, you know. How it happened.'

'I'm worried about you, Chris, is everything OK? I went to the garage and Ron said you were thinking about selling your car. Is that true?'

'Not selling. I was thinking about upgrading but I've changed my mind.'

'That's a relief. You need a car for work, don't you?'

'Yes. Look, I'm glad you rang, actually. I don't want us to fall out.'

'Me neither. I miss you.' I swallow hard. 'Are you still seeing this woman?'

He sighs. 'Just because we're talking doesn't mean I've changed my mind. I haven't been happy for the last few months, and this is for the best. I'm sorry, but it is.'

'What about marriage guidance?'

'I don't need to talk to anyone. I've made up my mind, Ella. You have to accept that.'

My stomach plummets. 'Geoff rang,' I say, trying to take control of the conversation.

'Geoff?'

'Yes, from swimming. Said he hasn't seen you there for ages. You never miss swimming. Can we meet, have a proper talk? I still don't understand what went wrong. Geoff said you owe him some money. Are you in trouble?'

'Of course I'm not in trouble. He had no right telling you that.'

'I'm your wife. He's worried about you too.'

'Well, he's got no need to be. I suppose you told him we've separated. I don't want everyone knowing my business.'

The word 'separated' stings. 'Why are you pushing everyone away? Can we talk, please?'

'I've got to go, this isn't getting us anywhere. And look, you should know, I'm thinking about putting the house on the market.'

'You can't. It's my home, too.'

'And I've given you plenty of notice. I won't change my mind, Ella. Don't make this difficult.'

The phone call leaves me reeling. He can't mean it about selling the house. This has to be *her* idea. I have to find out who she is, and what exactly is going on, starting right now.

CHAPTER THIRTEEN

ELLA

At five o'clock I'm parked outside Chris's office. I've taken the car, which I picked up on the way over, instead of the shop van as it has our distinctive logo on the side. Workers are scurrying out of buildings, hurrying ant-like along the pavement towards the tube. I'm paid up for the next hour, just in case. A parking attendant eyes me, one hand on his camera, and I look pointedly at the ticket displayed prominently on the dashboard. I almost miss Tanya, who emerges from the office door, chatting and laughing with a man. She's wearing a striking red suit. If she disappears into the tube this is a pointless exercise. But she crosses the road and aims her hand at her bright pink Fiat 500, making its lights flash. She slings her bag into the back seat and climbs in. I rev my engine and slide into the traffic two cars behind her.

We only drive for about twenty-five minutes before she pulls up outside a house in a tree-lined street in north London, Finsbury Park, not far from the park itself. Victorian houses stand to attention along this small street that backs on to the railway line. I drive slowly along the road, noting the door number – 12 – as she lets herself in. I drive out of the street and then return, noticing that this time the light has gone on in the front room downstairs. My guess is that the house is divided into flats, but I can't be sure without scrutinising the letter box. I park the car further down the road and walk back towards the house, pulling my jacket hood up.

I wonder if this is the first marriage she's wrecked. Anger quickens my pace and I hurry up the steps to the house before I can change my mind. There are three bells: Flat A is Barry Hutchinson, Flat B is T. Redmond, Flat C is Ali Hussein. *What would happen if I were to press the bell and confront her? Would she deny it?*

A loud clattering noise sends my heart racing before I realise it's a train trundling by. I hurry back down the steps to the safety of my car and drive off past Tanya's pink car, which looks like a blob of bubblegum compared to the other cars on the street. I've got what I came for. I have an idea.

The next morning in the gift shop is non-stop. It's my first time working with Sam and as Jamie said, she's a good worker. She deals with a steady flow of customers who are mostly buying greeting cards, chatting away with them as she takes payment and wraps gifts. My new card range is a hit and my cheeks flush as I hear Sam bigging me up to a customer – 'yes, Ella here makes them all herself'. Between orders she manages to tidy the shop and I'm free to get on with admin work in the back room, which smells of roses – Jamie has thoughtfully left a vaseful on the desk, a little card tucked underneath saying '*Smile, I love you xx*'. I stick it in my pocket as I don't fancy explaining my situation to Sam. I can't stop worrying about the house conversation I had with Chris. *She* has to have put the idea into his head. I add Tanya's name and address to our customer database before settling down to the accounts from last week.

The idea that was fermenting as I drove back from Tanya's is now in the front of my mind. I've got nothing to lose. I ask Sam to gift-wrap one of my premium notebooks with *Someone Special* embossed on it in gold letters. I'm banking on Tanya being chatty. It's a crazy plan, but I can't think of anything else. Doubt niggles at me: *what if it's not Tanya?* In that case, at least I'll know and I can eliminate her. Jamie is the ideal person for this task. He can make the delivery at the end of a working day. Chris never finishes work early; even in the beginning when he was smitten with me, he wouldn't stop work for anything. Although I also thought he'd never compromise about swimming. After Sam leaves I flip the sign on the door to show we're closed. But I stay inside, reluctant to go straight home to an empty house.

On the way home I hope that despite what she said earlier, maybe Alice will be in and I'll walk through the door to find heavenly smells in the kitchen, wine breathing on the side. But she isn't and my loneliness ricochets around the house. I take my laptop to bed with me, not wanting to sit in the silent, empty kitchen; the room that should be full of laughter and love. Sitting alone in the huge bed with only virtual company I can't help but remember the old days. I imagine Nancy bumping around upstairs, pipes clanking from the bath, a house full of life. I feel a pressure on my leg as Lady lands on it. She's taken to sleeping up here with me and I don't discourage her; I'm grateful for her presence. Chris used to insist on closing the door at night so she couldn't get in, but what Chris likes doesn't matter any more.

It was Lady who first alerted me to the fact that relations were strained between Chris and his mother. I'd not long moved in and was still pinching myself whenever I came home to Heath Street. Every time I stepped into the hall I'd pause and look up at the high ceilings, following the sweep of the red carpet with my eyes, up the spiralling stairs towards the beautiful bedroom we shared. On those first few days excitement woke me around six every morning and I'd drink a cup of steaming tea by the bedroom window, looking out over the misty green of Hampstead Heath. *Could this really be my life?*

One evening when Chris was out at swimming club, I'd made up a fire in the living room and I was looking at the tired paintwork, wondering if Chris would mind if I offered to decorate, restore the neglected interior, when I heard Nancy calling me from upstairs. She'd pulled herself up in bed on her twig-like arms, a hopeful look on her face.

'Would you read to me?'

Her request took me by surprise, followed by a flicker of joy – I was needed. She pointed me towards a book of Hans Christian Andersen fairy tales and I turned to the *Little Match Girl*, a favourite of mine since I found it during a lonely lunchtime in the school library at one of the many schools I attended. Nancy closed her eyes as I read, only to open them when Lady slipped into the room and jumped onto the bed before curling up on her chest. Once I'd finished the story I must have dozed off too, as I was awoken by the shutting of the front door and Chris calling out to me. Dozily I opened my eyes and imagined how pleased Chris would be when he found us like this. But all he saw when he came into the room was the cat on the bed.

'Mum!' His loud voice woke her up and Lady bolted out of the room, her fur brushing against my leg and making me shiver. 'What have I told you about that bloody cat?'

'Chris.' I'd not seen him like this before, and I was shocked at him waking his sick mother up.

Nancy's eyelids fluttered. 'Cat?' she said, attempting to push herself up.

'No, it's nothing, go back to sleep,' I replied, tucking her back into bed.

'She knows the cat isn't allowed in here,' he said and left the room. I settled Nancy back to sleep, holding her hands until her bony fingers went limp.

I found Chris at the bottom of the garden, staring out towards the pond. The garden wasn't so overgrown then. He appeared not to notice me until I touched him on the shoulder.

'I don't know what came over me,' he said. 'I should never have come back here.'

'What do you mean?'

He shrugged my hand away, but not before I felt a shudder ripple through his strong shoulders.

'Nothing.'

*

Snuggled up with Lady, remembering Chris's strange outbursts, I wonder about those moments when he'd flare up without explanation. Probing only made him withdraw, and Nancy feigned not to know what I was talking about. But there was something, I know there was.

Next time I'm in the shop I watch Jamie as he strolls back to work after his lunch break, crossing the square from his latest Tinder date. He's smiling, which is a good sign. The last guy he met turned out to be at least thirty years older than his profile and had a missing front tooth, although Jamie does like to exaggerate. I'm sending him out on this afternoon's deliveries, with Tanya neatly scheduled in the middle. Earlier this morning I'd logged on to her Facebook and she'd posted about how she was going to be stuck in all afternoon waiting for a boiler repairman. The timing couldn't be more perfect.

CHAPTER FOURTEEN

ELLA

I make a detour through the heath on my walk home, going the long way round, so I pass by the back of the house. I follow a trail that takes me up a steep grassy bank and leads on to a forestry path that twists its way up to the pond. I stop here, sitting on a bench that faces our house across the water. You can see our jungle garden from this point, the mass of weeds waving in the wind. I used to sit here when I first met Chris, pinching myself to make sure it was real. I knew then that I wanted to spend the rest of my life with him. I swallow back tears. *How quickly things change.*

Silence greets me when I enter the house and I wonder if Alice is out, but as I go through to the kitchen a breeze blows in from the open back door. For a moment I freeze. *What if Chris has somehow got in?* But I breathe in deeply, reminding myself he hasn't got keys. I catch sight of a flash of blue and I spot Alice sitting on the bench at the end of the garden. For a second I'm transported back to a summer's day before Nancy became bedridden, when I came home to find her sitting out there, gazing at the heath, her eyes glazed over. I'd taken a glass of iced water to her, and had gone to pull up a chair beside her when she'd shocked me by getting up and scurrying back across the garden and into the house. Her door had remained closed that evening and the next day she'd acted as if nothing had happened. That was the last time she ventured outside. I'd tried to talk to Chris about it, but he'd refused to engage.

I decide to surprise Alice, put the kettle on and make us some jasmine green tea. I slip off my shoes – it's warm outside and the grass feels soft underfoot as I carry the tray towards her. As I get closer, her voice carries in the breeze – she's on the phone, she's agitated, waving her hands about as she talks. I want to know who arouses such emotion in her, remembering the way she'd held me the other night, how safe she made me feel. I don't want to disturb her: it feels intrusive, her voice louder now. I step backwards, but a twig cracks under my foot and she spins around. She mutters into the phone and closes the call.

'How sweet of you,' Alice says. She takes the mug from my hand, and moves over for me to sit beside her on the bench. But I'm puzzled by the look of guilt in her eyes.

'I'd like to sort out the garden for you,' she says. 'It would be a perfect project for me to work on while I'm setting up my urban gardening business. I've had a look in the shed, there's some equipment there I can use.'

'God knows how old the stuff in there is. It must be full of cobwebs. My bike's in there, but I can't remember the last time I rode it. I'm not confident on the roads, and…'. Chris didn't like me cycling on the crazy London streets, but that's irrelevant now. I'm getting used to the stab of pain I feel every time a snippet of memory enters my head.

'So you don't mind?'

'No, not at all, you'd be doing me a favour. Chris wouldn't let me touch the garden. He said he'd hire someone but he never did.'

A blackbird hops onto the lawn, distracting me from my thoughts.

'Typical man, probably thought you weren't capable. I'd love to help out. And it would be great for my portfolio. I've got some design ideas – shall I sketch them out and we can talk it through?' Alice smiles when I nod. 'I'm excited to have something creative to do.'

'I can't help feeling guilty at making plans for the house without Chris. We should be doing this together.'

'It's bound to hurt,' Alice says and she glances at the blackbird. 'Are you sure you want to stay living here?'

'I won't leave.' My voice is loud and the bird shoots up into the clouded-over sky. 'You could never understand what it's like. You've got your parents, a family. Making a home was a luxury I never expected to have. If I can find out who this other woman is, I'll talk to her, make her understand. I think Chris is in trouble.'

I want Alice to like and respect me, yet my feelings seem to spill out when I'm with her. All I seem to do is burden her with my problems, but I'm so badly in need of a friend.

'I've misled you, haven't I?' I rub my hands over my face, sweep my hair back. A strand falls directly over my eye and she reaches over and pushes it away. The gesture is unexpected and it makes me want to cry. *Not again.* 'I should never have asked you to move in. Chris leaving, it's put me under incredible stress and it's not fair on you. I'm too needy.'

'Stop this now,' Alice replies. 'You're in a horrible situation. I've never been married, but I know what a messy break-up is like and I've had my heart broken too. Once. I'd never let it happen again.' She smiles ruefully to herself, rubs at a speck on her knee. 'I've broken a couple of hearts myself, if I'm honest. You told me about your situation when I moved in. I knew what to expect, I had a choice, I wanted to live here. I've chosen to cook for you, eat meals together, spend time chatting with you. I wouldn't do it if I didn't enjoy your company.'

'And the house,' I add. 'I've always felt it's a special place.'

'Wait until I've fixed the garden. Then it really will be special.'

*

Alice is home this evening and we watch a DVD together, a Spanish film with subtitles. After the movie Alice goes upstairs and it occurs to me that several hours have passed and I haven't thought about Chris once. *Baby steps.*

Alice's voice breaks into my thoughts; she's calling me from upstairs.

I haven't been in her room again since that first time. A lamp casts light on the woman in the photograph.

'Who's this?' I point to the photograph.

Alice looks over from where she's standing, 'My cousin. Look,' she climbs onto the bed and points at the corner where the wall meets the ceiling. A mushroom-shaped cloud covers the area, and I can't believe I've not noticed it before. She splays her palm on it and turns towards me. 'It's damp, it's spread all round the corner here.'

A sinking feeling swamps me. *More expense.* Another thing for me to deal with.

'I'm sorry, I honestly hadn't seen it.'

'Don't look so miserable, it's not that big a deal. You'll get it treated, won't you?'

'Of course,' I say, feeling queasy. Still, it'll give me a reason to call Chris; maybe he'll be missing me. Encouraged by the flash of hope I head back downstairs and call him immediately, but it goes straight to voicemail. *Why does this have to happen now?* It feels as if the house is taunting me, testing me, seeing how far I'll go to preserve it. Alice stays in her room but I can't relax. I go online to look up repair services. Mr Whiteley may be able to oblige; he did a good job on our kitchen in the summer. I leave him a message.

Unable to stop myself, I check Tanya's social media account. Instagram shows me she's in a bar with friends, all female, women wearing sashes round their bodies, one with a crown. Clearly a hen party. How I would love to be in a group of friends like that. When Chris asked why I wasn't having a hen party I made out it wasn't my style, too embarrassed to tell him I'd got nobody to invite. The couple of friends I'd managed to make got left behind when I was swept up by my feelings for Chris. My love for him consumed me.

I'm watching the news when Jamie calls me.

'It worked like a dream,' he says. 'I told her exactly what you said, that I was from Gorgeous Gifts on Cleveland Road, that her boyfriend was our one thousandth customer in the shop and his reward was for us to send a gift to a loved one on his behalf.'

'And?' I pace back and forth in front of the unlit fire.

'Well, it definitely isn't her.'

'How do you know?'

'From the way you've described him he doesn't sound like her type. She's way too high-maintenance – you should see those eyebrows close up.'

'Jamie—'

'Alright… I'm sure because when I mentioned her boyfriend she squealed "Ben, really?"'

'Ben?'

'Yes, Ben. She's a talkative type. Told me they haven't been going out for long, blah blah. She's pretty smitten, so I'd say it's unlikely she's having an affair.'

'Thanks, Jamie. You're a star.'

'Any time.'

So it's not Tanya. He's with *her*, this unknown vamp who pouts and poses in my head and makes me want to scream.

Trouble is, if it's not Tanya then who could it be?

Believing that Chris was with Tanya, however horrible, made me feel closer to getting to the bottom of what was going on. I felt like I was in control. Now I've taken a step backwards; not only is Chris having an affair, he's missed mortgage payments, stopped going to the swimming club he loves, owes Geoff money… Maybe something bigger is going on. *Could there be hope for us?* If only I still had Nancy to talk to.

Up in my room I give in to a wave of sadness, struck by a memory. I was on my laptop one evening, exhausted from settling Nancy after a chemo session but needing to complete an order. Chris had come up behind me and hugged me close. '*I love you,*' he'd said, '*for everything you're doing for Mum, and for just being you.*' I'd relaxed against his warm torso, luxuriating in his arms. I'd waited my whole life for someone to love me. Protected, that's how he made me feel. *How can it all have gone wrong?* There's a tap at the bedroom door and Alice appears in the doorway.

'You OK?' she asks.

I let out a long sigh. 'The usual, just driving myself mad, wondering where Chris is, who he's with, what he's doing.'

'This other woman will be just as insecure, remember that.'

'I suppose.'

'You're still hoping you'll get back together, aren't you?'

I bite into my cheek to stop myself from crying.

'You've got to stop doing that, babe. Never let a man take you over. It isn't going to bring him back. The best thing you can do is show him what he's missing, make it look like you don't care. You know, play hard to get. As soon as he thinks you're not bothered he'll come running back, trust me. Not that I want that, mind, I'll be out of a home.' She gives a rueful smile. 'Fancy a cuppa?'

I think how different the house would be without company. Silent, empty, lonely.

I nod. 'I'm so glad you're here, Alice.'

'Don't worry, I'm not going anywhere.'

DIARY

Kit went to the pub with his father tonight. Edward gave him no choice, said he was a man now. Kit hesitated at the door, looked back at me as if he wanted to apologise. It warmed me to see a fleeting glimpse of my little boy. He's all too familiar with the state his father is in when he staggers home after closing time, and I warrant he'll not be looking forward to that. I hope he's sensible and doesn't inherit his father's fondness for ale.

I went up to Melissa's room, glad of the opportunity to speak to her while the men were out. Men! How can my son be a man already? She was listening to music with her headphones in and jumped when I entered the room; she hadn't heard me knock. I perched on the blue-painted wooden chair she'd had since she was a girl, told her we needed to talk. I told her that her dad's been asking where she goes of an evening. It isn't safe for a young girl to wander these dark, tree-lined streets with the pond and the wilds of Hampstead Heath behind. I don't need to remind her of what happened to young Jodie Lawson last year; I shudder just thinking about it. For once I agree with Edward. Melissa tried to argue but she knows she can't disobey her father and I promised we wouldn't stop her going to youth club on Fridays, as long as Kit could pick her up. She scowled, but nodded in the end before sticking her headphones back in and shutting me out. I can't help thinking about Sylvia next door. Doris's daughter is a good girl, never any problem. But I wouldn't change my Melissa for the world. Her father, now that's a different story.

LATER

Kit arrived home before Edward, steady on his feet, my sensible boy. I was in bed already, but listening out, unable to sleep until I knew he was safely home. Edward says Kit is an adult now, but he will never stop being a child to me. There's no point waiting up for Edward. I hope he'll crash out on the sofa, as he often does. He's always up early, says only fools have hangovers. But the results are starting to show on his face: red, broken skin, hollow bags under his eyes and a scar on his cheek from falling and cutting it.

11 APRIL 1996

Edward left for work in the early hours; only Kit and I were up for breakfast, slices of hot toast and orange juice for him and a cup of weak tea for me. I can't remember the last time I had breakfast. Kit ate quickly, grunting at my attempts to make conversation, shrugging my hand away when I picked a crumb from his hair.

As he left the kitchen he hesitated at the door, throwing words at me like weapons: 'Best avoid Dad tonight. I've told him Melissa's secret. He's not best pleased.'

The word *secret* buzzed inside me. I knew it. I didn't even stop to clear the breakfast things before rushing upstairs to question Melissa. I knew she'd been keeping something from me. Silly girl, doesn't she realise women have to stick together? She blanked her face, feigned not knowing what I was talking about, until I said her father had found out and she might want to have me on her side. She ran from the room when I told her that, her face porcelain white, and I heard retching sounds coming from the bathroom. Her father is making her ill. Just like he's made me ill for twenty years and counting. I retched after dinner last night too, but unlike Melissa I voluntarily expelled the food from my body.

I waited for her outside the bathroom, folding my arms around my protruding ribs, counting them with my fingers.

I made sure I was tucked up in bed before Edward and Kit returned. It was so late but I find it impossible to sleep until both my children are home. I heard Edward stumbling through the front door, the low rumble of Kit's voice, footsteps ascending the stairs. Before I fell asleep I said a prayer for my son, asking God to protect him from becoming like his father. But I fear I am too late.

CHAPTER FIFTEEN
ALICE

Staying in the mother-in-law's room was tougher than I expected. When I found out that she had died in there I must admit that made me stop and think. *Did I really want to go through with this?* But I had no choice.

My room contains a bed, some shelves and a wardrobe. At first I just hung up my clothes and placed Olivia's photograph by the bed. But I quickly changed my mind and put it away. Unsure, I got it out again. I sat for a long while and looked at her deep brown eyes and cried at what I'd done. '*Running away*', she'd called it and she was right. But this time it was for all the right reasons, only I couldn't tell her that.

The first night was tough. Once I'd closed the door the room seemed to come alive. It was a windy night and the garden was a swaying mass down below, taunting me. I stood for ages looking out at the overgrown garden wondering how long it had been like that. It was going to make everything so much harder. I closed the blind, but that didn't stop the relentless swishing sound.

Ella had gone to bed, I made sure of that. But I still couldn't settle, images played out in my mind: *Nancy lying in bed, frail and dying. Dead.* Ella had only mentioned it in passing; of course she wasn't about to dwell on the fact that a woman had died in the room I was about to move into. She said she'd understand if

I wasn't comfortable with it and gave me the choice of the box room, a tiny square room which was used for dumping stuff in, but that was out of the question. Just thinking about it made me feel claustrophobic. Besides, it was no good to me as it didn't look over the garden. No, this was a challenge. One I was not sure I'd get through on that first night.

The wind intensified outside and the eerie whooshing sound from the garden grew louder and the window rattled in its frame. I plugged in the electric heater; the high-ceilinged room was freezing. Despite my thickest pyjamas I couldn't get warm. Ella had mentioned there was some spare bedding in the wardrobe so I felt around on the top shelf, pulling out what seemed to be a jumper. It was larger than expected and as I yanked it down, I saw it was a blanket. It was identical to one I'd had as a child.

I looked around the room with its freshly painted walls and sparse furniture. A room was not going to get the better of me. I picked up the blanket and pulled it around myself, inhaling the fusty smell, a hint of a fragrance. I closed my eyes, stood very still. Nothing bad happened. I got into bed. The window continued to rattle and pipes clanked around the house; the walls sighed and I wondered what they were trying to tell me. Eventually, I slept.

On waking I looked into Olivia's eyes in the photo I couldn't bear to part with. But all they did was reprimand me for running away. Unlike Ella, I'm not one to dig my heels in. Get out at the first sign of trouble, that's me, as Olivia so astutely told me. She should know. She was probably still wondering where I'd gone.

The second night, the room was less daunting. I unpacked my books and put a painting on the wall to make it more my own. I had a purpose and each day I intended to get that little bit closer. I'd made progress that day, the seed had been sown. I dropped it in casually, just a suggestion, questioning whether Ella really wanted to live here with all those memories. She didn't know what she wanted and that's what I was there for: to help Ella see what was good for her. And to sort out the garden, of course.

CHAPTER SIXTEEN

ELLA

Today time trickles by with few customers to speed it up. I'm relieved to see that Jamie has moved the chair from the window. I'm idly watching the street opposite when a man with a grim expression strides towards my shop. As he gets closer I sit up with a jolt. It's Chris, and the package in his hand takes on a more familiar form. It's the gift I delivered to Tanya from her supposed lover and my heart knocks against my chest. He pushes the door hard, crossing the shop in two deft paces. Sweat glistens in his hair and his jaw is clenched tight.

'What is this, Ella?' He slams the package down in front of me and the handwritten card flutters to the floor. I pick it up, hands trembling. *How dare he leave me for someone else? How does he have the audacity to do this to me, his wife?* These thoughts give me strength and I'm able to meet his gaze, keep my expression calm and neutral.

'How did you get hold of this?'

'Tanya brought it into work. What are you playing at, Ella? Me and Tanya, really? She's twenty-three. Do you realise what you've done? Tanya's boyfriend had no idea who this was from, and now he's convinced she's seeing someone else. They had a massive row about it. Pleased with yourself, are you?' He pauses to gather his breath as his words burst out in quick succession like carefully aimed bullets.

I swallow hard. 'Younger model, midlife crisis, isn't that what this is?'

'What?' Chris's eyes flitter about as he concentrates, then he lets out a sigh. 'I've had work drinks with Tanya, along with the other staff. That's the only time I've been out with her.' He runs his hands through his hair, and I notice with satisfaction that his nails are bitten to the quick. Let him suffer. But in that moment he looks lost, vulnerable, and despite everything I feel a pang of sorrow; even now I hate to see him hurting.

His voice is quieter when he next speaks. 'Honestly, El,' Chris's use of the familiar abbreviation makes me melt inside, so rarely do I get close enough to anyone to ever merit that kind of endearment, 'this has to stop. Snooping, spying on her, it's not like you.'

'I just want to know who she is. I still can't believe this is happening to us.'

Chris sighs and his shoulders slump. 'Look, I am sorry. You haven't done anything wrong. It's me, not you.' He laughs without humour. 'That old cliché. But it's true. Since Mum died we've grown apart and I've changed. The sooner you can accept that, the better. I'm not going to change my mind and you need to think about moving. You'll thank me in the end.'

Heat fills my chest and sweat pricks my skin. 'I'm going nowhere.'

'We'll see about that.'

A card has been pushed through the letter box when I get home that evening; there's a parcel to collect from next door. I go straight round without bothering to take my coat off. I've never been inside the house next door. The hanging basket swings as the door opens and I get a glimpse of a dark blue carpet; the hall is lit by a dim yellow light. The neighbour opens the door wearing a stiff white shirt and braces and the scent of lamb chops wafts through from the kitchen.

'Hello, lovey. You'll be wanting this.' He stoops down and picks up a medium-sized cardboard box. 'I'm Mr Mortimer, by the way. We've not been introduced. I know your husband, of course.'

'Thanks for taking it in. I'm Ella.' I wonder what it is, as I'm not expecting anything.

'Chris called round earlier,' he says, and I almost drop the box. I grip it to my chest, knuckles white. 'He made quite a commotion. I was having a bite to eat with the telly on and I heard him calling your name. I went out to have a look to see who it was.'

He must have come straight round here after calling at the shop and found out about the locks. *Why did I taunt him?*

'Oh God, I'm sorry. He isn't living here at the moment. We've been going through a bad patch—'

'Look, it's none of my business. I wondered if he'd left, as I haven't seen him around. I used to hear his car leave bang on seven every morning.'

'He's moved out. It was very sudden.' It's hard to swallow and I focus on the parcel, blinking tears away. The address is handwritten in capitals, no postage labels. Not Chris's writing.

'Did Chris… my husband leave this?'

'No. I noticed it on the doorstep, thought I'd better take it in. Kids messing about, cycling up and down, you can never be too careful.'

'Thanks. I'm so sorry for all the disturbance. I'll speak to my husband, make sure it doesn't happen again. I'm sorry to bother you.'

'It's not a problem. I can keep an eye out for you, if you like. I might as well, I'm always here.'

'Thanks,' I reply, shame flushing my cheeks.

The writing on the box isn't Chris's, but he could have got *her* to write it. The wrapping suggests a female touch: glossy silver paper with a dark length of red ribbon tied in a bow. I sit on the garden wall to open it, eager fingers making hard work of the ribbon. *How can I find out who she is?* The Sellotape is wound tightly and I use my teeth to rip the ends instead of bothering to get some scissors. The cardboard springs open and I scream as a putrid smell hits me. A fly buzzes into my face and maggots crawl out from feasting on what looks like was once a pork chop. I manage not to drop the writhing mass as I rush over to the dustbin and hurl it in. My stomach cramps and I throw up over the grass.

Alice is standing in the kitchen, a mug of tea pressed to her chest, staring out at the garden, when I rush in. She doesn't hear me come in until my shoes clack on the tiled floor and she turns, tea wobbling in her mug.

'Hi.' She grabs a cloth from the draining board and dabs at the milky drops. 'Weeds, weeds, weeds. The garden is so wild, it's hard to see where to begin.'

My chest heaves in and out. I describe the parcel to her.

'That's awful, who would send you that? Come here.' She pulls me into a hug, strong arms around my back, her hair tickling mine, a familiar hint of musky perfume. I'm reluctant to let go.

'It has to be Chris. He came round apparently, couldn't get in, obviously. He didn't know about the locks.' I relay Mr Mortimer's account to her, omitting the part about my gift to Tanya, too embarrassed to admit what I've done to a young woman who is most probably innocent.

'Bastard. I think if I ever saw him I'd want to do him an injury.'

My phone buzzes in my bag. It's Chris.

'Don't answer, let him calm down. It will only upset you further.'

I take myself up to my bedroom with a mug of chocolate and listen to Chris's message:

'I can't believe you've done this – locked me out of my own bloody house. I did you a favour letting you stay there. You'd better start packing because I'm moving back in as soon as I can. If you're not out in the next two weeks I'm taking legal advice.'

He calls again repeatedly and I switch my phone off, shuddering every time I think about the maggots, the stench. My skin prickles and it's impossible to stay still. *Surely Chris can't have sent it to me?* I go over and over the possibilities. The only other potential culprit is *her*. An image of them lying in bed, conspiring with each other brings a further flood of tears. I slump in Nancy's rocking chair, which I moved into my room after she died, and I rock myself back and forth, gulping down tears. The aching need to talk carves a dark hole inside me. I'm transported back to the children's home, with nobody to speak to. I scroll through my phone and stop at Kate, but she gave up calling me after I let her down once too often, not wanting to leave Chris and the new home. She wouldn't want to know now. I'm dreading night-time when no doubt the rancid meat will haunt me in my dreams. I've never felt like this before, here. This house has always been my safe space. I hear footsteps coming up the stairs and I forget my worry about Alice thinking I'm too needy. I meet her at the top of the stairs, my face crumpling.

'Oh, honey, come and sit in my room. You shouldn't be alone when you're feeling like this.'

'Thank you,' I say gratefully. Her lamplit room is cosy and the house settles around me. I catch sight of the photograph by her bed. 'Your cousin looks nice.'

She looks confused for a moment, sees me looking at the photo and nods.

'She must be special for you to have her photo on display.'

'Yeah, I guess she is. Family, it's important, isn't it? Like you and Nancy.'

DIARY

EVENING

Today was a frenzy of cleaning. Over and over I scrubbed the house, as it's the first thing Edward notices when he's in a mood. If only the bleach could cleanse my memories, make them go away. I've found an elaborate hiding place for this diary. If Edward were to find it I don't know what he'd do.

Lunch was another cup of tea, my stomach churning. Afterwards I went for a walk on the heath, sat on my favourite bench opposite the house, looking across the pond. Spring is with us, and purple and white crocuses carpet the ground, yellow daffodil faces smile in the gentle breeze. I can't smile back. I sat for a long time, unable to stop thinking of poor young Jodie dredged up from the thick green pond water, life sucked out of her. Suicide, the verdict found, but her family refused to believe it. Sitting out here on the heath I reflect on Melissa's words, trying to anticipate what Edward will do. She's a young girl, what she's doing is normal, but Edward won't see it like that.

I had the fright of my life when I arrived home to see Edward's van outside. He should have been at work. I couldn't turn my key in the lock with my trembling hands and twice it dropped to the floor. When I finally got in I smelt smoke; he was standing in the kitchen, cigarette between his lips, still in his paint-splattered dungarees, an open can of beer stood on the counter. When he saw me he picked up the can and squeezed it slowly until it crumpled. Asked me if I knew about Melissa's boyfriend. He didn't believe me when I said I didn't, said it didn't matter because he was going to find out who he was, where he lived and he was going to 'sort him out'. He ordered me to meet Melissa from school and bring her straight back to the house. I did as he said, of course I did, I always do, but waiting outside the school it occurred to me if ever there was a moment to run, that would have been it. Take Melissa far away from him. Somewhere safe. But I couldn't leave Kit, no matter how he's behaved towards me lately. He's still my son.

Melissa wouldn't talk to me on the bus, just said she wanted to 'get it over with'. Edward didn't shout at her, but spoke in a low, cold voice that made my blood feel like ice. At least he didn't hit her. That he saved for me, once she'd been sent to her room after promising never to see the boy again.

But he didn't notice the determined gleam in her eye. She won't let her father control her life like I do, and I'm glad. He knocked me to the floor and kicked me in the ribs. I curled up tight and small until he had finished. When he'd gone off to the pub, slamming the door so hard the windows rattled, Melissa came out of her room and helped me upstairs, bathed my face, washed away the blood and put me to bed without saying a word. She's locked in her head like I am. It's the only way to survive.

CHAPTER SEVENTEEN

ELLA

A battered old van pulls up outside the house and Mr Whiteley emerges. His shoulder-length grey hair looks as if it needs a good wash. He takes his toolbox from the boot of his car and whistles as he walks down the path.

'Morning,' he says, pulling his grubby white baseball cap off.

'Hi.' I move aside to let him in, inhaling a smell of sweat and stale tobacco. 'Thanks for coming so quickly.'

He takes a pair of glasses out of his pocket and puts them on.

'You got lucky. I was booked to plumb in a new toilet for a bloke over in Hackney but he broke his leg and had to go to hospital. Which room is the damp in?'

'It's up in the bedroom, I'll show you.'

He wheezes as he climbs the stairs. He looks to be about fifty, and is small and wiry. I'm struck by how cold the room feels and I shiver. I haven't noticed that before.

'Ah yes.' He looks up at the ceiling. 'It doesn't look too bad.'

'No?' I let out a long sigh of relief. 'I hope you're right.'

Alice has taken all the books off the shelves and piled them up by the bed. The room smells faintly of her musky perfume. My eyes are drawn to the photo of her cousin and I wonder why Alice appears reluctant to talk about her.

'Can I get you a cup of tea?'

'Ooh, yes please. Strong as you can with three sugars.'

I go downstairs, hoping we've got some sugar and after rummaging around in the cupboards I find an unopened box of cubes. I daren't check the sell-by date. While the kettle is boiling I text Chris to tell him Mr Whiteley is checking a problem with the roof, postponing the inevitable call I'll have to make later. I'm going to confront him about the meat left outside; my stomach heaves at the memory.

'Cheers, duck,' he says when I take the mug of tea up.

'I'll leave it on here.' I put it down on the bedside table. A box of unopened contact lenses sits next to a glass of water. I hadn't realised Alice wore them. Usually it's easy to see the tell-tale edges. Her eyes are dark brown, framed with long, dark lashes, the kind I've tried to create with mascara since I was a teenager, so I can't help noticing them every time she looks at me. They're the kind of eyes you can lose yourself in.

It's hard to settle down to anything with a stranger in the house, but I stick the TV news channel on with the sound turned low so that I can hear if Mr Whiteley calls. I make myself a coffee and sit with the back door open, wondering how long it will take for Alice to sort the garden out. I'm sick of it looking like this. I go back inside when I hear my name being called. Mr Whiteley's placed the ladder on the landing and is looking in the loft. He's scratching his head, peering into the corner.

'Can you pass my torch, it's on the shelf in the bedroom. I thought there'd be a light up here. I've found something odd.' I fetch it and hand it to him. 'Thought I'd check the attic, see the roof area, but when I was feeling around in the dark for a light switch I found a hole in the wall.' He disappears into the loft with the torch and then I hear a muffled exclamation. Eventually his legs emerge, jeans clinging to his scrawny waist, the red waistband of his underpants visible.

'The roof looks alright up there and the space is empty. But I've found something.' As he descends I see he's holding a packet.

'Where I was feeling about, my hand disappeared into a hole. I shone the torch inside and found this.' He waves something at me, chuckling as he folds the ladder up. 'You'd be surprised the things I've found over the years,' he says, handing me the package. 'Looks like it was in a plastic bag but it's rotted away. Must be pretty old.' It's a square packet covered with brown paper, tied with string. 'I'll get my stuff and see you downstairs. Let's hope it's a wad of banknotes, eh?'

I turn the package over in my hands; it weighs nothing. Mr Whiteley talks as he follows me downstairs.

'I don't think it's damp as such, but a water leak. I'll need to inspect the roof. I'll just have a smoke in the van then I'll get up there, see what's going on. I'll knock when I'm ready to come back in so you know it's me.'

The small, flat package is intriguing. The string is tied so tight it takes me ages to undo the knot. Opening it, I see it's a small piece of embroidery in a wooden frame. A pale yellow background with numbers stitched in black in the centre. I turn it up the right way and realise it's a date: 30 July 1997. The date means nothing to me.

A tap at the door makes me jump. I go outside, where Mr Whiteley is loading his toolbox into his van.

'There are some loose tiles at the edge,' he points vaguely, 'they need replacing.'

'Is that something you can do?'

'I can,' he scratches his head, 'but I'm pretty booked up for the next few weeks. The shelves in the bedroom will need to come down once I've confirmed what the problem is so I can repair the damage to the wall. That other job, I'll be starting it tomorrow, the delay has put me back a bit. But if you want to find someone else—'

'No, I'll wait,' I say. I'd prefer to use someone I know. The thought of more expense lodges like a stone in my stomach. Chris is going to have to help me out. There's no avoiding it; I'll call him as soon as Mr Whiteley has gone.

'What was in the mysterious package?' he asks.

'Oh, just an old piece of embroidery. It's probably fallen out of an old sewing box. Strange, really.'

'Remember who found it if it turns out to be valuable,' he says as he gets into his van and laughs wheezily as he drives off. 'I've got your husband's details on file, shall I send the invoice to him?'

'Yes please.'

'Problem?' A gruff voice makes me jump. I hadn't noticed Mr Mortimer appear in the garden next door.

We both look up towards the roof. 'Do you know anything about the roof?' I ask. 'Has it ever been repaired before?'

'Not for years. I wouldn't be surprised if it was leaking. Same happened to my house. Cost me a fortune to get it fixed. Had to use half my savings. That put paid to the cruise I was planning, although my wife died and that ended that plan anyway. Didn't fancy going on my own.'

He looks forlorn and I pull what I hope is a sympathetic face.

I'll make sure Mr Whiteley gets his money, but it won't hurt to give Chris a scare. I need to confront him about that parcel – it makes me want to vomit every time I think about it. It's the least I can do. My gut twists as I think of my husband.

CHAPTER EIGHTEEN

ELLA

Once Mr Whiteley has gone, I call Chris. He doesn't pick up. I try calling repeatedly throughout the afternoon. I pop out to the bank to get some money and I check the account while I'm there and see that Chris still hasn't made a payment. Irritation propels me home and it grows each time Chris fails to answer his phone.

No lights or sound welcome me as I step through the front door and I feel a pang of disappointment that Alice is out, remembering her kindness last night. The warm glow I felt in her presence has evaporated and the dull ache that is Chris's absence is back. I sit down on the chair in the hall and gaze at Nancy's portrait.

A breeze blows through the hallway and I hesitate. Surely the back door can't be open? The kitchen is in darkness but a light glows in the garden. As I move through the room it becomes clear that the light is coming from the shed. It must be Alice, but I'm clutching my mobile as I snap the kitchen lights on, the back of my neck tingling as I go into the garden.

'Alice,' I call, and she pushes the shed door open. 'What are you doing out there in the dark?'

A pale yellow scarf covers her head, her face is smudged with dark streaks and her beautifully manicured hands are filthy.

'Hi,' she says as she switches the light off in the shed and comes into the house. 'I didn't notice it had got dark outside. I've been clearing out the shed. There are some tools in there I can make use of. I've loaded that wheelbarrow up with stuff. I'll put it back again tomorrow once I've finished.'

'You gave me a fright. For a moment there I thought someone had broken in.'

'This will save me buying a new set of tools. There are a couple of trowels and a large fork and spade. Would it be OK to use those?' Her face is sallow in the harsh kitchen light, and I switch the lamp on.

'You look done in. I'm surprised you managed to get into the shed. How did you know where the key was? I'd have had to hunt for it myself.'

'I scoured the kitchen and found these in a drawer.' She holds up a key ring with two keys on, a Yale and a large, old-fashioned key.

'Oh well done, you've done me a favour. The other one is for the cellar – I was wondering where that was. I'll put them in here.' I drop the keys into the drawer that is stuffed with takeaway menus, loose coins and elastic bands: a mess that used to drive Chris mad.

Alice rubs her eyes, stifling a yawn. 'I'm off to bed, I'm exhausted. Are you working tomorrow?'

I nod. 'I'm tired, too, I'll be going to bed shortly.' *But first I'll try Chris one more time.*

'I'll make sure I put everything back in the shed and leave it tidy. I've had some ideas of what I want to do – we could go through them this weekend if you like.'

'That sounds great.'

I fix myself a hot chocolate and take it up to my room, wrapping myself in a blanket and curling up in Nancy's rocking chair, as if I can protect myself from this difficult call I wish I didn't have to make. Images flicker through my mind as I wonder whether Chris is snuggled up too, with *her*. I've convinced myself she's the one sending me nasty packages, and that he knows nothing about it.

'Ella.'

On hearing his voice the fight drains out of me. 'I've been calling you all day, Chris.'

'I was at work. What do you want?'

I swallow down the hurt, determined to keep this businesslike. 'I had to get Mr Whiteley round, there's some damp in Al... Nancy's room,' I correct myself. 'The roof needs fixing, so I've booked him in but he's not free straight away. I'll need to pay him, Chris. And I'm worried about the mortgage.'

'Shit, I forgot. I'll sort it tomorrow, I promise.'

'All this is so unlike you. Having an affair—'

'I don't want to talk about that. What we should be talking about is why you've changed the locks. I can't believe you've done that.'

'Maybe I shouldn't have, but I was angry. And scared. Strange things have been happening.'

'What do you mean?'

'My car got scratched. And yesterday someone sent me some rotten meat in the post. It was disgusting. Was it you?'

'You are joking? Are you sure you're not imagining things? We've been there before, haven't we? You getting anxious about everything,'

'That's got nothing to do with it. This is different. I'm not imagining things. Is that what this is about? You're trying to set me up, aren't you? Make out I'm crazy. Anyway, Alice was here, she saw how upset I was.'

'Who's Alice?'

'My friend from the gym. Or maybe it was *her*.'

'Your friend?'

'No, of course not. *Her*. Your other woman.'

'That's ridiculous. It was probably kids messing around. I'm sorry that's happened, but it had nothing to do with me.'

I want to believe him. 'Maybe you're right, I panicked and perhaps I shouldn't have changed the locks, but... my emotions are all over the place. I still can't believe this is happening. Worrying about money doesn't help, and I can't help worrying about you. Plus, I told you before, didn't I, Geoff rang and said you haven't been answering his calls. Why haven't you been at swimming club?'

'Not this again. Because I fell off my bike and injured my neck. I had to go to A & E and I was told not to swim or do any kind of exercise for at least a month. Geoff must have my old number. I'll ring him.'

'So you're not in any kind of trouble?'

'Of course not. Why would you say that?'

'He said you owe him money. Have you paid him back yet?'

'He had no right to tell you that.'

'Are you sure nothing is wrong? We have to make sure the mortgage is being paid, we don't want to lose the house.'

'I've told you, I've had a lot on my mind, what with the bike accident… You don't need to worry about the mortgage, I promise to sort that in the morning. But we do need to talk about the house. It might be best to sell up: that way we can both have a fresh start.'

'No, Chris, no way.' I sit up and throw the blanket on the floor. 'I thought we were happy here.'

He sighs. 'You have to face facts, Ella. Things haven't been right between us for a while. Since Mum died. Accept we're over, think about moving on. The house is too big for you on your own. Wouldn't you prefer a nice flat somewhere?'

'No, Chris. Besides, I'm not on my own. Alice is staying here.'

'Staying for a couple of nights, you mean?'

'No, she's staying for as long as I need her.'

'You can't do that.'

'I am doing it. I can't afford the bills on my own.'

'For God's sake, why are you making this difficult?'

'Me, making it difficult? It's not me who's having an affair. Who is she, Chris? Why are you doing this? Were you seeing her when Nancy was alive? Did Nancy know?'

'I might have known you'd bring my fucking mother into this. I will not discuss her with you. This is pointless. I need a new set of keys cut.'

'Pay the mortgage and then we'll talk about it.'

I put the phone down and collapse, sobbing. Sleep eventually descends but in the early hours of the morning hunger wakes me and I remember I didn't eat again last night. My stomach is too churned up to rest and I lie awake going over my conversation with Chris. *Why won't he tell me who she is?*

I hear Alice's alarm sound from her room when I eventually go downstairs to put the kettle on. As I pad down the stairs I rub my eyes, seeing that the postman has been early this morning. There's something waiting for me on the doormat. All I can make out with my blurry eyes is a fuzzy brown and red shape. But as I get closer the object comes into focus and I let out a cry, recoiling in horror. A dead, bloody mouse lies on the doormat, and I cover my mouth with my hand, shocked. My heart thuds as Lady appears in the hallway, staring at me with unblinking eyes.

'You bad girl, you scared me,' I say, going into the kitchen to get a dustpan. She's never brought anything like that into the house before, but I guess there's always a first time. Yet when I bend down to scoop the broken body into the dustpan, I realise it's lying on a piece of paper. Confused, I pick it up and see that there's one word scrawled on it: *LEAVE*.

CHAPTER NINETEEN

ELLA

Alice finds me on the bottom step, unable to move. I point a shaky finger to the mess on the doorstep. She bends down to look and then flinches, stepping back.

'Ugh, that's gross. You go into the kitchen, I'll deal with it. That cat needs training.' She hasn't seen the note.

'Look closer, underneath.'

'Bastards.' She shakes her head as she reads it. 'Unbelievable. Go on, you go. I'll sort this out.'

I rest my head in my hands at the kitchen table, sweat dribbling down my back.

'Someone's trying to frighten you,' Alice says after she's disposed of my disturbing gift.

'It's working.'

'You mustn't let them know that, that's exactly what they want. It has to be Chris, right?'

'I spoke to him last night and he denied everything. Surely he wouldn't do this.' *Would he?*

'You didn't think he'd have an affair, or try to force you from your home.'

Alice is right. I don't know him any more. The Chris I thought I knew, *my husband*, has gone forever. *Does he hate me that much?*

She fetches two glasses of water and sits opposite me. I twist my wedding ring around my finger.

'Maybe it's time to stop wearing that.'

I shrug, tears threatening to spill over.

She pulls a face. 'Is Chris still wearing his?'

'I don't know.' *Another thing I don't know*. 'Maybe I should go to the police.'

'I know it's horrible for you, but I'm not sure the police would bother with it. Besides, the dustmen were emptying the bins when I took it outside, so the evidence is gone.'

'You're right. It's too trivial. I'd like to think it was kids messing around, but what with everything else that's been happening that doesn't seem likely. It has to be her, the girlfriend. If only I knew who she was.'

'Whatever you decide, don't let Chris see that he's getting to you. My mother taught me not to tell everyone my business. If the wrong people know you're hurting they can use it against you.'

'It's the first time you've talked about your parents. Did they mind you moving in with me?'

'I'm an adult, of course they didn't mind.'

The shutter has gone back down and Alice turns away from me, her dark brown hair swinging in one neat movement. *You don't give much away.* I wish I had even an ounce of her composure.

'Right, work beckons.'

She heads outside.

I clear away the cups and glasses from the table and pull on my rubber gloves to give the kitchen a good clean. Scrubbing the counter down, I imagine the mangled mouse and rub the cloth so hard on the surface that I build up a sweat. Even though the mouse didn't get further than the doorstep, the house feels contaminated. I empty the cupboards and stack everything on the table, washing the insides, hoping the smell of pine cleaning fluid would erase the mouse from my sensory memory.

I take a hot, lingering shower, wanting to scald the stench off me. Chris's half-full shower gel is still in the cubicle and I throw it in the bin. I want him out of the house and out of my memory. Opening the window to let in some air, I see Alice bent over the rockery in the corner of the garden. Dungarees would look scruffy on anyone else but Alice has the height to carry off the cropped, casual look and the faded denim contrasts well with her dark hair. Her flowery gardening gloves make me smile.

To take my mind off everything I fetch the piece of embroidery Mr Whiteley found, sit on a cushion on the floor against the radiator and study it. *1997*. Chris's dad would have been alive then.

Chris mentioned his father to me once and once only. It was the first time he brought me back to Heath Street. His mother had invited me for afternoon tea. I'd spent ages choosing a new dress; it was a summer evening and I'd worn a cotton dress decorated with large red poppies. Chris had met me in Hampstead Village. He'd taken my hand and walked me down towards his house; butterflies fluttered in my stomach. Once we got to the wooded area which runs beside the street, he'd led me gently away from the path. 'You look beautiful,' he'd said, pushing me gently against a tree, kissing me hard. He'd brushed a little piece of bark from my back before we'd rejoined the path. 'The house is the first one you see when you go round this corner,' he said and propelled me forward so I saw it first. And there it was: number 46, an old-fashioned lamp post directly to one side, making the bright red front door shine. A tall woman stood in the front garden and waved, the light picking out the silver in her hair: Mrs Rutherford.

'Please call me Nancy,' she'd said, clasping my warm hand in hers, which was tiny, her bones delicate and birdlike.

The fire was burning in the front room where a table was set out for tea.

We ate tiny square sandwiches and cakes from a tiered stand decorated with flowers. Nancy poured tea from a bright red pot. I couldn't take my eyes off her. A regal woman, she bore no resemblance to Chris with her ramrod-straight back, tweed skirt and frilly, high-necked blouse. Her long, thin fingers, emerging from the ruffles around her wrists, betrayed how frail she was. She was as delicate as the china teacup and saucer she drank from. She asked me lots of questions and I found myself telling her the truth without the usual shame I could feel bearing down on me whenever I thought about being in foster care, and my birth mother, who at that point in time I hadn't tracked down.

There was only one awkward moment. Waiting with Nancy while Chris went off to get our coats, I admired a photo on the old-fashioned mantelpiece of Chris as a child and another of Nancy with an older Chris, scowling behind his glasses. 'Do you have any photos of your husband?' I asked. Nancy's face appeared to shut down.

'No,' she said, and left the room. Despite standing in front of the blazing fire I felt a chill sweep over me. Walking back down Heath Street with Chris five minutes later, I told him what had happened, asking him if I'd done something wrong.

'We don't mention my father,' he said. 'I should have warned you.'

CHAPTER TWENTY

ELLA

The doorbell rings. It's afternoon and Alice is out in the garden, so I wander into the hall hesitantly. Images of the dead mouse and the rotting pork chop flash into my head. I see Chris on the doorstep and step back in surprise. I will my face not to react, but my fingers whiten as I squeeze the door frame tight. For a split second I want to wipe out the past few weeks, fling my arms around him and welcome him into the home we've created together. I put the chain on, inching the door open. He forces the door, splitting the chain and barging past me. My urge to hug him evaporates as the door slams.

Chris holds his hands up. 'I didn't want to do that, but you gave me no choice. This is my house.' He shifts about on his feet, clearing his throat. 'Can we talk? Neither of us want to involve solicitors. I'm sure if we sat down and had an adult conversation we could sort this out.'

I don't move and he clears his throat again. 'Can we sit down?'

I'm stalling for time, grappling with the battle going on inside me. 'How do I know I can trust you?'

'For Christ's sake, Ella. We have to sort this out. It's my house too, remember.'

'I'm glad you said "too", because the last time we spoke you mentioned trying to force me out. Who knows what you might do?'

'Ella, please.'

The lines around Chris's eyes add years to him and his shoulders sag. This isn't easy for him. Besides, Alice is in. He can't do anything while she's here. I shrug and relent, walking into the house, leaving him to follow me.

'Alice is in the garden, I'll just let her know you're here.' *Warn her*, is what I mean. He doesn't need to know we're developing a relationship, a friendship that is getting me through this, making the precarious raft I am floating on easier to navigate. 'Put the kettle on.' I want him to see this new assertive Ella who won't let anyone boss her around. I almost believe my own hype, save for the weak feeling in my legs as I walk into the garden. I can't see Alice, and the ground is damp from this morning's rain shower. I slip my garden shoes on, not wanting to get my new mules wet crossing the muddy path.

'Alice!' I yell.

'Behind the shed,' she calls back.

I find her bending over a pile of weeds.

'Chris is here.'

She looks alarmed. *She cares about me.*

'It's OK, he's calmed down, wants to talk. I'm making a point of letting him know you're here, just in case. That way he won't try anything.'

'No worries. I'll respect your privacy, but if you need me just shout and I'll come to the rescue. Not sure I can promise to be civil, though.'

I laugh and I make sure I'm still smiling as I head back into the kitchen.

'Who's your friend?'

'I told you, Alice. You know, from yoga class.'

'I don't remember her.'

Because you were never here.

Chris has got the mugs out and he's sniffing the milk. His presumption makes me bristle.

'I'll have a green tea,' I say, looking pointedly at the mugs. He pulls a face.

'Since when?'

'You walked out on me, remember. Things change.' I don't want him knowing everything about me. I'm being petty and childish, but this small victory keeps me from dissolving into a puddle and begging him to stay.

'You're not scared to see me on your own, are you? I'm me. I'm still the same person, Ella—'

'No you're not. My Chris wouldn't have walked out on me, threatened me with homelessness, and most of all he wouldn't be screwing someone else.' My cheeks burn as I stare at him, but he doesn't deny it. He's still seeing her, kissing her red, pouty, glossy lips whenever he wants. I curl my fists up inside my pockets, not wanting to show my emotions to him, not willing to give him any part of me. Whatever he wants to talk to me about, I won't make this easy for him. Chris sits at the kitchen table, flicking through his post, tea in front of him. He's left my mug on the side. I never used to notice his selfish little actions. But I do now. He's slumped at the table, shoulders hunched, with a hint of a protruding belly, no longer the fitness-obsessed man I first fell for. He doesn't look happy.

'What is she doing out there?' he asks.

'She's working on the garden.'

He narrows his eyes. 'Doing what?'

'Redesigning it. She's developing her business as a landscape gardener. She's good.'

'How long exactly is she staying for?'

'A few months, not sure really.'

Chris slams his hand down on the table and the tea wobbles in our cups. 'What are you playing at? You shouldn't have invited her to stay. I want you out of here. And leave the garden alone. It's a major project. It will take months to sort it out.' *I hate the way he always flares up.*

'So what? What harm can it do to make a start? I'm sick of not having a decent garden. Anything would be better than that jungle. You never got round to it, no matter how often I asked, and now you've walked out I'm finally getting all those things done. So don't tell me what to do. Besides, I told you about the damp in Nancy's – I mean, Alice's room. Mr Whiteley inspected the roof and the tiles need repairing. He's not free for a couple of weeks, but you'll need to help me with the cost of the repairs. I can't manage it all on my own.' I'm gripping the table by the end of my speech.

He runs his hand through his hair and sighs. 'I don't want to undertake any repairs at the moment, which is what I've come to talk to you about. I want to put the house on the market.'

His words wind me. 'No, Chris. After all we went through to remortgage? You can't afford it on your own – have you forgotten how I stepped in to help you buy it? With the inheritance tax you would never have been able to afford it. I did it because I loved you.' My voice wobbles. 'Imagine what Nancy would think. She was so happy I helped you out – she told me so, more than once. You know she always hoped your sister would come back, so at least you would be here if she did.'

*

I remember Nancy sat in her rocking chair, a knitted shawl around her frail shoulders. Her cheekbones were increasingly visible, yet she still maintained her sparrow's appetite, despite my efforts to get her to eat. I was standing at the window looking down at the garden. The weeds were knee-high at that time.

'It used to be full of flowers, you know, when we first lived here,' she said. 'I spent hours out there, tending it. I loved the explosion of colour when I opened the back door, sunflowers smiling into the kitchen at me when I washed up.'

'I've offered to help restore it, you know, but Chris won't let me,' I replied. 'I don't understand it.'

'Don't bother him with it, he's a busy man.' Her eyes glazed over and she went somewhere far away in her head. That was happening more and more. 'Not the garden.' She reached for my hand, her cold fingers clasping mine, exerting pressure to make me listen. 'Promise me something, Ella. Never let Chris sell this house. It has to stay in the family.' Her thumbnail dug into my palm and the muscles flexed in her spindly arms. 'I've been getting my affairs in order.' It was my turn to squeeze her hand, scrunching my eyes tight at the same time, not wanting to face the inevitable. 'I've instructed my solicitor to look for my daughter. I had to try. If he fails to locate her then the house will go to Chris, and to you, of course, now that you're married. I see how you love it here. This house needs some love.'

*

'Did Mum really believe she would come back? That will never happen.' Chris drags me away from the memory.

'I wish you'd tell me why she left. Nancy wouldn't talk about it either.'

'Because there's nothing to tell. She was a selfish teenager, that's all. Will you at least think about selling?' Chris is looking at his tea as if he's just noticed it. He takes a quick drink and I watch his fingers as he drums them on the table. I stiffen; he's removed his wedding ring, and any notion I have of feeling sorry for him evaporates. Underneath the table I slide my ring off and put it in my pocket. I won't be wearing it again. My chair screeches as I get up and he looks surprised.

'I'd like you to leave now.'

'Will you think about what I've said? It makes sense for us to sell, especially with the roof problem. You don't need the hassle.'

Too right I don't.

He gets to his feet. 'Shame I didn't get to meet your room-mate,' he says, making us sound like students playing at house. 'She won't stay long, what with the damp and everything.'

'She isn't going anywhere.'

Alice doesn't appear and I'm relieved when Chris gets up, taking the pile of post I've been keeping for him: letters, circulars and junk mail, encircled by an elastic band. Let him deal with the rubbish; it's the least he can do.

At the front door he shoves the pile into his suit pocket and I notice a stain on his sleeve, his crumpled shirt, the crinkled lines around his eyes. I'm glad he's suffering, too. I fold my arms and wait, pushing away the seed of an idea that has me in its grip: *could I really lose this house?* I expect him to go to his car, but I don't see it anywhere. It must be parked nearby as the road is pretty full. I watch until he disappears from sight before I close the door. I put my gardening shoes on and head outside to join Alice; my legs are wobbly as I walk to the shed. My hand fiddles with the ring in my pocket; it feels cold between my fingers. The garden fork is laid across the wheelbarrow, but there's no sign of her. Lady lands on the shed roof, making me jump.

'Where is she?' I ask the cat. Lady stares, unblinking, before springing to her feet and following me back to the house. I notice that the lid on the rubbish bin has fallen off. *Must be the dustmen*, I think, remembering how Alice said the mouse had been taken away. But the bin is full. *That's odd.* The memory of the bloody mouse makes me shiver and in that moment a wave of loneliness engulfs me. I'm confused as to where Alice has gone and I can't help feeling let down. *What if Chris had turned nasty?* Maybe I can't depend on her after all.

Maybe I really am all alone.

CHAPTER TWENTY-ONE
ALICE

The husband came round yesterday. It was a close call. Ella wanted me to meet him, but I don't think it's a good idea. It's best if I keep myself nice and separate. That way, he can't associate me with her and accuse me of interfering. *If only he knew.*

Ella was stressed after his visit, so I made her a gin and tonic with a slice of lime. I stuck to tonic, my glass piled high with chunks of ice. Evenings are getting chillier as winter approaches, but I felt closer to her outside.

'He wants to sell the house.'

I rattled the ice around in my glass. I wasn't expecting that.

'He said we should both have a fresh start.'

'Don't do it,' I said, and she looked surprised. 'It's a trick. Think about it. Gorgeous house, worth, what, at least a million and a half, in one of *the* most desirable areas in London. He's having an affair. You've changed the locks and it's unsettled him. He didn't expect a fight from you, did he?'

'Probably not. He implied I'm falling apart, imagining things.'

'My point exactly. He wants you out and her in.'

Her pale grey eyes widened and her bottom lip wobbled. She was sat with her back to the garden and her white jumper glowed as the light faded and the plants and bushes around us morphed into indistinct shapes. Moonlight danced on her fine blonde hair, which hung to her shoulders. It has grown since I first met her and it suits her heart-shaped face. 'He'll deny it, but I bet that's his game.'

Ella drank eagerly, as if she wanted the ice-cold liquid to freeze out the problems piling up around her. I refreshed her drink twice more over the evening, and it was sweet the way she loosened up, got giggly; I'd never seen her like that before. Her face was beautiful when she smiled and it stirred up feelings inside me but I forced myself to focus on my real purpose. *Ella is an unexpected diversion I can do without.*

I spread my plan for the garden out on the table and talked her through my ideas: flower beds, a small vegetable patch, a lawn and a decking area. Wind raced through the garden and all the vegetation moved in a blurred mass. Ella's movements were jerky and she made enthusiastic noises. I went along with her pretence that she was taking it all in, ignoring the fact that she was obviously drunk.

'I just want lots of flowers, like Nancy used to have,' she said. 'There must be some photographs somewhere. Hidden in this house. So much is hidden in this house.'

'What do you mean?'

'Lots of flowers, that's what I mean.' Her voice was loud and the cat twitched awake and stretched before deciding it was safe to go back to sleep.

'Look at you,' Ella said. She clasped her glass between both hands and stared at me with those grey eyes framed by dark eyelashes. The intensity of her gaze made me look away.

'I wish I had your confidence. Have you always been like that?'

I crunched on an ice cube. 'A gap year travelling did the trick. I had a place lined up at university to study architecture, but once I'd had a taste of other countries and cultures, eternal sunshine, I knew it wasn't what I wanted. I liked the independence, learned how to look after myself. Rely on yourself, that's what you need to do. Stand up to Chris. I've got your back.'

'I'm so glad we're friends.' Her words sounded slurred and soppy. 'Chris never wanted to sit out here, I can't understand why.' A gust of wind rushes through the greenery behind her and the hairs on my arms stand on end.

Ella finished her drink. 'I've got to pull myself together. I've spent ages looking at property law online, but it's so complicated. Jamie said I have rights, but I can't help feeling guilty. Chris grew up here.'

'Yes, but how will you feel when he's moved her in? Will you care about his hurt feelings then?'

'No.' She stood up quickly and the cat scarpered into the bushes. 'I won't let that happen.'

After Ella had gone upstairs I sat out in the dark and wondered whether I was right about the husband's game. *Everybody has a game.* Even Ella, but she doesn't see it that way yet. *She will.* Her game is to get the house. And my game is – I can't put it into words, not even to myself.

I took action the following morning. The cellar key hadn't been used in a while and it was a struggle to get in, but I wouldn't take no for an answer. A scrabbling sound made goose pimples pop all over my body and fear rose into my mouth. *What if I'd got it all wrong?* The dark was impenetrable. Several steeps stairs stretched into the unknown and I steadied myself against the narrow walls as I descended, dread mounting. At the bottom my fingers crept over the cold brick, feeling around for a light switch, finding only cobwebs, dirt sticking to my fingertips. I took a few steps forward, the dark clearing a little as my eyes adjusted. I felt further along the wall and landed on a switch. A pop of yellow light illuminated the room: one light bulb hung from the ceiling. An old-fashioned desk in a corner was surrounded by cardboard boxes. A poke at one of them with my foot revealed a pile of books. Several old suitcases littered the floor, along with a couple of crates of wine. Dust coated most of the items and the musty smell tickled my throat, making me cough. This would take me far longer than I had anticipated. The scratching noise started up again, but it wasn't the creatures that I couldn't stand any longer. I picked up the box closest to me. It was heavier than I expected, but no match for my fitness. I groped for the light switch, shutting the room off from my sight, and went back up the stairs as fast as possible.

Once the box was safely stored in the now orderly shed I went up to my room and dug out the pack of cigarettes I kept for emergencies. I made a strong coffee and took it out into the garden. Smoking helped me control my breath. The darkness of the cellar had taken me by surprise and my mind had run away from me. Convincing myself it was due to lack of sleep, I thought about the best way to tackle the room. Because if there was the teeniest chance what I was looking for was in there, then I was going to make sure I found it.

The next day I went and had a nose around her shop. The colleague is only a boy, a pretty boy at that – Jamie. It's funny how he didn't have a clue who I was, considering he's heard so much about me – and it's thanks to him I got the room. He was too busy chatting on the phone, what was obviously a personal call. The store is a gorgeous boutique gift shop, and I love the way it's kitted out with retro signs and furniture. Ella said Jamie was responsible for all the branding – maybe he could give me a hand with my own business when the time comes. But then I remember: that won't be possible once all this is finished.

For someone who runs her own business, Ella isn't very good at the practicalities; she's relied on her husband to sort that side of things for her. *So different to me.* I like to be the one in control. Financial issues baffle her, like the mortgage. I've offered to go through the mortgage documents because I'm wondering why a man who runs a successful business is defaulting on payments. There has to be a reason for it. Either it's a ploy to get his wife out so he can move the mistress in, or he's in financial trouble. She'd told me how he built up Rutherford Carpentry single-handedly, the likeable boy done good, with his London accent and twinkling eyes. But I'm far more interested in her. And I can tell she is interested in me. She lapped up the tale I spun her yesterday, about my gap year and my abandoned university place. But lying in bed reading last night, the words on the page of my book lost focus, and not because they were in Spanish, but because I was seeing Ella's face imprinted like a hologram hovering over the page. I rubbed my finger over the page, as if to erase her. That was the point at which I threw the book on the floor, rolled over and looked into Olivia's eyes. It was happening again.

CHAPTER TWENTY-TWO

ELLA

Alice is out this evening and I wonder where she is and who she is with. She hasn't mentioned any friends in London by name, but I guess she's friendly with the guys at the garden centre. I sort out the relevant documents for her to look through and leave them out for her. The door to her room is open and I stand on the threshold, my eyes drawn to the photo of the woman she keeps by her bedside. '*A cousin*', she said. *Why is she so special to you?* I wondered. I want to be special to Alice, too.

Standing at Alice's window looking down towards the heath, I picture where we sat last night, recalling how my mind swam with alcohol, my thoughts becoming hazy. Alice's features appeared softer in the twilight, making me aware of her plump mouth, her deep brown eyes, so different to mine.

I choose one of the Spanish films she has left downstairs and spend the evening watching it, but reading the subtitles makes my eyelids droop and I allow myself to close my eyes for a moment.

The screensaver is jumping about on the screen when I wake. The house is quiet and Alice isn't home yet, even though it's almost midnight. I go round each room switching everything off, noticing Lady's untouched bowl of food, her full dish of water. I haven't seen her all evening. In fact I haven't seen her for hours. Reluctantly I open the back door and step outside.

'Lady,' I call, feeling conspicuous, even though everything is dark. The night is still and a dog barks in the distance. 'Lady, where are you?'

Silence. A bird calls out, a long, wailing cry, and I hug my arms around myself because of the cold. *Where is she?* After a few more seconds I give up and go inside, making sure the back door is firmly closed before going to bed.

Something wakes me in the night, and when I look at my phone it's four o'clock. Alice must have got home long ago. My bladder is full and I go to the bathroom before checking in on Alice. Her door is closed, so she's back. Darkness presses against the window, but a light catches my attention. Someone is in the garden moving around; the light snakes along the path, drawing circles. *Who is out there?* The light is moving along the path now, towards the house. I lean my face as close to the glass as I dare and I make out the murky shadow of a person moving slowly. Fear ripples through me. I grab my phone from my room. My fingers hover over the phone keyboard: *should I call the police? Should I wake Alice?* She won't thank me after getting home so late. As I stare the light goes off. I peer into the darkness, but no shapes crystallise in my vision. Going downstairs, I'm careful to step over the creaky stair, breathing as softly as possible. I stand for ages in the kitchen, my bare feet icy on the stone-cold floor; I watch the blackness outside, but the light doesn't reappear. A chill runs down my spine. *Did I imagine it?*

I make myself a tea and sit in the kitchen until my pulse has stilled and I'm sure there is nobody in the garden. I head back to bed, not expecting to sleep, but miraculously I do. When I wake light streams in through the window but the happenings in the night are foremost in my mind. Outside, the garden looks normal; nothing is knocked over or out of place. I tell myself my mind was playing tricks on me; I've been so tired lately, my emotions have been all over the place. But the fear persists, my hands shaky, spilling tea over the bed. *Get a grip, Ella.*

While I'm standing at the window Alice emerges in a pair of ripped denim jeans and a cashmere jumper, carrying a mug. She sits at the garden table and leafs through some papers, running her hand through her hair in a familiar gesture. I pull some clothes on and go down to join her. In the kitchen Lady's food remains untouched.

'Hey.' I slide into the green iron chair next to her, making her jump. The large silver ring she wears on her thumb glints in the morning sun. It's a beautiful, crisp autumn day. 'Have you seen Lady? She didn't sleep in my room last night.'

'No. I don't think so.'

'It's unlike her.'

'She's a cat. Cats like to do their own thing.'

Like you.

'Doing some work?'

Alice picks up the papers and taps them on the table to arrange them neatly, closing the folder. I catch sight of the familiar handwriting and reach out to take it from her.

She rakes her hand through her hair. 'Your mortgage papers – I presume you left them out for me.'

'Yes, I did. But you don't have to, you know.'

'You were upset about Chris defaulting on his payments. I don't like seeing you upset.'

Our eyes meet and I look away, an unexpected, warm feeling inside. 'I meant what I said. I'll stand up to him. There's a woman who often comes into the shop, she's a solicitor. I'll engage her if it becomes necessary.'

'Good. Don't let him intimidate you. I'll have a look through them anyway.'

'Thanks.'

A lone bird tweets from the roof and I'm reminded of how threatening the garden felt in the dead of night. I look around for Lady; I can't help worrying. 'Did you hear any noises in the night? I thought I heard someone in the garden.'

'I was shattered when I got back, crashed out right away. What kind of noises?'

'Footsteps, and I thought I saw someone with a torch. But without my contact lenses my vision isn't great – it was probably a bush, a trick of the moonlight. I'm sure it was nothing.'

'No, you're right to be alert.'

'What makes you say that?'

'This is London. I wondered about the anonymous note you got, the sender. If Chris's other woman sent it she's bound to be suspicious he's still seeing you. She might be a bit unhinged. Deep down she must know she can't trust him. Men don't change. He's cheated on you, he'll most likely do the same to her. Maybe not for a while, but…' Alice shrugs, leaves the thought hanging in the air. It comforts me, the idea of him hurting her too. It's so easy to blame her instead of him.

'Or maybe she feels threatened by me?' The thought glimmers into a flame of hope inside me. *Why can't I let him go?*

'Don't get your hopes up.' Alice's voice is gentle. 'I don't want you to get hurt.'

I nod, but my hands cup the flame of hope, nurture it, willing it back to life.

'Right,' she says, 'this garden won't organise itself. I need to start working.'

She pulls on her flowery garden gloves and I laugh. 'What?'

'Everything you wear looks so stylish. Look at me in this old sweatshirt.'

'You look lovely.'

I smile, blushing as I gather our mugs together. I'm about to go inside when Alice lets out a cry. I turn, tea slopping everywhere.

'What is it?' I put the mugs back on the table. 'Alice, what's the matter?' Her face is buried in her hands.

'No, Ella, don't come any nearer. It's Lady.'

I rush forward despite Alice's protests and stop dead when I see Lady lying on the ground, rigid, flattening the long grass. I drop to the floor and lean over her. 'Lady, no, poor Lady.'

Alice kneels beside me and puts her arm around me. 'I didn't want you to see,' she says, her voice raw.

'But what's happened? She doesn't look hurt.' There's no sign of any injury, no blood. I burst into tears.

'Come inside,' Alice says, leading me indoors. 'Was she old?'

I nod. 'About eighteen. She was Nancy's cat.' Tears roll down my face.

Alice pushes a box of tissues in front of me. 'You're shaking. Put this on,' she says, handing me her jumper. 'I'll go and… look after her. We'll do something nice for her later.' She rests her hand on my head before she heads back outside. I bury my face in Alice's jumper, breathing in her musky perfume.

Something about Lady's death doesn't feel right.

DIARY

8 MAY 1996

Doris has been to the hairdressers'. They've cut and straightened her hair – *à la* Princess Diana, she told them. I fussed over her hair hoping she wouldn't pay attention to the thick make-up I was wearing on my cheek, thick like cement to hide the bruise Edward gave me last night. The pain almost made me pass out when he knocked me against the edge of the door. I can't face questions from the doctor, not after last time when I was convinced my rib was broken, and he asked all sorts of probing questions as if he didn't believe me. I came out shaking, terrified Edward would find out.

But Doris had something else on her mind. She insisted I eat a fairy cake that Fred had baked the day before. She pretended not to watch me break it into bits and push the crumbs around my plate, but I knew she was watching. After an unusual silence she put her cup down with a bang that made the crumbs scatter in different directions. 'I have to say something, Nancy,' she said, 'cos you're my best friend and that's what friends are for. Look at you.' Doris grabbed my wrist and curled her fingers around it. She asked me how much weight I'd lost, but the voice in my head warned me not to say anything. I told her I'd got a headache and I had to go for a lie-down. It upset

me, because I wanted to talk about Melissa and now I'll
have to wait another week.

12 MAY 1996

Melissa refuses to tell us her boyfriend's name. She holds
herself tight, as if she thinks Edward is going to hit her
the way he does me. It kills me to see her frightened
like that. When she refused to speak he told her she was
grounded until he was satisfied she wasn't seeing the
boyfriend any more.

I heard her crying in her bedroom this evening, deep,
uncontrollable sobbing that made me want to break down
too. This morning I waited until Edward and Kit had left
for work before I took her a breakfast tray. A soft-boiled
egg and toast cut into soldiers, with freshly squeezed
orange juice in her favourite glass. I told her she didn't
have to go to school, but in return she had to talk to me.
When she came downstairs in her old grey tracksuit, tears
running in lines down her face, I held her hands in mine
and told her she could always trust me. Anything she
told me would be in confidence, but her face remained
as closed as her mouth.

At dinner tonight Edward ate his food fast, as he usually
does, shovelling it in in great mouthfuls. A blob of gravy
congealed on his chin. How different we used to be.

Thinking back to a meal out in the early days, I remember touching my flicked-back hair nervously, wanting to
please the young man with the flared trousers. We ate ice
creams at a table with a red-and-white checked tablecloth,
me leaning over to wipe a splash of cream from his cheek

with my fingertips, letting my hand linger there, enjoying the warm feel of his smooth skin. How brave I was then.

Edward's face is craggy now, deep lines driven into it by his perpetual bad mood. Melissa ate slowly, her long hair hanging down over her plate, almost tickling the potatoes. Edward wiped his face with the once-white handkerchief he keeps in his pocket, then handed me his empty plate even though I was still eating, or rather pretending to. I welcomed the tiniest moment of respite from the cloying smell of the meat, the grey-looking potatoes.

Once I'd sat back down Edward made an announcement. His voice was low and cold but his words were clear enough. 'No daughter of mine makes fun of me.' He never says Melissa's name, I've noticed that now. 'I went to see your teacher last week.' That made her look at him. 'Messing around in class, not listening, wasting everybody's time. Your mother will be picking you up at the school gates from now on. That will teach you.'

I was screaming inside at him. My hopes for Kit had already been dashed and I'd wanted so much more for Melissa – women can do anything these days, no matter what Edward says. My daughter didn't say a word; she sat with her hair covering her face until he stopped speaking, then she bolted from the room. I went to go after her but Edward put a hand up to stop me. I obeyed; I know too well what damage that hand can do. The words I wanted to say tangled in a sticky mess of spaghetti in my throat; I knew the consequences if I tried to untangle them.

CHAPTER TWENTY-THREE

ELLA

I don't go into work the next day, too reluctant to leave the house. Alice buried Lady out in the garden and marked the spot with a circle of tea lights. *How long had Lady been lying out there, hidden in the long grass?* I walk past the seating area, to the middle of the garden which is a mass of bushes and weeds, but just beyond that a square patch of soil has been dug over, little green shoots peeking out from the soil. A tiny fence runs around it.

'She's done a good job, your mate.' Mr Mortimer's voice makes me jump.

'Oh, hello, I didn't see you there.'

I'm not in the mood for conversation, but I make an effort. He must be lonely and I know how that feels.

'Alice, that's my friend. She's staying for a bit.'

'I've seen her around, never close enough to say hello.'

'I'm sure you'll cross paths with her soon. How are you?'

'Oh, mustn't grumble. I find it hard to sleep. Then those pesky birds start up. Although the last couple of nights I was woken up by noises out here. When I looked out, I thought I saw a light, like a torch. It's hard to tell with all the shrubbery.'

'I heard something too. I'm glad you said that, I thought I was going mad.'

'Yes, I'm easily woken, though.'

'Thanks for telling me. We always lock everything, but I'll make doubly sure now. I don't like the thought of anyone roaming around outside at night.' I act calm, but inside I'm quaking. *What if the noises were someone harming Lady?*

Back inside, I remember the embroidery. With everything that's happened I'd forgotten it. The Mortimers have lived next door for as long as Chris can remember. I'll ask Mr Mortimer about that date next time I see him.

Later that day I get in touch with Jess, Chris's PA. I doubt Chris will have told his colleagues about the split. He's a private person and he hates anything that might show him up. My heart accelerates as the dialling tone rings, as if I'm doing something wrong.

A woman with a husky voice answers the phone. 'Good morning. Jess Taylor-Scott speaking, how can I help you today?'

'Jess,' I say. 'It's Ella, Chris's wife.'

'Oh, hi, how are you? Chris is in a meeting, I'm afraid, he won't be free until… actually he's got a lunch, too, so he isn't actually free until…' I hear a tapping sound, 'four o'clock this afternoon. He's mostly out of the office these days. Maybe you should ring his mobile?'

'It isn't Chris I want to speak to, it's you.'

'Me?'

'Could we meet for a coffee, on me, of course? I'd like to have a chat with you.'

'I'm not sure—'

'It would be in the strictest confidence. I promise if you don't want to answer any of my questions, you don't have to. It's just that I've been worried about Chris.'

'I suppose I could.' Jess sounds cagey and I imagine her looking over her shoulder in case anyone is listening in.

'What time do you finish work?'

'Six.'

'Forget coffee, how about I buy you a drink? There's a bar in town not far from your office, Myrtle's, do you know it?'

She laughs. 'A bit too well, unfortunately. I'll see you inside, round about ten past.' A series of clicks sound. 'Better go, there's another call coming in. I'll catch you later.'

I recognise Jess as soon as she comes through the door. Golden-brown tan; no make-up; naturally, effortlessly pretty. She hooks her backpack off her shoulder and dumps it on the chair.

'This is weird,' she says, straightening her shoulders. 'I want to be upfront with you. After you rang, I had second thoughts. Chris is my boss, and it feels wrong to be going behind his back, meeting you like this. Although part of me is intrigued, obviously.' Her voice has a rich tone to it and I recall in the back of my mind Chris saying she used to be an actress. This means she might be playing a role. *God, I'm getting paranoid.*

'Please don't worry, I asked you to meet me, I'll take responsibility. I've got a few questions I want to ask about Chris.'

Jess frowns.

'Let me get some drinks in. What would you like?'

'Vodka and soda, please.'

'Be right back.'

Once we're settled with our drinks, I feel the familiar prickling of nerves, not knowing how this is going to go.

'You haven't been to the office for ages. Actually, I wondered if something was going on with you guys. He's not been himself lately.'

'In what way?'

'I dunno, kind of distracted, not as cheerful as usual. And a bit scruffy – you know how he likes his clothes, always looks neat, for an older guy, even if he does favour a lumberjack shirt.' She covers her smile with her hand. 'No offence meant.'

'None taken.' Jess can only be in her early twenties, an age when anyone slightly older appears geriatric. I smile back to reassure her; I hope she can't tell I'm lapping up her words. 'Look, I appreciate you meeting me, I really do.'

She's staring into her drink. Her eyes flash when she looks up at me. 'Don't think I'm being disloyal to Chris, it's not what you think. He's a good boss, but lately it's not just him I'm worried about. The only reason I agreed to meet you is because I'm concerned about the company. I'm not supposed to know this, but my mate does the invoices and some of them haven't been paid. Chris keeps making excuses but he looks like he's falling apart. Are you guys having problems, is that what this is? Because he needs help, and if he doesn't pull himself together I'm worried the business will go under. I've got my rent to pay, I can't afford to lose this job.'

I place my hand over hers. 'That's why I'm here, too, I understand more than you can know. Chris has left me for someone else. I'll be honest, I've been wondering if it's someone at work. I thought it might be Tanya.'

She bursts out laughing. 'You're joking, aren't you? Tanya's into young, fit blokes, no offence intended. Plus, she's got a boyfriend. But if that's what he says is going on, maybe it's one of the clients. It must be tough for you, I'm sorry.'

'I'm trying to get used to it. He won't tell me where he's living or anything.'

Jess wrinkles her forehead. 'There is one thing. The other day I noticed some washing-up in the sink and I was puzzled as I'd done it all the night before and I'd been the last one in the office. And Tanya mentioned her shower gel had disappeared from the work shower.'

'So do you think he's been staying there?'

'I do now. I guess that explains his slightly dishevelled look. And if he's short of money, then that would explain why he isn't living in a hotel.'

Jess's words worry me.

'This might sound like an odd question, but have you seen his car lately?' I ask.

'No, he hasn't had it for a couple of weeks, it's been in the garage, being fixed. He had a minor accident.'

This is news to me.

'Doesn't he have any mates who could talk to him?' she asks. 'If he is in trouble, he can't just bury his head and hope it will all go away. I need this job, and I'm not the only one in the office who's worried.' Her eyes flicker to her phone. The music in the bar notches up a level and the chatter around us increases in volume accordingly. My head spins with Jess's words.

'Don't worry, I'm on it.' I make myself sound businesslike for her sake. Aside from Geoff, and Ted and Sadie, who live a few doors along Heath Street, he has a couple of good friends, but would they talk to me? Most of the times Chris was out with his friends I chose to stay at home and keep Nancy company. Why would I want to go out when I could spend an evening in my own home?

Jess's eyes dart to her phone again.

'I really appreciate you coming, and I promise you Chris won't find out about it.' Jess doesn't need to know he's barely speaking to me as it is. What she's told me makes my shoulders sink with worry. The image of the endless lines of transactions on his credit card, betraying his affair, is imprinted on my brain. *Are there other credit cards I don't know about?*

She loads her bag onto her back.

I hug her but her shoulders are stiff and she looks thoughtful as she pushes her way through a group of women coming into the bar. Her words reverberate in my head.

Exactly how much trouble is Chris in?

CHAPTER TWENTY-FOUR

ALICE

For a few precious seconds after waking I had no idea what day it was. Then it hit me: *Olivia's birthday*. On this day last year the past caught up with me.

Everything went wrong after I heard the news. At first I didn't let it affect me. After all, it had been so many years, and I'd changed so much. Olivia knew something had happened but I couldn't tell her because how could I expect anyone to live with that? I didn't want to be that person any more.

Little things gave me away. Lapses in concentration. Taking too long in the shower, the only place I could be truly alone, hoping the water would wash it all away and when it wouldn't, trying to burn myself to blot out the never-ending pain. I couldn't hide my reddened skin from Olivia; she wanted to scoop up cold white cream with her long brown fingers and smooth it onto the screaming scars. *How could I tell her I wanted them, cruel reminders of what went before?* Not letting her touch me any more was painful in itself. She'd curl up on the sofa and make herself small in an effort to take herself as far away from me as possible.

Her birthday was ruined and I couldn't tell her why; I had to keep the devastating news to myself. The year before Olivia and I had slipped out of the house at first light and gone down to the sea. The waves lapping the shore were the only sound as we held hands and ran into the water, swimming until the day broke. We had breakfast on the terrace, where sun poured down through the trees, picking out gold strands in her hair. I traced the sunlit pattern on her face with my eyes, never tiring of looking at her.

I opened my eyes and gazed at her photograph; her eyes hurt me with their reproaches. I placed it face down on the side table, swung my legs out of bed and forced those memories away. But I could still feel those dark eyes watching me from across the room: *what would she think of me now?* A muffled sound from the room next door alerted me to Ella: her radio alarm cut into the silence and the moment was broken. *Enough.* I removed Olivia's photograph from the table and placed it out of sight, deep among my personal papers, in a box under the bed. I turned my thoughts to Ella and the events of last night. *Surely she wouldn't be going into work today?* I hated to see how vulnerable she looked. I hadn't shown Ella how freaked out I was too.

Getting upset only made my thoughts swing back to her. I'm trying to switch my thoughts off and realign them. Ella has to be my focus now. Not her, no longer *her*.

When I went downstairs Ella was pouring milk into a jug, the muscles straining in her thin arms. I needed a strong shot of coffee to revive my tired brain, and a cigarette to still my breathing and switch off the thoughts that had risen to the surface during the long night. In Spain I'd sit out on my little balcony with my tomato bread dripping with oil, but I slept better back then.

'Coffee?' Ella's eyes looked red, as if she too hadn't slept much afterwards and a spike of anger rose in me. *How dare he do this to her?*

'Please.'

'Shall we go outside – might as well make the most of this mild weather before winter properly sets in.'

The table was covered in dew and I wiped my hand across it, enjoying the cold against my skin. My back was sore from all the hours I'd devoted to the garden but from this viewpoint the hours of work were barely in evidence. Ella appeared, holding a tray with two mugs of coffee and a plate of chunky biscuits.

'You look tired.'

'I didn't sleep at all.' She picked up one of the mugs and blew on the steaming liquid. 'I can't stop thinking about Lady. Do you think it was an accident?'

I sigh. 'I've been wondering the same. What with the other things.' The thought of the dead cat made me feel queasy.

'Thanks for helping me. You look like you haven't slept much either.'

As if I ever did. Every night is haunted by the same old dreams. Trying to find her, almost there, and then the crashing disappointment when she slips out of my reach. Long, restless hours taunted by the idea of sleep, while it forever escapes me. 'You're right,' I said.

'The night before when I heard noises, it sounded like somebody was out here. I'm convinced now I was right. Mr Mortimer heard something, too.' Ella looked around the garden with a wary gaze, as if someone was still lurking behind the bushes. Her eyes looked bruised from tiredness.

'You're already stressed, and this is only making it worse. I wish I could help you get over him quicker but time is what you need. It's a cliché for a reason.'

I hated the words as they came out of my mouth. I was trying to convince myself as much as her. It was a question of priorities. Some things had to be remembered, kept alive. Otherwise…

CHAPTER TWENTY-FIVE

ELLA

I pace around, unable to settle. A walk on the heath will help clear my head. I turn right out of the house, away from the lane that leads to the main road, where traffic is a distant mumble. As I walk down the street I'm aware of a car passing me and it pulls up alongside the curb. Ted from number 42 unfolds his long body from the driving seat and strides to his front door, deliberately facing forward as he lets himself into his house. I shove my hands in my pockets, trying not to feel hurt that he's snubbed me. Chris must have told him what's happened between us.

I put my head down against the blustery wind and continue towards the heath. The wind strengthens and my breath quickens as I turn the corner to be confronted by the inky black surface of the pond. Alice was right about the mild weather we've been having lately coming to a close. I cross to the bench and sit by the pond, trying to get my thoughts in order. I have a good view of the exterior of number 46 and a ripple of fear cuts through my exhaustion, imagining a dark figure prowling around the garden. *To scare me? Or to hurt me?*

The white walls of the house glow against the dark slate of the roof and the tall chimney pot. I study the area behind the garden. There's a small wooded copse between the garden and the pond, which leads through to the heath. It's accessible from behind, if someone was determined enough. I can't get the sight of Lady's rigid body out of my head.

The sky is darkening and I continue on my walk, taking fast steps, needing to keep moving, wishing I could push my thoughts away. The path becomes a track and I find myself in a clearing surrounded by a dense curtain of trees. A twig snaps, a bird shoots towards me and I duck. Feet approach, a quick tread, and I breathe a sigh of relief as a runner overtakes me, his breath visible against the now-dark sky. I hurry back to the path, pulling the hood of my sweatshirt around my head. I run along Heath Street to number 46, slamming the door behind me with a gasp of relief. The grandfather clock ticks as I pant into the silence.

I've just settled down in front of the television, hoping a bit of mindless viewing will send me off to sleep, when the doorbell rings. Through the frosted glass I make out a blurry shape with rounded shoulders and a flat cap: Mr Mortimer. He'll have seen me come in so I can't pretend I'm out. Besides, I'm curious, I can't remember him ever calling round at the house before.

'Mr Mortimer,' I say as I pull the door ajar.

He nods and removes his cap, twists it around in his hands.

'I'm terribly sorry to disturb you, lovey. You looked like you needed cheering up, so I baked you some biscuits.' He hands me an ancient-looking tin.

The kindly expression on his face warms me. 'That's so sweet of you. Would you like to come in, have a cup of tea?'

He blinks hard again. 'That's kind of you. Just a quick one then. I eat my supper at six o'clock and watch the news while I eat. I like to stick to a routine, and it's important to keep up with what's going on.'

He follows me into the kitchen and I boil the kettle. He looks around, his eyes bright. 'Three sugars,' he says. 'Doris only let me have two, but now…'

'I wish I'd met her,' I say. 'I think Chris remembers her.'

He nods. 'He would do.'

Mr Mortimer is silent as I set out the cups and make a pot of tea in Nancy's red teapot. I put some of his delicious-looking shortbread biscuits on a plate.

'Have you lived next door long, Mr Mortimer?'

'Fred. Please call me Fred.'

'Fred, then.'

He nods, stirs a heaped spoonful of sugar into his tea. 'When we first got married we lived in Kentish Town in a rented flat. My wife inherited the house when her parents died, and we moved here in the summer of 1975.'

'You've got a good memory.'

'Some things you don't forget. It was a happy time, despite my mother-in-law's passing. Setting up our first proper home. And we appreciated how lucky we were, such a pretty street with the heath on our doorstep. It wasn't such an expensive area at that time.'

I pass the plate of biscuits to him and he takes one in the shape of a Scottie dog. I push away a thought about Lady.

'Do you remember Chris's parents, the Rutherfords?'

'Oh yes. My Doris was great friends with Nancy. I was so sorry to hear she'd passed away. She was a lovely woman.'

'She was.' To my horror, tears well in my eyes. I drink some tea to distract myself.

'I'm sorry, love, I didn't mean to upset you. Me and my big mouth.'

I shake my head.

Fred finishes his tea, pats at his mouth with a handkerchief. 'I was thinking about those noises in the night we were talking about,' he says. 'It has to be a fox. Those foxes are a bloody nuisance, pardon my French. I don't want you worrying yourself about it.'

I wonder if foxes attack cats. I don't want to ask him, I'll only get upset again.

He glances up at the clock, puts his cap on. 'Right, I'll be off then.'

'What's for dinner tonight?'

'Shepherd's pie. I've not cooked it myself, though, it's courtesy of Waitrose. And thanks for the tea, very kind of you. I'll keep an eye out for any more intruders.'

'Thanks so much, Mr Mortimer.'

'Fred.'

'Fred.'

He whistles to himself as he goes down the path and I wipe my eyes, feeling a spurt of affection towards him. As soon as he's gone I curse myself for getting upset. I completely forgot to ask him about 1997. *But really, what would I have said?* At least I haven't been thinking about Chris for half an hour.

In the evening, I stick a pizza in the oven and take a shower, hoping Alice will show up and join me for dinner. I imagine her in a sophisticated restaurant sharing secrets with a close friend, laughing, her glossy hair shining as she moves. Then I visualise myself with her in the restaurant as I rub my hair dry with a towel; I wish I could rub out these feelings of jealousy towards her phantom friend.

But Alice doesn't come home. I eat the pizza, leaving the crusts, then light the fire, sit on the sofa and pick at the skin on my fingernails. I call Jamie for a chat but the call goes to voicemail. Tears spring to my eyes when I think about how it used to be, me padding softly down the stairs after reading to Nancy as she drifted off to sleep. How I'd curl up in front of the fire, Chris reading in an armchair. Cocooned in number 46. Dozing and dreaming about the children we'd have one day, children who would never know what it was like not to have a mother. 'Happy?' Chris would ask me, stroking my leg, smiling, knowing the answer from my face.

I give up trying to relax and go to bed.

Upstairs, I check the window is closed, but it doesn't settle my unease so I go back downstairs and take the oversized umbrella from the hall to bed with me for protection.

In the middle of the night I wake with a start and my heart pounds as I listen to what sounds like something being dragged outside. *Not again.* I jump up and go over to the window, peering out into the darkness. Once again, torchlight bobs back and forth leaving a silver trail as it moves. Someone is definitely out there. I switch my phone into torch mode, keeping it against my leg to shelter the light in case anyone has got into the house. I go to warn Alice but her bedroom door is ajar.

'Alice?' My voice is a loud whisper.

Silence. I repeat her name, then with a shaking hand, white in the dark, I push her door and it swings open. A lamp glows in the corner of the room.

'Alice,' my voice is a normal pitch now and the stillness in the air tells me the room is empty. The duvet is cast aside as if thrown off in a hurry, a paperback lies open, face down on the floor. I cross the room and peer out through the window, still concealing the light from my phone. Outside, the light bobs like a rabbit's tail. *What if she heard the noise and went down to help and is in trouble? Or could it be her in the garden?* I glance across at the house next door but Mr Mortimer's house sleeps – the windows are black.

The floorboards are cold against my bare feet and I shine the light on the floor and follow it to the back door. The rooms downstairs are empty. *If I put the light on suddenly, would this startle whoever it is? I should protect myself.* Too late, I remember the umbrella under my bed. I daren't go back upstairs, my legs are like jelly and I'm trembling, and not from cold. The back door is closed, the key still in the lock. I remember locking it last night, but I always leave the key on the window ledge. *Did I forget?* With a shaking hand I turn the key, but it isn't locked, and I swallow hard, my breath loud in the silence of the room. A sharp pain digs into my foot and I smother a cry, hopping up and down as I grab my foot and pull out a large splinter. I pull the door open, shining my torch in front of me, and take a deep breath.

'Hello?' I say, my voice shaking.

CHAPTER TWENTY-SIX

ELLA

'Hello?'

My gut feeling is that I am the only person in the house. Emboldened, I shine the torch over the grass; the light is surprisingly strong. *Is that dew already, catching the light, shimmering at me?* I slide my feet into my garden shoes and tread ahead, waving the torch around like a student with a glow light at a rave. The shed is empty and so is the garden. A light switches on upstairs next door and satisfied I'm alone out here, I hurry back inside. The last thing I want is Mr Mortimer haranguing me about why I'm outside in the middle of the night when I should be tucked up in bed. I wish I was. But there's no way I'll sleep now.

Back inside I make sure the door is locked and this time I leave the key in the sitting room. My torchlight catches the amber glow from a bottle of whisky on the shelf. A present from one of Chris's first clients; the memory is sour in my throat, like the taste of whisky. *Back when Chris was successful. Back when he was my husband.* Chris is the only one who ever drank it but he's not here any more and I hope the small glass I pour will stop my hands from trembling.

The unpleasant, harsh taste makes me wince, but the warmth I feel as it trickles down my throat is welcome. I pour a second glass and I'm about to take it into the sitting room when I realise my foot is throbbing. I lift it up to look at the underside – it's covered in blood and there's a bloody trail smeared across the kitchen tiles. Grabbing a cloth, I soak it in cold water and hold it to my foot until the bleeding abates. I haven't got the energy to clean the floor for the moment. Instead I hop into the living room, turn the chair to face the door and collapse onto it.

'Ella.'

A loud whisper jolts me awake. I wince as I go to stand and I fall back into the chair, my foot still throbbing. Alice peers down at me.

'Ella, are you OK? What's happened? There's blood all over the kitchen floor and the back doorstep. I thought…' Her almond eyes roam around my face and I see genuine concern. A flicker of warmth is stoked inside me.

'It's just my foot, looks far worse than it is. I should have cleaned up but—'

'Forget about that. What have you done to it? Are you OK?'

'Trod on a splinter, that's all, but it felt pretty big.'

She kneels down and lifts my foot onto her lap. Her fingers are warm against my skin. 'Have you got a first aid kit?'

'In the cupboard under the sink.'

'Keep your foot still and I'll see if I can find something. What were you doing down here in the middle of the night anyway?' Alice disappears off to the kitchen where I hear her rummaging about in the cupboard before she emerges with a green plastic box.

'I could ask you the same thing.'

Alice doesn't reply; she's kneeling on the floor and staring intently at the box.

'What is it?'

She jumps to her feet. 'This looks ancient, but the dressings will be fine.' She cleans the wound and removes a small bandage from a paper wrapping which has gone yellow with age. 'This should be OK, I think. Maybe check when you last had a tetanus injection.'

'I don't think I can remember. Alice, where have you been? I was looking for you, that's why I was wandering about down here. I heard a noise again outside and I went to see if you'd heard anything. But you weren't in your room. Someone was out here with a torch.'

She sighs. 'I was hoping you wouldn't wake up. I know how frightened you've been. I heard a noise too, so I went down to investigate. It was my torch you saw.'

'You shouldn't have gone outside on your own. What if something happened? Weren't you scared?'

'Like I said earlier, I'm not easily frightened. Living alone in an isolated hill dwelling in Spain is a lot more dangerous than this, believe me. Where I lived was pretty remote, no Wi-Fi or phone signal. At least here you've got the emergency services a phone call away, even if they don't hit their seven-minute target or whatever the latest ridiculous government guideline is.'

'But I locked the back door.'

'Lucky I had my key on me, wasn't it?'

'Did you see anything?'

Alice shakes her head. 'What kind of noise did you hear?'

'A dragging sound.'

'Me too.'

She gets to her feet.

'It was probably a fox. I'll check properly in the morning. The plants I brought home from the nursery yesterday are still outside the shed. They're worth quite a bit of money. Anyway, you look shattered. You should rest that foot.'

My phone screen shows it's just gone four. 'But the kitchen floor…'

Alice takes my arm and helps me out of the chair, 'Forget it, I'll sort it before I go to bed. I'm wide awake now.'

*

Back in my room I get into bed and pull the duvet around me. A sharp pain throbs through my foot. Thuds from downstairs as Alice moves about reassure me but after a while the stairs creak and her bedroom door closes. The wind has picked up outside and I can't get warm, my hands are icy. I picture Lady, stiff and cold outside. *Did she suffer? Did somebody deliberately hurt her? Was it the other woman?* The garden rustling becomes a whispering in my head and I bolt out of the room and hammer on Alice's door. She pulls it open and my whole body trembles.

'I can't bear to be alone, can I sleep in your room?'

Alice closes the door behind me and wraps me in an old-fashioned knitted blanket.

'Where did you find this?' I ask through chattering teeth.

'At the back of the cupboard.'

'Nancy must have made it. She used to knit a lot.' I hug the blanket around myself, warmed at the thought of Nancy being close to me.

Alice pats the bed and I get in, enclosed by the blanket.

'Here, take this.' She passes me a hot-water bottle.

'What about you?'

'I'm fine. You're in shock, you need it. You'll warm up in a minute.'

Alice climbs into the other side of the bed. She's wearing navy silk pyjamas with a gold trim. She's looking after me and it feels precious; her actions make me feel valued. Her affection is a tiny compensation for the care Nancy gave me that was so cruelly snatched away. *Maybe it isn't a mother I need, but a friend.*

'OK if I turn the lamp off?' Alice asks.

'Yes, thanks.' Darkness descends. Despite the wind roaring outside I can hear the comforting sound of Alice breathing beside me.

'Alice?'

'Hmm?'

'I'm so glad you're here. Especially with Chris being such a bastard.' My words sound soppy but I want her to know how grateful I am.

'No worries.'

The window rattles in the wind, but I'm warm now, under Nancy's blanket. Alice is lying on her back; I'm wide awake.

'Alice?'

'Yes?'

'Do you have a lot of friends?'

'No, I'm a loner, me. Friends weren't high on my list of priorities. I hated school, left as soon as I could.'

'It's a terrible place if you don't have friends. I went to too many different schools to make roots anywhere. I'd make a friend, then I'd be off and I'd have to leave them behind. It hurt more each time, until I realised it was easier not to get attached to anyone in the first place.' My eyes are adjusting to the darkness. A slither of light shines under the door – she must have left the hall light on. 'Your cousin in the photograph. She must be a good friend.'

'Olivia. She's… she's not really my cousin.'

I stare at the ceiling, waiting for Alice to continue. A noise shatters the silence and it takes a moment for me to realise it's the house phone.

Alice's hair tickles my face as she jumps out of bed and goose-bumps erupt on my skin. 'What now?'

She runs downstairs and I sit up, rubbing my arms. Her face is drawn when she comes back into the room. I pull the patchwork blanket around me.

'Who was it?'

Alice bites into her lip, hesitating.

'Who was it, Alice?' My voice sounds high, hysterical.

She hesitates. 'Nobody there. Wrong number. Try and get some sleep.'

I lie for hours listening to Alice's soft breathing and the wind howling over the heath. I go over the events of the night in my head; I think about Alice going outside alone, not wanting to wake me. The concern I saw in her eyes, I'm sure I didn't imagine it. *But I'm such a light sleeper, why didn't I wake up when she got up and went downstairs?* The stairs creak, no matter how softly you tread. Lying here, in Alice's room, I suddenly feel vulnerable. Am I right to trust her?

Thoughts in my head clamour to be heard. That was no wrong number. Lady's death is too much of a coincidence. *Somebody is out to get me.*

DIARY

5 JULY 1996

Last month Doris told me I needed to see a doctor about
my lack of appetite. I wish she'd stop going on about my
health. This week I wear a baggy cardigan over my dress,
to stop her looking at my shrinking figure with that
worried look disturbing her face. When I left her house
she said she'd noticed I had a black eye, and she asked if
everything was OK. I pictured the look on Edward's face
when he swung his belt at me and I gave her my brightest
smile. 'Of course it is,' I told her.

Edward was waiting when I got back from next door,
sitting at the kitchen table gripping a bottle of beer. I've
long stopped wishing he would use a glass. He asked me
why Doris didn't come over here any more. The question
took me by surprise. I said she didn't mind where she went
and I enjoyed going there. He accused me of wanting to
get away from him. Said he didn't want me going over
there any more. I tried to stand up to him, I really did; I
told him Doris was my one friend and the only person I
have any kind of social interaction with. I explained that
he gets to go to work and mix with other people while
I'm stuck at home all day long, day in day out, doing
housework. I shouldn't have said that, those words were
what set him off. His nostrils flared as they always do

before he takes the first blow; I had just enough time to curl in on myself so his punch landed on my side. I closed my eyes and stayed bent like that until he had finished, not making a sound. Melissa's got enough to worry about.

Doris called round the following Wednesday when I didn't show up, and she came again the week after and the week after that. I expect she would have tried to phone too, but he's got rid of the house phone, said we don't need anyone else. I cried when I heard him speaking to her, heard him say 'difference of opinion' and 'spending more time with her family'. She knew I didn't have anyone else.

I made a plan today. I'd hang around in the garden until Doris came out, but when I went downstairs this morning Edward was there at the table. Said he'd jacked his job in to keep an eye on me. I pleaded with him about Doris, but he said he didn't think she was a good influence, with her modern ideas and fancy ways. Just because she went on holiday abroad and came back with golden-honey skin. My heart feels squeezed at the thought of not being able to see her any more. Edward is diminishing my life, making it smaller every day. He won't even let me tend the garden now, said he'll get a gardener in. My flowers are dying, too.

Every night I feel around under the mattress for the letter I've written to her, telling her about the diary and where it's kept. I'm going to have to post it soon. I'm not sure I can wait much longer.

CHAPTER TWENTY-SEVEN

ELLA

An alarm is buzzing over and over, but it's distant, as if muffled under a mattress. I'm clutching a woolly blanket with colourful squares: Nancy's blanket. I'm in Nancy's room. But Nancy's gone. And so is Lady. The swoop of pain that follows the realisation is familiar. I sit up, jolted back to reality.

The house creaks and sighs but I can't hear any sign that Alice is here. The grandfather clock chimes and I count each chime: it's ten o'clock. Alice must have gone to work.

I sit up feeling hot with shame. Getting so scared last night was pathetic. *What must Alice think of me?* Olivia's photograph is no longer by the bed. She said she wasn't her cousin; *why would she lie about that?* I stand under a hot shower and will myself to wake up. I need to get myself together, focus on my business. The shop is my livelihood and it's all the more important now I'm single. One business going under is bad enough. Tears prick my eyes and I turn the water round to cold and blast them away.

I'm washing the mugs in the sink, thinking about my conversation with Alice, remembering my doubts about her last night when the doorbell rings. A young man stands at the door brandishing a mobile phone and a bunch of keys. A red Mini Cooper is parked outside the house. As I open the door he zaps the keys towards the garish car, which has *SUTTONS* written on the side, next to an image of a crudely drawn house.

'Good morning. You must be Mrs Rutherford. I'm from Suttons.' He twiddles with his tie.

'Suttons?'

'The estate agents. Your husband arranged this visit. Did he forget to mention it?'

He adjusts the jacket of his expensive-looking grey suit.

I tighten my grip on the door frame. 'My husband isn't living here at the moment. I'm not sure—'

'Oh yes, he explained all that. Said I needed to organise viewings with you. Which is why I'm here.'

'Viewings?' I wrap my cardigan around myself and step forward onto the doorstep: the guardian of my house. 'The house isn't for sale.'

Mr Suit waves his mobile at me. 'It's all in here. Your husband has signed a contract, asked us to put it on the market as soon as possible. A house like this in such an exclusive area, we're the agents for you. I assure you, I can get you the best deal. A house in the next street sold last month for over three million—'

'You aren't listening. Whatever Chris has signed isn't valid. We're joint owners of the property, he can't do this. This house is my home.'

His confident expression falters for a second before he's smiling again, displaying his teeth like a wolf, ready to pounce. 'Mr Rutherford didn't mention anything about that. How about I get him on the phone for you to discuss this? I wouldn't mind a coffee, and I really do need to measure up, take some photographs. These properties don't come on to the market very often and we've got a waiting list for anything that comes up in this area. It can't be easy to run – these houses are what, late-nineteenth century? The upkeep must be pretty expensive.'

Ted from number 42 walks out of his house and looks over. I know that Chris used to go for a drink with him occasionally and I wonder if they're still in touch. I'm sure he ignored me the other day.

'You'd better come in. I'll speak to Chris, get this charade sorted out.'

I lead him through to the sitting room, but he doesn't sit down, wandering round appraising everything instead.

'What a view,' he says. It's windy today and the red and gold leaves which are dropping from the trees rustle en masse across the heath, where the water ripples in the pond. 'That alone will push up the price.'

'Please sit down. Will you listen to me?'

He contemplates me for a minute, shrugs off his jacket and sits down. 'OK,' he says. 'I'm sorry, I'm just doing my job. Obviously there's some kind of dispute going on here. Shall I get your husband on the phone?'

I nod. 'Yes please. I'm sorry for taking this out on you, but it's a huge shock. I'll get that coffee you asked for.'

'My name's Warren, by the way.'

My hands tremble as I slot the pod into the machine, glad for something to occupy me while he calls Chris. Having a third person to witness our conversation is probably a good thing; it might stop me from losing it completely. Tension is pulsing in my head and I get myself a glass of water. My stomach churns and I'm not sure whether I want Chris to pick up or not. I can't ask him what's going on with his finances while the estate agent is here. But he does eventually pick up and I place the coffee, fingers trembling, in front of Warren.

He puts the phone on speaker. 'Chris, Warren from Suttons here. I'm at the property now with your wife. It appears you haven't had a chance to discuss the sale with her.'

Chris clears his throat. 'That's right. Is she there?'

'Yes, we're on speaker right now.'

'Chris, of course I'm here. It's my home. Why are you doing this? I've told you, I'm not going anywhere. The house isn't for sale.'

'I know you don't want to sell, but listen for a moment. I popped into the estate agents just to see what the market is like. I'm sure Warren will tell you but the amount we could get for the house is astronomical. Of course we'd divide it fifty-fifty, you could buy yourself a decent place, you'd be sorted for life. I know you're attached to the house, and it's where Mum died… but Warren doesn't need to hear all this. We could put it on the market, see if there's any interest—'

'I've got viewings arranged already,' Warren says. I'd almost forgotten that he's here; my mind is in overdrive. Chris is right, but how can I explain the way my gut wrenches at the thought of losing this house? *Why doesn't he feel it too?*

'Ella, are you still there?'

I attempt to swallow, but my throat is so dry. I look at Warren, who takes command. 'Chris, I'm going to ring off now – I can't go ahead without Mrs Rutherford's say-so. We'll have a chat now and I'll get back to you first thing in the morning, I promise.' He closes the call, takes a sip of coffee.

'Mrs Rutherford, contrary to public perception, estate agents aren't monsters and I can see this situation is somewhat delicate. You have a think about everything overnight and let me know what you decide in the morning. I'm not going to do anything against your will – obviously I don't want to put the house on the market with you still living here if you're not in agreement. But this house would sell easily, I promise you. As I mentioned earlier, we have a reserve list for any houses coming up in this area as it happens so infrequently. I'd love to come and measure up and do your beautiful house justice. But only once you're in full agreement. Here's my card, give me a call once you've slept on it. And I'm sorry for any upset I've caused.'

CHAPTER TWENTY-EIGHT

ELLA

I need to talk to someone to stop me from going insane, so I call Jamie.

'Sorry I didn't return your call,' he says. 'Remember that guy I went out with? He's gorgeous and I've seen him every day since our first date. I've neglected you, I'm so sorry.'

'It's OK. You've been holding the fort at the shop for me. And it's thanks to you that Alice is living here. I don't know what I'd have done without her.' I recount the events of the last few days. Except for Lady, I can't talk about that without crying. As I'm speaking, the niggling doubts about Alice surface. The night-time goings-on are getting to me, but it feels wrong to discuss them with Jamie. I'm worried I'll look crazy.

'I can't believe Chris sent an estate agent round without telling you.'

'Neither can I. I'm actually quite worried about him.' I tell Jamie about Geoff and the swimming club. 'What with the mortgage and the car, I'm wondering if Chris has got himself into debt by spending so much on this woman. Perhaps he can't face telling me. If only I knew who she was, I'd confront her. She must be pushing him into selling the house.'

'Maybe I could help you, to make up for my neglect. Jason is going away next week and I need to keep myself occupied. I could follow Chris, see what he gets up to?'

'It's a bit stalkerish, isn't it?'

'So what. Chris deserves it. And if it helps rule out who is tormenting you it will be worth it.'

Talking to Jamie makes me feel better. I ignore my twinge of guilt at the idea of him spying on Chris. It's for Chris's own good. I am genuinely worried about him.

'Have you had a visitor?' Alice is looking at the mugs in the sink.

'Yes, an unwanted one. An estate agent turned up.'

'An estate agent? Why?'

'Bloody Chris sent him. He's decided it's a good idea to put the house on the market. Without consulting me – and I have a joint share in the property. This guy was ready to measure up and everything. Thankfully he was quite reasonable, phoned Chris and agreed to give me time to make a decision. He wasn't as bad as estate agents are made out to be.'

'Is that reasonable? It's your house. Don't let these guys push you around, Ella. How have you left it?'

'I said I'd let him know what I decide in the morning.'

'I'm not condoning the way Chris is going about things, but do you think he has a point?' Alice asks.

'What do you mean?'

'Putting the house on the market, what with everything that's been going on. This house is turning into a bit of a hassle for you, isn't it? The damp, the roof, and you don't seem that comfortable. You get nervous when you're alone, don't you? Maybe it's for the best.'

'I thought you liked living here.' My words come out in a pleading tone and I hate myself for sounding so needy.

Alice looks straight at me. 'I do, why ever would you think otherwise?'

'Advising me to sell up, that's all. I didn't expect it.'

'Forget me, this is about what is best for you. I care about you, Ella, you must have noticed. I'll get by, I always have.' She averts her gaze and a bitter expression crosses her face.

I swallow hard. I hate Chris for putting me in this position.

'Look, it's good of you but I'm not letting Chris get away with this. It's the principle more than anything else. I won't sell up. I'll ring the estate agent in the morning and make that clear. This is my house. I'll raise the money and buy him out if I have to.'

But it's bravado talking. I could never afford that, and who knows what debts are piling up around Chris. We're still married, after all. Alice goes out to work in the garden before it gets too dark, leaving me rattling around in the house alone. I haven't mentioned Jess's concerns about the business to her or Jamie. Up in my room, I take out the piece of embroidery from the attic and look at the date, wondering why it was hidden. The thirtieth of July was a Wednesday. *Probably a birthday. Did Nancy make it?* I wonder if Chris would recognise it. Tomorrow I'll visit Mr Mortimer, find out more about the house, ask him about the dates.

It's a silent evening, save for the shifts in movement of the old house as it responds to the weather outside. At around nine a slow patter of raindrops increases steadily until rain pounds the roof. My legs are stiff from sitting on the floor with my computer on my lap and I go into Alice's room to look at the damp. It has spread, forming a dark, cloud-like pattern and creating bubbles under the wallpaper. I was praying it wouldn't rain before Mr Whiteley comes to fix the damaged roof.

Listening to the rain makes me feel cold. One hot shower later and I'm tucked up under my duvet with a mug of hot chocolate. I play some soothing music, determined to get a good night's sleep. Despite trying to empty my mind of thoughts, I'm wondering where Alice is as I drift off.

A scuffling noise wakes me. I sit upright, my body rigid. *Somebody is in the house.* My heart thuds as I try to convince myself it's Alice. But my gut won't settle. Fear stops me from calling her name, getting up and going downstairs. I'm familiar with the noise she makes when she comes in after a night out; her tread is fairly heavy and she moves fast. The shuffling sound gets quieter and the living room door gives off its familiar squeak as it's opened. I've intended to oil that hinge so many times.

Bolder now that the sound is further away, I tiptoe out of my room and go to the top of the stairs. I hear the back door closing and I let out the breath I hadn't realised I was holding.

The landing is lit by moonlight, which spills through the small window. Alice's door is slightly ajar, and in a repeat of the other night I gently slide it open. The clothes she was wearing earlier, a black cashmere jumper and grey trousers, are folded on a chair. Black Dr. Martens boots stand beside the bed as if she's about to step into them. The duvet is cast aside once more. My heart rate steadies. It's Alice; she must have heard the noise before me and gone downstairs. *But why didn't she call me?* I'm sure I've told her what a light sleeper I am.

At the window I watch the torchlight drawing patterns. With the glow of the moonlight I'm able to see a figure down by the shed, crouching over something. It doesn't look like Alice. Is she in danger? Cold blood circulates around my veins and a scream lodges in my throat. I recall last night, the terror that drove me to Alice's room. *Now she needs me.* Shame at the memory of my behaviour fires me up. I hurry down the stairs, but this time I grab the tall umbrella. I turn the knob on the back door, but it doesn't open: the wood sticks. My hand shakes and I need both hands to finally get it to turn. *Why won't it open?* Freezing air rushes in and my cotton nightdress billows around me as I open the back door. It's no longer raining. I hear a tapping sound: *tap, tap, tap.*

'Alice?' my voice rings out through the darkness. The tapping stops. Silence. I clutch the umbrella so hard my knuckles tingle.

'Who's there?' My voice is louder now, filled with a confidence I don't feel.

The person turns towards me and lifts their arm. Nancy? It's her coat. Confused, I step backwards. *Should I run?* Torchlight hits my eyes and I move my head away from the glare. A hooded figure stands in front of me and I squint at the bright light, raise the umbrella with shaking hands.

'Ella, stop.'

It's Alice.

CHAPTER TWENTY-NINE

ALICE

The last thing I expected was Ella to wake up and cause a scene. I've been making mistakes. *Too many, lately*. Letting myself be caught out by things. Two nights ago it was the first aid box that made me catch my breath: I had to hold myself still so that she wouldn't notice. She'd already given me a fright, surprising me like that in the middle of the night. I thought I'd been so quiet. Then there was blood all over the floor: that horrified me. I thought she'd really hurt herself and I hated the idea of that. Feelings are creeping up inside me, spreading out their tentacles and catching me unawares. But it was only a splinter; it made me want to laugh out loud with relief, but Ella was hurt and scared and I didn't want to add any more worries to the dung heap that her husband has already created. *What is it with these men?* She told me Chris had sent an estate agent round to put the house on the market. *What was he playing at?* Of course I told her to think about it. But it did mean one thing – time is running out.

Ella looked knackered this morning. Dark bags had formed under her eyes and I had to force some breakfast down her. She's so frazzled I thought she'd be knocked out at night. I told her I was looking for someone in the garden too, and it's the truth; I just twisted it a little so that it fits my story.

I don't scare easily, as I've told Ella before, but when I shone the torch in her direction and saw her looking like a ghost, wearing a huge white nightdress and holding an umbrella, I almost yelled out loud. My heart pogoed up and down and in the end I just had to tell her.

It wasn't ideal. I found it embarrassing. Being out of control is the ultimate failing as far as I'm concerned. It's bad enough me knowing, but having to tell someone else about it is embarrassing.

Olivia couldn't handle it. For a while she developed insomnia herself because she was convinced I'd fall out of the window onto the unforgiving concrete below. It's not as if we were in one of those hotels on a Spanish party island that you read about, where a drunken British tourist out for a good time takes one step too far over the balcony and ends up having no kind of time left at all. Our balcony was a small drop. So she'd prevent herself from sleeping just in case I had 'an *episode*', as she called it. Eventually she got used to the idea and it only happened once when I was with her. That was bad enough. She wouldn't believe I wasn't awake; she said my eyes weren't glassy like she'd imagined they would be; my arms weren't rigid in front of me. You shouldn't believe everything you see in the movies, I tried to tell her. She did love her films so. That's where I get my passion from. And now I'm passing it on to Ella. *Like a daisy chain.* But that's a pretty image, and I'm talking about something ugly. I have no control of my faculties; worst of all, I couldn't tell you what I get up to when I'm under the spell, as I like to think of it. It's a bit like being under the influence, which is more fun, but that's not a state I allow myself to get into.

Up until now, I think I was justified in not wanting to share my secret with Ella. Olivia was healthy and well adjusted, but it's fair to say that Ella's not exactly in tip-top condition. Telling her about my sleepwalking won't have helped her state of mind one iota.

There, I've said it: I sleepwalk. I have done for as long as I can remember. Ever since, well… That's another story.

I was wearing a raincoat that hangs by the back door, one of hers, presumably. My arms and legs were covered in mud, which looked worse because it had started to rain.

Ella's face went white when I told her, making her grey eyes stand out. She drank a glass of water and said she'd had such a shock because I was wearing Nancy's old raincoat. She couldn't bear to throw it out. I took it off straight away, wanting to run upstairs and get under a hot shower, trying with all my might not to scratch at my prickly skin or to think about that.

I really, really wanted to sleep, but Ella kept me up talking, wanting to know more about my condition and what she could do to help me. I emphasised that it normally only happened a couple of times a year, but that didn't convince her because, as she pointed out, it's happened three times this week. I let her think that was the case because I didn't know how to explain otherwise. I was too tired for clever arguments. Ella said she was going to google it first thing tomorrow.

Just as I was going into my room she called my name and I turned and she pulled me into her arms and held me tight. Her body moulded into mine and I had to draw away. I drew back a little more roughly than I intended and she looked hurt, then closed her door in what was almost a slam. I stood staring at the door for ages; the last thing I wanted to do was hurt Ella, but the truth was too complicated and it was four in the morning. So I tried to sleep, and I imagine she probably did the same in the next room. I was thinking about her a lot, you see, and that disturbed me.

CHAPTER THIRTY

ELLA

The next morning I wander out into the back garden, clutching my mug of tea. In the fresh morning air it's hard to imagine the chill and terror I'd felt the night before, peering through the black gloom. But there was nothing to be afraid of. I'd discovered Alice sleepwalking, covered in mud, her shirt torn. It must have been terrifying for her. If I hadn't caught her in the act I don't think she would have admitted to it; it was like she was wrenching the confession out of herself, while I waited like a fisherman reeling in his catch, desperate for the tiniest slither of information. I feel closer to her now. And relieved, if I'm honest. It explains her slightly odd behaviour. Covering up for it must be exhausting.

The mug warms my fingers as I look around the garden. Alice is making progress; there are fewer weeds, and a vegetable patch is taking shape. *Or is it?* On closer inspection there are piles of earth behind it and a deep hole has been dug. I look up to my window and picture me looking down at night, terrified at the strange happenings in this garden, where torches dance and sleepwalkers roam. *Was someone else here?*

Mr Mortimer is in his front garden watering his hanging baskets when I get home from work. His front porch pops with colour. I feel a little tug of affection. Since our conversation the other day I've warmed to him. His movements are slow and he puts his green watering can on the ground when he sees me. Rubbing his back and taking his cap off, he walks to his side of the path that separates our tiny front gardens.

'Shouldn't be bending at my age. Gives me aches and pains in all sorts of funny places. I like to keep the garden looking nice, though. It's only what Doris would expect from me.'

'Doris has nothing to worry about. You can always ask me to help if it gets too much trouble. Or Alice, I'm sure she wouldn't mind.'

'Not sure I'd trust her. I've been watching what she's getting up to out the back.'

'What do you mean?' I can't help remembering the other night: the muddy shoes, the trail she'd left.

'I've been watching her progress. Not being nosy, just interested, like. She looks strong, capable, like she knows what she's doing. Works fast, too. But what's she's been doing is digging holes, then filling them back in.'

'Planting seeds, you mean?'

He shakes his head, silver strands quivering with the motion.

'No, she just chucks the earth back in. Real quick, like, as if she's in a hurry. People are these days, mind, aren't they? Rushing around yelling private conversations into phones, holding office conversations on the bus. Crazy.' His hair bounces about some more. 'Not that I'm against these mobile phones – I've got one, you know. Don't carry out my business on it though, especially not on the bus.' He chuckles and I fake a smile, my mind still on Alice.

'You're probably mistaken,' I say. 'Alice knows what she's doing. She's been planting vegetable seeds, she showed me. She'll be adding flowers later.' He's already told me his eyesight isn't great and he must have been looking out from an upstairs window. 'I'm sorry the garden has been such a jungle for so long, but she is working on it.'

'Aye, I expect you're right. Wouldn't make sense now, would it, digging a load of holes and filling them back in. Unless she's looking for treasure.' He chuckles again.

An image crosses my mind. I've stood at the window watching Alice, admiring the fluid way she moves and her strong, tanned limbs. *Have we both been in our windows at the same time, our gaze on her? Can she feel our eyes watching her?* I won't do it again, I tell myself. *Why do my thoughts always return to her?*

Then I remember the embroidery.

'Mr Mortimer—'

'Fred.'

A memory stirs whenever he says his name. I remember why. 'Fred. You won't believe this, but there's a sign in the garden that says "*Fred's bakery*".'

'Is there really? Well I never! I used to own a bakery in the village. I wonder what it's doing in your garden. I sold the business years ago.'

'I wanted to ask you about something else I found in the house. It's a piece of embroidery, with a date on: 30 July 1997. Does that date mean anything to you?'

'Ninety-seven, that takes me back a bit.' He scratches his head. 'Let me have a think about it. I'll do some baking, that always helps me concentrate. I'll make some cakes and you can come over for tea. How about that?'

'That would be lovely.'

The knot of anxiety inside me loosens after our conversation, making me feel emotional. Mr Mortimer – Fred – goes inside and I go through the house into the back garden and walk over to the shed. I haven't looked in here since Alice cleared it out. It's tidy now and the shelves are lined with packets of seeds and small plants that she's been bringing home from the garden centre. I almost trip over a cardboard box and it opens. I frown as I recognise Chris's handwriting. The box contains a load of files and I grow increasingly puzzled as I realise it's Chris's old paperwork. His tendency to keep everything drives me mad, but at least he agreed to keep it out of sight in the cellar. *The cellar. So what is this box doing in the shed? Surely she would have told me if she'd been in the cellar? Why would she want to go down there?*

I take the box down to my craft room. It's sealed with thick tape and it takes a while to hack through it with my large scissors. Inside are bank statements, bank letters, MOT certificates. A valentine card. The first one I'd sent him. A house on the front with hearts as windows. A lump forms in my throat. I'd made it in the shop. He'd have known it was from me but I'd drawn a question mark inside all the same. I was trying to tell him I loved him and his home. I sit for ages looking at the card, remembering how in love we were – how different things are now. I put it to one side and finish going through the box. A few more cards, a postcard. It looks old; the photograph is of Notre-Dame in Paris. I turn it over and read the simple message:

Arrived safely, spending a few days in the sun.

I squint at the little red stamp, try and decipher the postmark: July 1997. I jump to my feet, pacing about: *1997 again. But why has he kept it?* I take the last few cards out of the box; they're old Christmas cards. The doorbell rings and I stuff the card in my pocket and hurry downstairs. It's Sadie from number 42. When I see she's holding a baby in her arms I want to slam the door in her face. I smile instead, cooing at the baby, who makes my insides cramp.

'Hi Ella.'

'Hello Sadie. I haven't seen you for a while.'

'I know.' She's jigging the baby up and down. It hurts to watch. 'Ted told me about Chris moving out and, well, I—'

'It's fine, Sadie, really. It's awkward, I know, and you were Chris's friends first.'

'Gosh, thanks for being so sweet about it. Anyway, I'm here to make it up to you.' She hands me an invitation. 'We're having a party on Friday. Do say you'll come. And please bring a guest. I hope you can make it.'

'I'll do my best.'

My phone rings as I watch her go. It's the estate agent, so I let it go to voicemail. I mull over Sadie's words as I take the box upstairs and stash it in my room.

At first I dismiss the idea of the party, but it could be just what I need. I display the invitation on the mantelpiece. Something is missing. Chris's photo as a boy. *Odd.* Alice must have moved it, tidying up probably. I straighten the party invitation. It was nice to be asked along. I'll take Alice. Have a drink, forget babies and mortgages and unknown temptresses just for one night. And if Chris is there, I'll show him I don't care. Besides, I'll be with Alice.

DIARY

It was so difficult to get out of bed today. My ribs were still aching, the pattern of dark green clouds on my skin a constant reminder. As if I could forget. This time yesterday morning Kit was still here and I hadn't been punished for his departure.

I'd woken to the sounds of the front door closing, Kit leaving for work, or so I presumed. I'd gone downstairs for breakfast, a boiled egg with a slice of toast, but I didn't manage a single mouthful. My daughter was upstairs in bed, off sick from school. Food poisoning, I told Edward. But my gut told me otherwise. I went upstairs to see if she wanted anything, but she was asleep, or perhaps she was pretending but I let her be.

Kit had left his door ajar and I stuck my head into his room to see if he had any clothes that needed washing. He has a tendency to leave his clothes on the floor and Edward gets mad at me for not cleaning up after him, not doing the housework properly, not being a good enough wife. The boy needs his privacy but Edward gives me no choice.

But Kit's bed was made and the air felt curiously still. There were no clothes abandoned on the floor and a white envelope sat on top of the green quilt. My stomach lurched as if I was on a boat, out at sea. I stood for a while, not wanting to know yet knowing already.

I could hear the clock ticking in the hall downstairs and I counted five hundred ticks before I opened the note. It used to be one hundred that I counted up to, to put things off, but that doesn't satisfy me now. This is what he wrote.

I'm sorry Mum, I can't do this any more. Dad wants to keep me here working with him. It's not what I want, but saying no to him isn't an option, you know that. If I stay I won't be able to protect you, so I'm leaving home and I promise one day I'll let you know where I am but I'm too scared of Dad finding out so it won't be for a while. Destroy this note as soon as you've read it. You should get out too, Mum, take Melissa and run. Love you.

My vision blackened at the edges and I had to grip the back of the chair to stop myself from fainting. The dizzy spell appeared to go on for ages, my heart thudding in my chest. I can't bear to think that my boy has left me.

Much later when I'd composed myself I went to see Melissa. She was asleep and I didn't have the heart to wake her; she adores her brother. Or used to. Before this family fell apart. I didn't know what to do about Edward, but I couldn't keep still so I took everything out of the kitchen cupboards and scrubbed until the air smelt of lemons and my hands were sticking to the rubber gloves from sweat. After that I cleaned the fridge and polished the table. My face looked back at me from the shiny surface: an old woman with tired, sagging skin and jagged lines around her eyes. I didn't recognise her; I wished she wasn't me. For a second I remembered how I looked when I first met

Edward, my slim figure, my excitement at life. He used to take me dancing and treat me like porcelain – precious. That was before he made me his wife.

Edward liked me to look my best, so I had a bath and put one of my nicest dresses on – the one with the red flowers. My dress looked cheerful and I tried to pretend I was, too, plastering a smile on my face. I baked him a steak and kidney pie, his favourite, and it turned out not too bad despite the way my hands trembled like twigs in the wind. But when we sat down to dinner, just the two of us as Melissa was still in bed, tension crackled between us. My throat was so dry, I was unable to speak. The sound of Edward eating made my stomach turn. The last thing I wanted to do was eat. The grandfather clock ticked although time appeared to stand still, and when nine o'clock came and Kit still wasn't home Edward said he knew I was hiding something and when he dug his fingers into my shoulders and spat words in my face I couldn't hold it in. I never can, that's the trouble.

When I told him Kit had gone he hit me so hard I fell to the floor. He kicked me in my ribs again and again and again. I clenched my mouth shut, praying Melissa wouldn't hear anything and I bit so hard into my lip that my mouth bled too, but that was nothing in comparison to the marks he left on me. Black and blue and purple. All over my body. Everywhere. Each time it's worse. He went upstairs and I heard him bashing around in the spare room. He never sleeps in the same bed with me after an episode. It was the only good thing to come from that awful evening.

The sound of retching woke me again this morning and I attempted to get out of bed. I'd forgotten. Pain made me cry out and I wrapped my hands around my ribs, pressed the skin lightly with my fingers, feeling for the damage.

I rubbed cold cream into my bruises and dressed in my loose cotton dress, worn soft with use. I walked around the room until I'd got used to the places it hurt; I think one of my ribs on the left side is broken. That's how it felt the last time one broke. I worked out the best way to move so that Melissa wouldn't notice. I've got used to having to prepare myself, slip into a mask, so that other people don't ever see the truth.

When I was prepared, I went to Melissa's room. She was sat on the edge of the bed, hair limp around her pale face, arms folded. She told me she was sick. I wondered aloud about what she'd eaten the night before but the expression on her face was fear. She uncrossed her arms and her nightdress shifted, settled over a bulge.

We both looked at the bump and she burst into tears, a terrible howling of anguish. She knew what this meant, too, and she begged me not to tell him. After the terrible scene Edward caused when he found out she'd got a boyfriend I didn't think she'd dare see him again, but she assured me she hadn't broken her word. This was from before she broke up with him – the forbidden boy she loved – but the damage had already been planted inside her. We talked in whispers and she realised how foolish she'd been, but I couldn't waste time in recriminations. We had to act. I should have given her a lecture but terrifying images were playing in my mind. We had to make a plan while Edward was out.

Melissa said she wouldn't get rid of it. That was when the nightmare began. I got to my feet without making a sign that my ribs screamed with pain. Her face crumpled when I told her Kit had gone and we cried together, holding onto each other. She'd told him about the baby, which made it worse for her.

I looked at her stricken face and I decided then. I told her we had to go too, we had to get out before her father came back. I didn't say the words but I didn't need to. I saw hope on her face for the first time in months. She knew what he would do if he found out. She knew it wasn't worth the risk.

CHAPTER THIRTY-ONE
ALICE

Ella was waiting for me to come home from work today. Just like Olivia used to: different setting, same motivation. Olivia used to sit at a wooden table outside the flat, chopping vegetables for supper, her long dark hair standing out against the white cliff behind her. She said she liked to watch me coming down the cliff path, home to her. The slow smile she used to give me was like a present to come home to.

Ella had a different energy, rushing in from the garden the moment I walked in from work, accosting me. This afternoon she made me a cup of tea, gestured for me to sit down opposite her, asked about my day. For the first time in ages I felt wanted.

Then she sprung it on me. She wanted me to mediate. The husband would come round to discuss what they were going to do about the house and I'd make sure they were civil. Her eyes burned. Her spark was back. The fire she'd lost when Chris betrayed her was being lit once again. Her features were reanimated and she glowed. I flickered, too.

Of course I couldn't do it. *No way.* I pointed out that I was hardly impartial, forced to see how she had wilted like a plant without water when Chris left. How I hated him for doing that. Ella's cheeks flushed and she wore a hint of a smile, pleased, but not wanting to show it. She needn't know the real reason. I almost got carried away watching her, acknowledging for the first time a jolt of attraction. I sipped at my tea, which had cooled, hoping to cool my insides too. I was right not to tell her about Olivia.

Getting sloppy, I am. Emotional nonsense, forgetting my purpose. Why I am here. I soon forgot any fancy notions when she told me what she'd been doing. Looking into Chris's affairs, the boxes and files he kept in the shed. Isn't it funny how emotions can change so quickly? I asked Ella if she'd moved anything and she said she hadn't. *I hope not.* The cold tea couldn't help, what I needed was hard liquor, a shot of fiery whisky to my belly to keep me on the right path.

Ella told me she feels differently now; she has accepted the situation. That explained her new glow. She'd talked to a solicitor and was actually considering selling. I didn't let my alarm show; I tried my hardest to hide it. I suggested a glass of wine to celebrate but ice swirled inside me as it hit me that I'm running out of time. Too many obstacles are rising up: the estate agent, the nosy neighbour and, of course, *him.* The husband.

The neighbour is out there whenever I am. Lurking, watching, following. He should get the hint that I'm not going to speak to him.

At night my compulsion keeps returning, as if she's calling me from wherever she is. *Why not, so what if it's dark?* I've spent enough time out there now to know the layout well enough.

But I'm not getting anywhere. I've been focusing my attention around the shed: digging, digging, digging. *Nothing.* At night I do it in my sleep, pull up weeds and search. Maybe my focus has been wrong. The clue has to be inside the house itself.

My defences are down in this creaky old house, late at night. It's making me weak. Letting Ella sleep in my room the other night was a mistake. She acted as if I were some kind of saviour. What would she think if she found out she reassured me that night as much as I did her?

Ella is getting under my skin. *Big mistake. Or is it?* Maybe she can help me get what I want.

DIARY

It happened again today. There's no stopping him. Since our aborted attempt to flee he won't let us out of his sight. I'd lain awake for hours listening to the rain hit the windows, trying to batter its way in. Some of it penetrated the side window; I could tell it was open from the loud drip that kept me from sleeping: *drip drip drip*. I counted thousands, it gave me something to focus on.

My limbs were seized with paralysis, I hadn't known it was possible to be so frightened. Despite it being summer I was wearing my thickest pyjamas, I trembled all over. I rubbed my hands over my body in an attempt to get warm, my hip bones sharp against my hands. My one small victory over Edward is that he doesn't know I've barely eaten lately; I stash food in carrier bags under the bed where it festers until he goes out. I've been flushing what I can down the toilet, it's my 'fuck you' to him. He doesn't know I swear either, the names I call him in my head. It helps, a little.

The bed pressed against the knots of my spine and I twisted about, wishing I could scream, let the pain out into the cold room. The drip lessened and I held my breath between drops until it stopped altogether. There was movement downstairs: a shuffling, a scraping. He was getting ready.

I heard the slam of the back door, he didn't care who heard him. I couldn't believe he was going out again. Even though he couldn't hear me I tiptoed on my bony feet over to the window, watched the golden blob of torchlight as it drew patterns over the lawn, up the bushes, towards the pond beyond.

The first night he went out I asked him what he was doing and he grabbed my shoulders and exhaled his sour whisky breath over my face, digging his dirty nails into my skin until blood crept over his fingers. I've watched him every night he's been out there, digging in the dark, my eyes getting accustomed to the blackness. The realisation of what he is doing has crept over me, beginning as a dread in my gut, coursing through me with the blood around my veins, until it strikes horror into my heart. Because I know what he plans to do and I'm too frightened to stop him.

Melissa sleeps downstairs, unaware. Or at least, I hope she's sleeping because if she isn't she might be watching from her window, too, her body growing as mine shrinks. She might have worked it out, like I have.

What he plans to do to her.

CHAPTER THIRTY-TWO
ALICE

Ella was different tonight. She had a wistful air. My skin tingled with anticipation. I was getting closer to her now, I could feel it. A feeling was no good to me, though; it needed to translate into something tangible. But enough of that.

Ella had received an invitation to a party from the couple who live across the road. She said it was awkward as they were originally mutual friends of hers and the husband.

'Chris won't be there,' she said. 'And if he is, well, I'm ready to face him.' That made it easy for me to decide. I'd been toying with the idea; I saw it as a challenge. And I wanted to be with her.

Her face lit up when I offered to accompany her and she threw her arms around me. Pressed her curves against mine; I couldn't deny the frisson I felt. I pulled away somewhat hastily and hurt flickered in her face. She really should learn to hide what she's feeling. But I was flattered, of course I was.

There was only one sticky moment when Ella asked me about a missing photo of her husband as a child. 'I don't remember ever seeing that,' I said.

It was fun getting ready together, like being a teenager again, although what would I know about that? I wore my new Armani trouser suit over a navy silk blouse; my pressed trousers were just the right length to show off my soft leather boots. Ella coincidentally matched me in a fitted blue dress that showed off her figure. She looked stunning, but she didn't realise it. I wish I could wash all her insecurities away.

A man with a flushed face opened the door to number 42 and tried to hide the bolt of embarrassment that crossed his face when he saw Ella. *Surely Sadie had told him she'd invited Ella?* He hugged her and went to hug me too, but I stuck my hand out and he got the message. Ted led us into the kitchen where he said, 'It's Ella,' in a loud voice to a woman with red hair who was ladling out punch from a bowl, but if it was a warning it was lost on her. She released her ladle into the bowl so that drops of what looked like blood spattered the table, before she squealed with delight and held out her arms to Ella. Alarm bells clanged in my head.

'Ella,' she said, 'I'm so glad you could make it. Have some of my super punch. It's lethal.' She handed us each a glass, giggling. 'And delicious.'

'Christ,' Ted said, rolling his eyes at her and leaving the room.

Ella introduced me and Sadie looked surprised when she heard I was her flatmate. I prefer lodger; 'flatmate' makes me sound like a fresh-faced student living in digs. Ella had drunk a glass of wine before leaving the house; she'd put music on and danced around the kitchen. I'd seen a playful side to her I haven't witnessed before. But it was alcohol-induced bravado, she couldn't hide her nerves from me: the anxious flutter in her hands, the clearing of her throat. It made her talk even more than ever.

'I thought Chris would have called you,' Sadie said, lilting her voice to phrase it as a question. 'I guess it makes sense. Chris said he'd put the house on the market.'

'Did he now?' I said.

Sadie's cheeks flushed a shade of red almost equal to the punch she was suddenly stirring furiously.

'It's OK, you can tell me.' Ella's tone was jaunty but her clenched jaw gave her away.

'I haven't seen him,' Sadie said. 'You needn't worry about that, it's just that I've been so busy with Charlotte starting nursery, getting her settled in. I can't bear to be apart from her. And she couldn't care less – loves it, typical. She cries when I pick her up. So embarrassing.' She looked at Ella, who had her head cocked to one side, hands twisting together. That would be from the mention of the child. I know Ella. Certain things hurt her.

'You were saying about Chris…?'

'Oh, yes. Ted's seen him, not me. They met for a quick drink last week. That's how we know the house is on the market. You'll get a good price. You know how rarely houses like these go up for sale.'

'Chris wants to put it on the market.' Ella drained her punch and stuck her glass out for more. 'I haven't decided yet.'

But that's not what she told me.

Sadie opened her mouth to speak but she was interrupted by Ted ushering more guests in, another couple. While he was introducing them to Ella, I slipped out of the kitchen and went into the garden. Plants in marble pots were strategically placed around a decking area and a twisty path snaked through the neatly cut lawn. A few chairs were set out on the grass, a chill hung in the air and the garden was lit by fairy lights which twinkled in the trees, anticipating Christmas. It was so different to the jungle at number 46, where Nancy's tree grew. I thought about my room, looking down into the garden below. My mind strayed to Nancy being in there and everything that happened. A large gulp of the deep red punch helped me wipe the thought from my mind, then I poured the rest onto the lawn. It was too strong and I needed to stay alert.

Laughter tinkled out from the kitchen and I made my way back inside. Ella was deep in conversation with Sadie, whose hand was resting on her arm. Seeing me, she broke off the conversation.

'Oh, there you are. Come for more punch, have you?'

'I'd rather have a glass of water, if that's alright.'

'Coming up, sparkling OK?'

I nodded, watching Ella, who was biting her lip. I took her by the elbow into the other room, where a small group of people were chatting. Two men were smoking in the garden and a couple were having an earnest conversation on the sofa, leaning close to one another, oblivious to the rest of the party. Ella and I sat on the sofa at the far end of the room. I asked her if she was OK and she assured me she was. She pointed out who some of the people were, but I wasn't interested in them. I was completely unprepared for the tall man with an Afro mop who came over and asked Ella if she wanted to dance. She was on her third punch by then and swayed a little as she jumped up to join him. The Rolling Stones were playing, 'Jumpin' Jack Flash', so there was no danger of a smoochy kind of dance, but I felt as if my blood was hot when I watched them. Like when I used to watch Olivia salsa-dancing with José. The record changed and I willed Ella to come back but they carried on dancing while I drummed my fingernails on my empty glass. A group of about six people streamed into the room and began dancing, encouraging others to join in. It became more like a party then.

The doorbell rang and Ted, who looked like he was auditioning for *Saturday Night Fever* in his white suit, stopped his dad-dancing and went to answer the door. Male voices rose from the hall and Ted came back in, taking Sadie aside. They had a hurried conversation in urgent whispers. I realised what was happening but it was too late to do anything about it. It was Ella's husband.

CHAPTER THIRTY-THREE

ELLA

It's Chris. I swear the room goes quiet even though the Bee Gees are playing. The man I'm dancing with, Gary, looks ridiculous – his arm movements are following a different rhythm to his feet. I look to Alice for reassurance but I can't see her through the crowd. My heart stops as I wait for Chris's girlfriend to follow him in but it looks as if he's alone. I turn away so that he can't see my face.

Sadie is pushing through the crowd towards me with a knotted expression. She takes me into the kitchen. 'I'm so sorry. I thought he wasn't coming. God, this is a mess, bloody Ted must have invited him because I certainly didn't.' Her hands are clenched together and her fingers are dancing. I wish she would stop talking.

'It's OK. It's not as if we haven't seen each other since the split, but it's so difficult at the moment. At least he's on his own.'

Sadie's eyes widen and she throws a quick glance over her shoulder. 'That's what I wanted to warn you about. He isn't alone. His – er – friend…' she hesitates, 'has gone to the bathroom. Awkward.'

I swallow hard and the door opens with a squeak. I hold my breath as an immaculate-looking blonde woman walks in wearing a tight red dress and spiky stilettos. She heads straight to Chris. It's just how I imagined. So this is the 'friend'. She's not one of the women who work in his office. I look for Alice, but can't see her. *Where is she?*

'Let me get you a drink.'

Sadie has a purpose now and she takes my elbow and guides me into the kitchen. I dip my glass into the punch and fill it to the brim, slopping liquid all over the table, a splatter of pink landing on the fresh white tablecloth. *I don't care.* Sadie is making sympathetic noises while looking guilty and talking quickly about how she's sure it's nothing serious and she's not even sure they're dating. '*Wittering*', Nancy would call it. I refill my glass and imagine a zip drawing Sadie's mouth to a close, the edges digging into her skin. A noise is roaring in my head, but I'm the only one who can hear it.

I push past her, through the people in the living room, knocking against the woman in the red dress whose strong perfume catches in my throat. She gasps and moves closer to Chris, who's seen me, and I run upstairs to the bathroom, looking for Alice. The bathroom is occupied and I hammer on the door calling her name, distantly aware that I'm making too much noise.

'For Christ's sake, can't I have a piss in peace?' The door is yanked open and the tall man I'd been dancing with emerges. *Gary.*

'Oh, it's you. Fancy another dance?'

I ignore him and check the bedrooms for occupants, but this isn't a teenage party and there are no writhing couples hiding under the coats, and there's no Alice, either. *Where is she? She'll know what to do. Alice always knows what to do.*

She must be in the garden. I hold the bannister tightly as I sway downstairs, coming to a stop in the living room doorway, but Chris is right in front of the patio door, his girlfriend hanging off his arm. *How could he?* I gulp at my drink. I focus my eyes on the exit, lower my head and push forward, but I'm too slow.

'Hey.' His hand lands on my forearm and grips it. I let out a cry and pull away. He shifts so his body blocks my path. The girl at his side tosses her hair back: long, glossy blonde hair that shines under the spotlights. *Definitely not Tanya.*

'Let me pass.'

'You can't avoid me, Ella. We need to talk about the house. I'm putting it on the market. You can't stop me.'

'I need more time. It's my home too.'

'In theory, but it's been in my family for decades. I can't believe you would do this.'

The girlfriend, who is standing at his side pouting at me, puts a hand on his arm, but he shakes it off, causing her thickly painted eyebrows to disappear under her fringe. She doesn't know him as well as I do; Chris hates being touched when his temper is simmering.

'How do you think Nancy would feel if she could see the way you're treating me?'

'How dare you bring Mum into it?' He takes a step forward. 'I'm selling the house and you can't stop me.' His voice shakes with anger.

I have to get out of here.

'I want you out, Ella. Your little flatmate, too. I've had enough of being nice.'

I'm aware of the pulsing music of the track fading, the buzz of conversation fizzing out like a dying wasp and heads turning at the sound of Chris's shouting.

'The only way you'll get me out is if you physically remove me. Do that, and I'll call the police.' I'm aware that I'm talking like I'm a character in a television drama, but nothing feels real any more. 'Show's over,' I say to the gawping faces and open mouths before I disappear into the garden.

CHAPTER THIRTY-FOUR

ALICE

The two men were standing too close together as I pushed out through the doors and inhaled deeply. They shifted apart as I emerged. The smoker said hello and flashed me a smile as his friend waved his empty glass and went into the house. The smoker ground his heel into his cigarette butt and I bummed a cigarette off him before he followed his friend inside, leaving me alone in the still garden. This garden had a neat lawn and you could see straight on to the heath, where the wind raced through the trees and a dog howled from somewhere in the heart of the forest. But unlike 46 Heath Street, this house wasn't in need of protection.

The sound of a glass clattering to the floor, followed by a cry, filtered out through the back door and I didn't want to go back inside. It had been a narrow escape. I didn't want to see him; I dared not trust myself after the way he'd treated Ella. *Ella.* As if I'd summoned her, she emerged in a flash of blue through the patio doors, a little unsteady on her feet, and scanned the garden. *Was she looking for me?* My heart jumped at the thought. Of course she would be, I'm her confidante: sensible Alice, the one who knows what to do in a crisis. Why had I agreed to come here when I should have dissuaded her from coming? We could be settled at home with a bottle of wine, curled up on the sofa, legs grazing…

I stood just outside the house, looking inside but obscured by a curtain hanging inside the window. A man's laughter rang out, a loud laugh that made me shiver. *The husband.* I couldn't help looking, watching him flirting with her, the other woman. Rage rendered me rigid. *How dare he bring her and flaunt her in front of Ella, in front of me?* The woman sipped her drink and ran her tongue around her lips as if she were putting on a show for him. Ella was still looking out into the garden, but she turned her head as he laughed and the siren made eyes at him. A look of anguish played over her face. He'd just made a big mistake, hurting her like that.

I took one last look at him from behind the curtain, bile rising in my throat.

I'd make him pay.

CHAPTER THIRTY-FIVE
ELLA

I burst into the garden to look for Alice, but I only see darkness. I knock over a chair and spot half a glass of red wine on a green garden table; I pause to drain it in one go before walking further down the garden. *She can't have left me here, surely, not with Chris turning up.* Then I remember that Alice hasn't actually met Chris, so she won't have recognised him. I'm stuck here, looking out into the darkness of Hampstead Heath, faced with either going back inside and seeing Chris and his young blonde sidekick, or climbing the fence and escaping through the park. I look back at the house. Music pours out through the windows and mingles with the buzz of chatter, laughter, a yell. At this moment in time the heath looks like the most attractive option.

A figure stands beside a tree, watching me, emerging from the shadows. *It's Alice.* Relief floods me. I trip down the path, stumbling towards her, and she reaches out to catch me. Warm hands on my cold skin, concern in her almond-shaped eyes.

'What's the matter? You're shaking.' Alice wraps her arms around me and holds me tight, the heat from her body seeping into mine. Her back is hard, muscular, strong. I feel protected.

My lips are against her ear; it's easier to speak without her seeing me. 'Chris is here with *her*. How could he, Alice, why would he do this to me?'

Alice's firm hands grip my shoulders and she pushes me back gently, holding me at arm's length. Her brown eyes fix on mine and I blink the tears away. The volume of the music from the house increases and it reverberates through the garden. The bass beat pounds with the anxious rhythm of my heart.

'He said he wants me out of the house. He shouted at me, right in front of everybody.'

'Bastard.' Alice's fiery eyes are glaring in the direction of the house. 'Listen to me. It's a shock for you, seeing her for the first time, it must hurt, but you're stronger than that, remember? What's happened to the Ella who told me – what – two days ago that she was moving on? Where's that strong woman gone? You've been so much better the past few days, Ella, don't let him get to you. He can't force you to sell, you've got rights.'

'I'm sorry, Alice, none of this is fair on you. You must be worried you'll have to move out, too.'

'You can't worry about me.' She relaxes her hands, looks towards the house where a peal of laughter punctuates the air. *Her, I bet. Talking about me.*

'But I like living with you.' *There, I've said it.*

Her hair swings as she turns back to me, a streak in the dark as it catches the light. I reach out and touch it without thinking. She holds herself very still, her lips slightly parted, a tiny puff of breath between us.

'I like living with you too.' Her eyes are back on mine, asking a question.

Yes.

Alice leans forward, pressing her lips to mine. The noise of the party fades away and I am only aware of the surge of excitement inside me. Her arms stretch around me and I don't know if the heartbeat I can feel is hers or mine. But it feels right, natural, to be kissing her, and my worries float away with the evening breeze. Until footsteps, voices, interrupt us and we're forced to separate.

Alice takes my hand. 'This way,' she says. 'You don't need to see him again.' She leads me towards the fence where the heath waits in darkness.

DIARY

27 JULY 1997

He was out there for two hours this time. I only dared spend a few minutes at the window watching the torch-light dance around in the black of night; I was too afraid he'd look up and spot me, even though that should be impossible with our bedroom in darkness. Fear makes you illogical. The rest of the time I laid still, pretending to be asleep, although if he'd touched me he'd have felt how rigid I was: on alert. But he never usually touches me on those nights, he's too preoccupied with whatever he's been doing. My energy is spent making sure I survive this. Because I have to be strong for her.

I cried with relief when he went out to the shop this morning. I drank tea in the kitchen, ignoring the rumble in my stomach, and looked out of the window. I wanted to check the garden but Doris was hanging her washing out and I couldn't possibly speak to her. Instead I looked in on Melissa, hoping to find her sleeping, but she was sitting up in bed, one hand rubbing her stomach, which grows daily. Dark patches underline her eyes and her sallow skin is far from blooming. Eczema has flared on her arms and legs and her lank hair is plastered to her head. Pregnancy is not being kind to her.

Melissa's wardrobe door was open and I caught sight of her school uniform – it pulled at my heart. The green-and-red kilt she so hated, the bottle-green jumper and red tie. It wasn't so long ago she was doing handstands against the back wall, tumbling and laughing, her tie hanging down. A lump in my throat stopped me from speaking but I had to be strong for her, so I swallowed it down.

I asked her how she was feeling and she looked at me with sad eyes and shrugged. I told her it was only a matter of weeks before this would be over and she burst into tears. I lost count of how long I sat with my arm around her, her slight body burdened with the huge load she carried. Carrying her was so different for me. I was young and in love and excited for the future. Hard to imagine now.

Once Doris had gone indoors, I ventured outside. He'd tramped through my flower beds in the dark, his footprints tracking his progress: he'd left a trail of broken stalks, petals littering the ground. The broken flowers resembled my heart, sliced into pieces and stamped upon. The soil around the shed had been dug over, but I couldn't see what had occupied him for two hours. I crouched down on shaking legs and peered at the ground. My heartbeat felt as if it was pounding in my ears. What would I find? I said a prayer when I saw he hadn't been digging as deep as I feared. Maybe I'd got it all wrong. Mother used to tell me I had an overactive imagination.

Doris suddenly appeared next door and I was trapped. I couldn't go back inside without talking so I made sure the mask was in place, kept the conversation safe. We discussed how the foxes were ruining the garden. She reckoned they kept her awake at night. For her own sake I hope she's not snooping around when he's out here. I wouldn't wish that on her. She asked after Melissa, why she hadn't seen her for weeks. I didn't look at her when I told her she'd gone away for a while, and she hovered about, prodding and poking me with questions that I won't – can't – answer. She narrowed her eyes when I was talking, as if she didn't believe what I was saying.

Melissa managed some soup and a slice of bread today. It took her ages to finish the feeble meal but it's better than nothing. My childcare manual doesn't cover what to do if the mother won't eat. Yet I was in control of myself – the one thing in my life I have got control over – and this gave me strength.

I know the chapter on childbirth off by heart, just in case. I tried to ask him what would happen when the baby came and he laughed in my face, said I was a woman, wasn't I, and I'd been through it before. When I protested he slapped my face. Red stripes marked my cheek and my face throbbed for days. I have to think of a way to get Melissa away from here. Away from him.

CHAPTER THIRTY-SIX

ELLA

Heavy curtains block out the light. Sunlight peeps through the slits; even these mere slithers are like glass shards scratching my eyes. I'm lying on my side, my right arm dead underneath me. I shift my weight and lift my lifeless limb, dropping it down on the bed. I knead my arm until it moves from unresponsive to limp, my mind blank until I massage a bruise to life and suddenly remember banging my arm as I climbed over the fence. Sitting up, my dead arm is forgotten along with my blissfully ignorant state of mind. The party, Chris, the argument, the house, Alice. *Alice.*

What happened? I close my eyes, my head banging in time with a branch that the wind is blowing against the window. My phone tells me it's mid-morning, so Alice should be at work, *thank God.* I screw my face up when I remember what a fool I made of myself. I curl up into a ball, wishing I could make myself disappear, squirming at my behaviour, my drunkenness.

This time yesterday the row with Chris would have been uppermost in my mind. But my focus has shifted to Alice. The memory of kissing her is the one thing that doesn't make me squirm, because she responded. *I'm sure she did.* I feel again the fluttering in my stomach: *did she feel it too? She wasn't drunk, was she?* I rewind back to earlier on in the evening when we arrived. *No, I'm sure she stuck to sparkling water.*

My phone beeps. A text from Alice. She wants to cook for me this evening. I drop my head back on the pillow, taking a deep breath. At least she hasn't run for the hills. I jump out of bed, instantly regretting the swift movement, which makes my head pound. I wonder where she is, what she's doing, unable to stop thinking about her.

Chris leaves a series of angry messages on my phone but I don't pick up. His red, bloated face at the party, yelling at me that he wanted me out of the house, pulses in my mind. *Should I sell up? Get away from all this?* My love for him is being eroded, piece by piece. But mostly my thoughts revolve around Alice. I need fresh air. A walk on the heath.

Autumn is definitely on its way out. I kick at conkers on the ground as I plough along the familiar track back to the house. A dog races after a ball, scattering dead leaves and twigs. It's not just the house I would miss if I moved away, it's all this: the heath on the doorstep, the view I can lose myself in, the feeling of being outside the city. The whole time my mind is on Alice. *Maybe she could stay in the house more permanently?* The idea excites me.

Mr Mortimer is watering his plants again. He makes his way towards the gate when he sees me; he looks at my muddy boots.

'Been out on the heath?'

'Yes, I needed some fresh air.'

'I've found something I'd like to show you, if you've got a minute?'

'Lovely.' I've always wondered what the house next door looks like inside. 'I've got something for you, too. I won't be a minute.' I fetch the bakery sign from the garden. He beams at it.

'Well I never. Didn't think I'd see that old thing again. I'll put it up on my shed. Come on in. What you said the other day, I've been thinking. Rang a bell somewhere, you know how it is when something's niggling in your head and you can't quite tease it out. So I've done a bit of digging.' He indicates his front door, winks. 'I might even stretch to a cup of tea, if you're lucky.'

'Tea would be great.'

Mr Mortimer's face flushes and I wonder if he's lonely. Loneliness is something I've come to recognise. I've never noticed any visitors to his house or him getting out much. I find myself wondering what he does for Christmas. I've always been too wrapped up in my life with Chris to even notice. *What else did I miss out on in our sham of a marriage?*

He leads me through his narrow hallway; the house is a mirror version of ours, but his home exists in a different period. The kitchen has a 1950s air to it, with a Formica table and pale yellow cupboards. It's spotless and there's a comfortable, lived-in feel to the place.

'I've only got ordinary tea. None of that fancy herbal stuff you get nowadays. I went into a café the other day, young chap serving, terribly polite he was, asked me what I wanted and I told him a coffee and he asked me what kind and pointed at this board. Well, it was like being in a foreign restaurant, like when me and Doris went to Majorca once. That was a long time ago, mind you. I told him coffee with water and a dash of milk. Not too hot. Very nice it was, in the end.'

I smile. 'Ordinary tea is fine, thank you.'

'Sit yourself down.'

He hums to himself as he puts the kettle on and makes a pot of tea. He's like the kindly grandfather I never had.

Once the pot is on the table he excuses himself and comes back carrying a photo album. 'Like I said, it got me thinking, our conversation the other day. That date you asked me about, 1997 wasn't it? Something was niggling at my mind, I couldn't quite work out what. So I thought I'd jog it along a bit. Doris used to like photographs, and she was meticulous about organising them. Because of her work, you see, she was an archivist for the museum. Used to collect things. All the photos of the family were very precious to her and she kept them all in albums, clearly labelled. And like I told you before, she used to be right friendly with the neighbours, we used to hold street parties and all that kind of stuff – very different in those days, it were. So if she had any photographs of the people next door I thought it might help me remember.'

He places an album in front of me. Black-and-white photographs are fixed onto the black pages with corners. Small photographs, four to a page, each with a neatly handwritten caption underneath. He opens the book to the beginning, traces his gnarly finger over the face of a woman. 'My Doris.'

'She looks lovely.'

The young woman he's gazing at has wavy ginger hair and a shy smile; she's wearing a flowery dress that nips her tiny waist in. She's leaning against a railing looking over a beach, an ice cream cone in her hand.

'Used to be able to get my hands right round her waist, lift her up in the air and swing her round.'

'You must miss her.'

'She's always with me, don't you worry. Listen to me, wittering on.' Mr Mortimer clears his throat. 'Enough of me being sentimental. This is what I wanted to show you.' He turns a couple of pages.

'There. Your in-laws. Long time ago, mind.' It's the first photo I've seen of Chris's father – there were never any around the house. I draw in a sharp breath at the unexpected facial resemblance to Chris. But there the resemblance ends, as I look at the tall man with a moustache, wearing a tweed suit, legs astride as if he's a soldier on duty. A young man. And Nancy. She looks even younger.

'Oh, look at Nancy, isn't she lovely?'

'Doris and Nancy were good friends when we first moved in, like I said. Something happened, I don't know what, she wouldn't talk about it. They stopped being so friendly. Very upset, Doris was.'

'That's a shame,' I reply. 'Do you know what year this party was?'

'Let me think. We'd been here a few years then, so I reckon it must have been around 1990. It was the summer street party they had every year.'

I do the maths. Chris would have been about ten.

'There are more.' He turns the page. The photos show the same long table set out in the middle of the road. White tablecloth, bunting. A group of children smile up at the camera, spoons raised, some kind of trifle in their bowls.

'Honey pudding,' he says, pointing to the food. 'Doris made it specially.'

'There.' I point out Chris, a serious-looking boy wearing shorts and a knitted tank top. Next to him a dark-haired girl, back to the camera.

'Was that his sister, do you know?'

'I'm not too sure, to be truthful, I don't recognise any of them in particular. There were that many kiddies living in this street, used to play out all the time. Doris knew all their names, of course. She'd have written them on the back if they were known to her. There might be some further on in the book.'

I turn the page, eager to see more.

'Can you tell me more about the people who've lived in the house before?'

'Another young couple lived there, had a baby – a girl, I think. But the wife wasn't happy living down south – she came from Newcastle I seem to remember. They moved back up there. The Rutherfords moved in after them with their two children, Chris and… the little girl, I forget her name. I haven't seen her in years. How is she?'

'I don't know. I've never met her and Chris doesn't talk about his family much. I don't suppose you remember anything about it?'

'Like I've said before, Doris would have been a lot more help than me. They were a very organised family, if that's the right word. Edward was an army man, used to keep his family a bit regimented was the impression I got. He had impeccable manners, although Doris reckoned it was a bit of a front. But the world was different then, most families had values like that.' His eyes take on a faraway look in them and he nods.

'You've got me thinking now, it's coming back to me. Doris came home once from shopping in town, she always used to go in on market day, have coffee with her friend, what was her name? Betty, that was it. Well, one day she came home, said she'd seen the young girl from next door all over a boy. Canoodling on a bench in the graveyard, they were. She wanted to tell Nancy, the girl's mother, but she decided against it in the end, said the father was so strict with the poor kiddies she'd better keep it to herself.'

'Chris won't talk about his father.'

'He went out to work every day, barely saw the kiddies. I was the same when our daughter was little. Doris stayed at home with her.'

'I didn't realise you had children.'

'Just the one. Sylvia. I don't see her much, she's busy with her own children. Two boys.' He shakes his head. 'Besides, she lives in Scotland, so it's not as if she can pop round, is it? And you won't catch me going up there, it's far too cold. Snows all winter. My old bones wouldn't be able to cope with that. Fiona from the church pops round every now and then to check I'm OK. I'm sure Doris put her up to it, but she's a lovely girl.'

'Could I borrow these photo albums, have a proper look?'

'Of course you can. They're only gathering dust on the shelves. Your Chris might like to have a look.'

'Thanks.' I gather up the books. 'And for the tea, too. I'll have a look through these and return them when I'm done. I'll make you a cup of tea in return, Mr Mortimer.'

'Fred, please, you'll make me feel like a teacher otherwise.'

*

Later at home I go through the album, my fingertips tingling, eager. I examine pictures of Chris with long legs and a gawky adolescent pose, and I briefly wonder again about what happened to the photo from the mantelpiece. Returning my attention to the photos, the dark girl from the earlier image is visible in others, always turned away from the camera, as if hiding. *Is this the mysterious sister, avoiding the camera like a typical teenager?* I've almost got to the end of the book when a photograph flutters to the floor. My back jars as I stoop to pick it up. A young girl with long, dark hair and deep-set eyes glowers at the camera. Full lips in a sulky mouth. There's something familiar about the pose, the way she leans against the wall, arms crossed defiantly. Something from the photo speaks to me. *I'm sure I've seen this girl before.*

My phone buzzes. It's a text from Alice, telling me to get dressed up for dinner. Excitement shoots little fireworks inside me. The idea of a future at Heath Street with Alice is a sparkler coming to life. I'll show her everything I've found tonight, and together we can try and figure it out.

CHAPTER THIRTY-SEVEN

ELLA

I'm fizzing with adrenaline and Alice won't be home for ages yet. I decide to take a quick trip to the shops followed by a workout. I sling my gym kit into my bag and head out the door. It's time I picked up my life again.

The dress I choose is a low-backed, calf-length black silk number. I can't afford it but I refuse to think about the expense; it's ages since I bought anything for myself – and I want to look good for Alice. My pulse rises and I can't help recalling how Chris maxed up his credit cards behind my back.

When I arrive home, Alice is wearing silk culottes and a white vest which contrasts with her brown skin. I dump my bag in the hall and follow the smell of chicken through to the kitchen. Garlic lingers in the air and the table is laid with lots of small dishes. Alice is washing up.

'Hi, Ella. Tapas tonight.'

'Great. I'll just nip upstairs and get changed.' I'm excited as I slip into my new dress.

'This weather makes me wonder why I ever came back from Spain,' Alice says as I go back into the kitchen.

'Yes, why did you come back?' Alice has never actually said. She turns from the sink and we smile at each other. Her eyes flicker up and down, taking in my dress, and I'm glad I made an effort.

'Let's not do small talk.'

I smile. 'I want to get to know you, that's all.'

'We have been, or haven't you noticed?' Her eyes meet mine and I bite my lip, but I can't look away.

'You look lovely,' she says. 'New dress?'

I nod, my cheeks hot under her scrutiny. 'You're making an effort with the food, it's the least I could do. I need to apologise for my behaviour last night.'

'Stop that right now. You've been stressed, and it's already forgotten. Sit down and I'll get you a drink. You're my guest this evening.'

'What's the occasion?'

'You deserve it after last night. I should never have let you go to that party. Chris is unbelievable.'

'You've got him sussed, and you don't even know him. Weren't you curious to meet him?'

Alice opens a bottle of red wine and brings it over. 'A Spanish Rioja,' she announces before saying, 'I'm not interested in Chris.'

'Fair enough. I'm not sure I should be drinking, though, after I made such a fool of myself last night. After this one I'm sticking to water.'

She pours us both a glass, then holds hers towards me and we clink glasses. After the first sip the dark lipstick Alice is wearing leaves a smudge on her glass. The wine is smooth as it slides down my throat.

'I'm sorry about last night.' *Best to get it over with.* 'I don't know what came over me.'

'I do,' she says.

I raise my eyes to meet hers. The wine has stained her lips even darker and I'm struck by the urge to wipe it off. The sharp lines of her hair frame her face.

I focus on my drink, remembering my talk with Mr Mortimer earlier. 'Let me show you something.' I run upstairs and get the embroidery. 'My builder found this, it was hidden. What do you make of it? I wondered about the date.'

She looks down at it, turns it over. 'I doubt it's important, it looks like the kind of thing you do in school needlework lessons when you're about twelve. The date is when it was embroidered, I'd guess.'

I'm disappointed, but she's right.

'I've been thinking about Lady's death and the scratch on your car,' says Alice, changing the subject. 'It has to be Chris's new woman.' The way she curls her lip on stressing the words makes me smile. I love that she hates her as much as I do.

'My other theory is that she's behind the attacks, wanting to drive me out, and he doesn't know about it.' I don't share my biggest fear, that he's told *her* about his sister, a confidence he could never share with me, and together Chris and his new woman are driving me out.

It couldn't be her, surely? After the way Alice dismissed the embroidery, I keep that thought to myself.

'Whatever the truth is,' Alice says, 'you've accepted, haven't you, that you and Chris aren't right for each other? Accept that, and move on. You never know what's round the corner.' She takes a sip of wine and runs her tongue around her lips. Her smile reaches her deep-set eyes and I'm close enough to see the outline of her contact lenses. An impression is flickering in my mind but I can't quite grasp it. A sharp pain cuts through my head and I gasp.

Alice mistakes it for emotion and leans over to kiss me. My head begins to sway and I pull back, my heart beating so hard I'm unable to speak.

'What is it? I thought…'

I try to form words but the room begins to move, darkness rushing in from the corners, and I lose myself.

DIARY

30 JULY 1997

I'm so worried about Melissa. She's barely moved all week and she's only eaten when I've forced her to. More than ever she needs a doctor, but Edward won't countenance anyone coming into the house. I suggested it might be better if I slept in the same room as her; I tried to make it sound like I was doing him a favour, but he just looked at me as if I were a worm that had crawled in from the garden. At least a worm has the freedom to wriggle outside.

One good thing happened this morning. A postcard arrived from my boy, Paris emblazoned on the front. A sky so blue it hurt my eyes behind a photo of an imposing building. *Notre-Dame* it said, in small print on the back. A large church with evil-looking gargoyles keeping watch across the city. I hope he went into its cold interior and said a prayer for his sister. I hid the card from Edward, not wanting to make him angry. 'Christopher is not my son any more,' he said. Since he left, he's never called him Kit. He got mad when Christopher was mentioned, didn't like not being able to control him now. The one that got away. I showed the card to Melissa, hoping it might cheer her up, but she stared at me with blank eyes before she rolled onto her side, facing the opposite wall, writhing with the weight of her stomach. She must be due any day now. Just thinking about it made my skin shine with sweat. I kept my childcare manual close by, just in case.

At least I have my own experience to draw on. My children were born at home, but the midwife was present, Edward pacing around downstairs until she ordered him to go out, get some air. Of course he went to the pub, and he's been going there nightly ever since. Having the children changed everything.

My daughter came first, my son three minutes later, my precious twins, and I held them on either side of my heart. Melissa always was a step ahead of Kit in everything she did. He idolised her, until he found out about her boyfriend Tommy and went straight to Edward. Tommy was a decent lad, although no boy would have been decent enough for Edward. Kit betrayed his sister – he should have known better. Even I found it hard to forgive him for that: he knew what his father was like. As a child, sometimes I would see a flicker of similarity between him and Edward, the odd sign, and I'd feel a trickle of fear that he might grow up to be like his father. They look so alike. I prayed it would never happen, but I can't deny the evidence.

'Arrived safely, spending a few days in the sun.'

He never was one to give much away, but I held the card to my heart, grateful he was letting me know he was safe, glad he hadn't been specific about his whereabouts.

EVENING

Her first cry came this afternoon around three o'clock, a shriek to rival Doris's fox in its intensity. It ripped through me and I dropped my knitting to the floor, a pale lemon bonnet for the child. Edward sneered when he saw me with my needles clicking, but didn't say anything. Moving the needles methodically and winding the wool kept me from dwelling on the fact that we had no access to a midwife or medical help. I continued as any grandmother-to-be would, for deep down I can't believe Edward would harm a child. He is a cruel man, but he wouldn't, would he? The spare bedroom was big enough for a nursery, I'd told Melissa. I wanted to let her know my plans to help her, but she wouldn't talk about the baby. I hoped she knew I was on her side.

At the first cry, Edward sent me up to deal with her.

She's having a child, I wanted to say, *your grandchild. Have you no heart?* I rushed to her room. She was crouching on the floor in a puddle of water. Somehow I knew what to do – we women do. I was first the first person to touch the child as it slid out of her, a little girl.

I held my breath for the longest time as I waited to hear hers, and when it came, a huge, wrenching wail, I cried too. I dealt with the cord and wrapped her in a white sheet before handing her to my own child, whose hands were outstretched. Seeing her like that lifted my heart.

'Kit wanted me to have a boy, but I always knew she was a girl.' Melissa registered my surprise. 'He guessed I was pregnant. He'll never see her now. I begged him to take me with him when he left, and he laughed. I'll never forgive him.'

My heart felt as if a fist was squeezing the life from it. Both my children planned to run? What a life I'd brought them into.

Sweat and tears poured from Melissa's face and I put my arms around my daughter and my granddaughter.

*

That was how Edward found us. The room felt smaller with his large presence blocking the doorway, the smell of tobacco and whisky mixing with the tang of blood and sweat. They say your heart can stop in fear, and I swear mine did in that moment when Melissa let out a piercing wail, crying out that the baby's lips were blue. Frantic, I turned my back on Edward, regardless of the consequences I knew would follow. My fingers stroked soft skin, searching for a pulse and finding none; I massaged her tiny chest, puffing breath into her rosebud mouth while Melissa sobbed, knowing it was to no avail. Melissa fell back on the bed and Edward snatched the baby from my arms, his mouth curled upwards in a smile. I hadn't the energy to stop him.

CHAPTER THIRTY-EIGHT

ELLA

The sound of the front door slamming wakes me. Alice has gone out. I open my eyes and blackness swoops over me again. Next time I open them I feel sick, and I rush to the bathroom and heave. Crouching over the toilet, I shiver. *What's going on?* I don't remember going to bed. I was downstairs with Alice, drinking, then… nothing. She must have helped me to bed, not wanting to disturb me. *Was I drunk?* Something important lurks at the edges of my mind.

I splash my face with cold water, stare into the mirror. Dull grey eyes look back at me, limp hair hangs around my face. Yesterday they had been sparkling with the possibility of… of what? *Me and Alice? What was I thinking?* My priority is to get myself sorted, clear up this mess with Chris. A walk will clear my head. I put on my old duffel coat.

Light is fading over the heath. The sky broods, as if the clouds are going to spill over at any second. I walk fast, shivering despite the coat, cold wind on my neck.

My hands are tucked into my pockets to keep them still and I stand and look across the pond at the dark house: all the lights are off. I think about all the times I've paused here, often choosing to cut through the heath, a part of this city that feels, magically, like the countryside. This is the one place where I am able to be mindful. Today I am anything but. I squeeze my hands tight in my pockets, worrying about the house. *Will I be able to hang onto it? What is Alice up to?* My head pounds in a way it never has before, but I'm certain I hadn't drunk that much. The cold air shocks my nerves alive. The light is disappearing fast. I pull up the hood of my old coat – it smells of bonfires. We haven't had one of those for a while. Chris used to set them up outside the back door, but I persuaded him to move them halfway down the garden, so Nancy could see from her window. He took some convincing, which I never understood – it was always me that had to make allowances for Nancy, little kindnesses to make her life easier. *How well did I know Chris, after all?* I drag my gaze away from the house and set off on my walk. I should get home before Alice arrives back. *Where has she gone? Is she thinking about me?*

A couple run past, following the path to a more wooded part of the heath surrounded by trees. It would be easy to get lost if you didn't know where you were going. Finding my way around is a skill I've developed over the years, out of necessity as a child, when I was forever on the move. I'm tramping down a path through piles of amber leaves when my phone rings. It's Jamie.

'Hello.' The link clicks and Jamie's voice cuts out. My phone rings again, but cuts out immediately. I check the signal but there's barely any reception; thick trees are forming a roof overhead. I walk a bit further and the phone buzzes with a text. Jamie again. I stop and read it:

> *I'd have preferred to tell you this in person but you need to know. I've found out who the other woman is. Be careful. Here's proof.*

The text is followed by a photograph. I haven't spoken to Jamie since the party. He doesn't know I've met her already. Still, I'm curious, struck by the masochistic desire to torment myself by studying her model-pretty face. The photograph takes forever to open, the signal is still patchy. I walk quickly up the track, until I'm practically running. As I emerge out from under the trees, I hold the phone inside my coat but the signal bar is still low.

I hear a rumbling in the distance. Thick raindrops land on my head, sliding into my eyes, and I brush them away. My breath quickens. I trip over a loose paving stone and my foot twists under me. Forced to stop, I rub my ankle and hobble the last few steps. The white facade of number 46 glows against the dark sky, swathes of rain battering against it. On the doorstep I take out my phone again as the pixels flicker and finally form a photograph. It's a shot of Chris's office door. Chris with a woman who has dark hair. Confusion cascades through me. The woman at the party was blonde. *Who is this?* I grab hold of the doorpost to steady myself, rain slithering down my arm.

I zoom into the woman's face. The woman with him is Alice.

DIARY

31 JULY 1997

He was sitting in the front room, smoking. The wallpaper was yellow from the number of cigarettes he sucked on, one after another while he listened to the radio and read his newspapers and drank his whisky. He lives in that room, eats in there too. He shunned the dining table months ago, leaving his discarded tray on the floor for me to deal with. Smoke spiralled up to the ceiling, where our daughter paced up and down, making the cord holding the light bulb swing.

When I asked him where she was, where he'd taken her, he didn't answer, so I raised my voice a little. He jumped up from the lumpy sofa, ash spilling onto the carpet, and seized my wrists. His smoky breath was hot on my face and made my eyes sting. He knows I knew nothing about the pregnancy until it was too late. Melissa was so terrified I had to wring the word from her. My wrists burned with pain as his big hands covered mine, fixing me in place. His words chilled me. 'I've dealt with it, like you should have done months ago, before it was too late.'

Sobs burst from my throat and he pushed me to the ground like a rag doll.

He sneered, 'I was going to do it anyway. She saved me a job. Never mention it again.'

*

Edward moved the rest of his things into the spare room this afternoon. I hope it means I won't have to suffer his monstrous body sweating over mine any more. He's getting so fat I find it hard to breathe, but I have no choice in the matter. The spare room is adjacent to the kitchen so he'll be down there all the time. He said he wants to 'keep an eye' on everything. He's drinking more than ever: dark, evil-smelling spirits which knock him out and make him snore like the fat pig that he is. I wish he was dead. There, I've said it.

He still won't talk about the poor baby, about what he did to her. It's been almost twenty-four hours since she was born. My fingertips are red raw where I've chewed at my nails and the skin around them. I should go to the police, but I'm too terrified. When I think about my granddaughter an uncontrollable shaking takes over my body and all I can do is wrap my arms around myself until it goes.

I didn't see Melissa for the rest of the day. I sat for hours outside her room, calling to her, and when it became clear she wasn't going to respond I just spoke in whispers to her every now and then to let her know I was there. I heard her pacing around, crying; there was a terrible bang and I feared she was doing harm to herself. But her door remained locked.

That night I didn't even pretend to try to sleep, I just sat in the chair in my room, rocking, wishing I had the courage to take my life, but I can't leave my children, and Melissa needs me now more than ever. I must have dropped off eventually as a noise woke me: a thud and the creak of a door. But I stared down at the garden and I couldn't see him. Though I swear he was there.

1 AUGUST 1997

He got up early today and clattered about in the kitchen, dropping something that smashed on the floor. He wouldn't let me clear it up. I waited until I heard him go back into his room before I crept downstairs. I made a decision during those long hours in the night: I'm getting Melissa out of here. Today. And I'm going straight to the police to tell them about the baby; it's the right thing to do, and we owe her a decent burial. If she'd been in hospital, as she should have been, maybe she'd have stood a chance.

CHAPTER THIRTY-NINE

ELLA

I stumble into the house, tears blurring my vision. Alice and Chris? It can't be true. I thought Alice was gay. Was she lying the whole time, about her, about Olivia? Was she just playing a game?

In my mind I run through the possible meetings between Chris and Alice. She wasn't here when he came round – she expressly said she didn't want to see him, because she hated him on my behalf. She disappeared at the party when he turned up.

I drop down on the sofa, sinking into the cushions, wishing they would swallow me whole. But if Alice is his girlfriend, then who was the blonde at the party? My head throbs and my cheeks flush with shame when I think about the kiss. Has she been playing me all along? How could she?

Feeling the sting of betrayal, I decide I need to find out what she's been up to. Is Chris somehow behind her being in the house? Suddenly, her guilty look when I saw her on the phone in the garden makes sense; her sleepwalking takes on a different meaning. I jump up from the sofa, energised.

Answers to what Alice is up to have to be here somewhere. I've looked in her room and the shed. *What about the cellar?* I collect the cellar key from the kitchen drawer and switch my mobile's flashlight on as I open the door, wrinkling my nose at the smell: more damp, which isn't surprising, given the proximity of the pond. I descend the cold wooden steps and another familiar aroma mingles with the damp, woody smell. Peering at the scene before me, what I find makes me stop dead.

The boxes that Chris left down here have been ransacked. Papers lie strewn across the floor, discoloured from the damp. I grab a half-open box to move it out of the way and a spider runs across my hand. I cry out in surprise and stand up, shaking. My hands tremble as I riffle through the contents. I come across a school letter detailing the poor attendance record of Christopher Rutherford, dated 1995. He would have been fifteen. I look around the rest of the space, clutching my arms around myself. But it's not the cold that is making me shiver, it's the sight of a pair of flowery gardening gloves. *Alice's.* As much as I don't want Jamie's evidence to be true, the reality is sinking in. A space has been cleared away from the spilled contents of the boxes and a row of plant pots and a bag of soil rest against the wall. The familiar smell I noticed on coming down the steps is stronger here. Chanel No. 5, Alice's perfume. *Alice has been down here. Why hasn't she said anything?* I recall the conversation in the kitchen where I pointed out the key, telling her where I was going to store it. I didn't make a secret of it. *What was there to hide?* My skin prickles with unease at the feverish searching that has gone on down here. *What is she looking for?* Suspicion creeps into my mind along with cold dread. What if they are planning to drive me out together? Images assault me. I can't bear the thought of them being a couple. Kissing. Sharing a bed. *My bed.* Then flashes of the meat and the mangled mouse torment me. Another spider scuttles in front of me and I can't get out of there quick enough. I lock the cellar and slip the key into my pocket. There's another place I can search: the box room.

All of Nancy's paperbacks are on a shelving unit in an alcove. I'm looking for a sign that Alice has been in here, but everything is as it was last time I was here. As well as the books on the shelves there are a couple of piles on the floor. I sort through those first, then try the bookcase, where the books are double-filed with another row behind. I don't know what I'm looking for. On the top shelf, some of the books are stacked higgledy-piggledy so I tidy them up a bit, arrange them as Nancy would've liked them. The row at the back isn't flush against the wall and I stick my hand behind; something is stuck there, another book. I squeeze my fingers into the gap and push until it lifts, pulling it out. It's a notebook with a black cover. Inside the pages are full of sweeping, swirling handwriting. Small with loops, written with a fountain pen. *Nancy's Parker pen.* I gasp. She wouldn't write with anything else. My hands tremble as I sink back down on the bed, push the books aside, no longer interested in stacking the shelves neatly. *Nothing else matters.* My pulse quickens as I turn to the front of the book, delicately handling the thin white pages. The black ink bursts from the page. A date is inscribed on the inside cover: 1997. The date 30 July 1997 flashes into my head.

Maybe she wrote it down.

This will take me closer to Nancy than any work of fiction ever could. This is her story. A sheet of paper is tucked inside the cover. It's typed, no address.

So you're back at 46 Heath Street. I might have known you'd return. Back to claim the house, which is rightfully mine. But I forgot, he brainwashed you, girls don't count, right?

I'll never forgive you for abandoning us. She needed you as much as I did. But unlike me, she would never escape. I always knew you'd get away, but I thought you'd take me with you. First you told him about my boyfriend – that was the beginning of the end for all of us. Second, you abandoned me to him, knowing what he was capable of. You condemned my child to death, and for that I will never forgive you.

*You'll never be able to leave 46 Heath Street, because
she is there, your niece. And you can't run the risk of anyone
finding her, because you let it happen, and I'm watching you.*

Your sister,

Melissa

It doesn't make sense to me at all. Chris told me he tried to find
his sister, but he never mentioned a child. Plus he denied ever
hearing from her. *More lies.* I turn to the first entry in the diary
but a loud banging makes me jump to my feet, and the doorbell
rings: the continuous sound of a finger holding the bell down. I
shove the diary under my pillow and run to the top of the stairs.
The shape of a head pushed up against the glass makes me recoil,
even though I know you can't see into the house through it.

'Ella, are you in there?'

Chris. I sink down onto the top stair and hug my knees to
my chest. He can't see me up here. I close my eyes and count my
breaths as I wait for the noise to stop. I can't face him, knowing
about him and Alice, how they've fooled me. I feel so stupid. The
incessant ringing suddenly stops.

'Fuck you, this is my house.' Something thuds against the door
and I hear footsteps heading down the path, away from the house.
I peep out through the blind and see Chris walking away. The
image of him with Alice shimmers in front of my eyes, making
me feel sick. I run upstairs and peer out at the garden.

The area where Alice has been digging is awash with mud,
and the spade lies across a hole as if it was abandoned suddenly.
Mr Mortimer mentioned she was digging a series of holes. *What
is she looking for?* Despite the full-blown storm raging outside, I
want to see for myself. I put my coat back on along with some

wellies and go out into the rain. Wind blows the long grass which swishes back and forth, but further back the grass has been mown and Alice has been digging a large area in front of the shed. Mud squelches over my boots and I lose my balance as my foot sinks into one of the holes. My hands slide into the slimy brown mud as rain pelts me from above. Something pink stands out against the dark earth and I scrabble around to grab hold of it. It's made of wool but it's too filthy, too sodden to make out what it is. I shove it in my pocket and extricate my feet from the mud before heading back inside.

I rinse it in the sink, hands shivering, a realisation gradually dawning. It's a knitted baby's blanket, and I have an identical one upstairs. Knitted by Nancy. *But when did she make this, and who for?* The child in the letter creeps into my mind. I wring the damp blanket out, wishing I could squeeze the answers out along with the water.

CHAPTER FORTY

ALICE

I needn't have worried; I didn't have to cajole Ella into drinking at all. She drank eagerly as I abstained, unsure how long it would take. At first she was talkative but when it happened it was quick. A slowing of her speech, a look of bewilderment, then suddenly she was unconscious.

I only needed a few hours. I could have waited until she was at work but my need was too pressing. A frantic, urgent pulse drove me forward. She'd sleep through the night and she'd never know it wasn't the wine. I left her on the couch and went up to her bedroom.

Straight away I saw the box. *Had she been in the shed and taken this one?* An icy finger tickled my neck. *Did she suspect me?*

But the box only contained paperwork belonging to Chris, and my pulse returned to normal. I was overreacting.

There was nothing under Ella's bed or hidden in her wardrobe. Mum must have left me some clue as to what he did with her. I made sure not to disturb anything. Under a neatly folded pile of T-shirts in a small plastic bag I found the embroidery Ella showed me. I couldn't react then. *Who would have thought a piece of embroidery could cause such pain?* Mum was always sewing or knitting, making things while she sat downstairs in the evening when he was out. It kept her calm, I realise now. At the time my head was full of my baby and what was going to happen to us. Mum gave me the square I now held in my hand after she was born, a tiny piece containing the date of her arrival – 30 July 1997 – the day of her death. I thought I'd packed it when I left, but I'd been in such a hurry, taking my one chance of getting out and running. I felt bad leaving Mum, but what choice did I have? I had to get out after what he did. *To me, to my baby girl.* Seeing the piece of fabric again, it's as if the needle Nancy used to embroider it is digging straight into my heart.

After a thorough search, I turned up nothing else. Only one option remained: my twin brother. He would know where she was.

Kit was the one person who could help me. *Chris, not Kit;* he no longer deserved that old, affectionate name, a gift from his kid sister. Chris, who betrayed me by telling our father my secret, who went abroad to escape, leaving me behind to suffer under our father's reign of terror. His chest was puffing in and out from where he'd run down the stairs to answer the bell: an action he clearly regretted by the way his face dropped at the sight of me.

'What are you doing here again?' he said when he saw me outside his office. 'I told you not to come here – we shouldn't be seen together.'

'You shut the door in my face last time, which I don't take kindly to. I'm not the kid sister you can push around any more. I'm coming in. We need to talk.'

'You're right about that. I know what you've been doing.'

It was still a shock for me, seeing my twin brother like this again, but of course I didn't show it. I'd had glimpses of him when he came to the house, then at the farcical party, but on both occasions I had managed to keep out of sight. *Boy, he looked rough.* His shirt was crumpled and spattered with tea, and his hair needed a good cut. His beard wasn't the carefully crafted type cultivated by hipsters, but neglected stubble. A pang of sympathy came from deep inside for the brother I used to know, the brother who was born just minutes after me, but I tossed my hair back and threw the treacherous thought out of my mind. This was Ella's husband, the man who had made her so unhappy and who'd threatened to take the house away. *Our house, my house.* And I wasn't finished there yet.

*

After Nancy died they didn't try hard enough to find me. She always said she would change her will and leave the house to me; she used to whisper it to me on those occasions when Dad had one of his rages and had stormed off, giving us a few hours' respite while he downed Guinness at the pub on the corner, before coming back for round two. We'd huddle by the fire and she'd stroke my hair, she said they'd both get their comeuppance, because Kit was already taking sides and he hadn't chosen the right one. Although he made a mistake when he copied Dad and tried to bully me. That was the point at which he lost us. Nancy and I huddled under a blanket and she told me she'd get her own back, she would bide her time and leave the house to me. But that depended on Edward dying first. She always seemed convinced he would; after all, he was considerably older than her and he was killing himself slowly with drink.

*

'Shall we go up?' I asked Chris, who had clearly lost the power of speech. We walked into an open-plan office space. Me following behind, feeling a pang of emotion at seeing his oh-so-familiar gait, just like when we were kids. But I was no longer in awe of my brother. Quite the opposite. Through an open doorway to a room at the back I could see a suitcase on a bed. Chris pushed the door to when he saw me looking. A smell of tomato soup hung in the air.

'You're living here, aren't you?'

He stood and stared at me for what felt like ages, then opened a filing cabinet, extracted a bottle of Jack Daniel's and poured himself a hefty slug. *Just like our father*. He didn't offer, and I didn't ask. He gestured to me to sit down.

'What are you playing at, Melissa? I've agreed to your plan, I'll happily split number 46 with you, but getting Ella out of the house hasn't been as easy as I thought. As you know only too well, *Alice*.'

His knowledge of my alias was a shock. I thought I'd managed to avoid him. We'd only met once, briefly, to talk about the plan. It was painful for both of us, seeing one another again after so long.

'Oh, I know you've been living there. The next-door neighbour told me. Good old neighbourhood watch. He was concerned about this woman who'd moved in, seemed obsessed with the garden and didn't appear to know what she was doing. I had my suspicions, Ella told me about her flatmate. Funny how you disappeared when I called round, wasn't it? I saw you at the party, that's how I knew. Ted pointed you out to me. We had a plan – why couldn't you stick to it? She'd have moved out sooner if she'd been living there on her own. She hates being alone.' A look of sympathy crossed his face. 'What are you even doing there? I told you I'd get her out. Why are you there?'

'I can't believe you're asking me that. To find where he buried her, of course. I've waited years for this. Getting Ella out of your way is taking too long. That's why I befriended her, took her into my confidence, just in case you tried to double-cross me. Do you think I trust you? After what you did, abandoning me, leaving me to Dad? Ella told me about her wonderful husband but when she told me about your affair, alarm bells went off. That wasn't part of the plan – you didn't mention any of that to me. You were going to move this other woman in, weren't you? You would never have let me back in. As soon as Ella told me you hadn't paid the mortgage and you'd stopped keeping fit, I knew something was up. The estate agent was good, though – you almost fooled me there. It was just another means of driving her out, wasn't it? But it backfired, didn't it, made her even more determined to stay.'

'Hang on a minute. You're accusing me of not sticking to the plan, but what about you? Moving in with her? That was never part of the plan, either. What are you playing at?'

'One word, Kit… Chris: *Trust*. Why should I trust you after what you did? You said you'd take me with you when you left home and when the time came you laughed in my face and left me behind to fend for myself.' I paused to take a breath; I didn't want him to see me get emotional. 'I thought if I befriended her it might come in handy. And I was right. Even better, her colleague had heard all about me and suggested I move in. It helped me start the search earlier.'

'What are you searching for, exactly?'

'I'm sure Mum would have left me some kind of clue. And I was right, only Ella found it. A piece of embroidery, with a date on it: 30 July 1997.'

'Is that when…?'

I nodded, couldn't meet his eyes. 'Mum made it for me. But it's not enough, there has to be something more. I already know the date. What I need to know is where my baby girl is.' I got up and paced around the small space.

'It's too much of a risk. Snooping about like some kind of spy. She'll catch you, won't she?'

'She won't. We're pretty close, and she needs me. Anyway, it turns out I was right to move in. Look at you. You're in trouble, aren't you? Admit it. Why are you staying here? Tell me what happened.'

He stared into his drink. 'I tried, honestly I did. When Mum died I instructed the solicitor to try and find you. We waited months. We had no idea where you'd gone. We were forced to remortgage and I had to accept help from Ella because I couldn't afford it on my own. It was a mistake. Ella was too needy. She was more interested in Nancy than in me; she wanted to have a mother figure in her life. The stress about what happened in that house has never left me. Living there, knowing what Dad did, my part in it. Knowing I could never sell up apart from to you – I couldn't take it any more.' He drained his glass in one, then immediately refilled it. 'You can have the house, I don't want it.'

'I don't understand why you moved back in the first place, after everything.'

'I was out of work and Mum asked me to come back. It was only meant to be for a few weeks. She told me what Dad had done, how we could never let anyone move in, she guilt-tripped me into staying. That's why I resented her, burdening me with that knowledge. She told me Edward had left the house to me, but omitted to tell me she'd changed the will. Left it to you. Bitch. But I don't care. That place is cursed. And as long as it stays in the family, I don't care. We can never sell with… well, you know. We can't risk anyone digging up the garden.'

'Why does it concern you?'

'Because I'm responsible, an accessory to the fact, don't you get that? Or at least that's how Dad made me feel and I couldn't get that old fear out of my head. It's haunted me my whole life. I know I should have stopped Dad from bullying you and Mum. But I was too weak. I ran away, just like I'm running away from Ella. I never planned to sell the house – it was a lie, a way to get her out, that's all.'

'There's one small problem – your wife. She's *very* attached to that house.'

'I've done my best, but nothing seems to scare her.'

'Oh, she's scared alright, just not enough. Scratching the car, she assumed it was your other woman, couldn't bear to think it was you. With the mouse and the meat, she wasn't sure, she began to waver. But the cat? Did you have to go that far? Or have you been trying to scare me too?'

'Bloody thing was always in the way.'

I hadn't really expected him to confirm it. My throat felt dry, making it hard to swallow. A memory of our father bludgeoning a limping pigeon to death made me shudder and avert my gaze.

'Could I have a glass of water?' I needed time to think.

Chris tapped his hand on the wall as he crossed the office to the sink and a memory hit me with powerful force. Ten-year-old Kit taking ages to get out of the house because he insisted on counting the tiles on the floor. Over and over. The kids in his class at school made fun of him, mimicking him on the bus. I wanted to go and shout at the mean boys, but I was a ten-year-old girl; they'd only have targeted me. I wasn't fierce back then. Although years later, when it was time for him to step in and protect me, he failed. *But could I blame him?* Now I can see that our father's behaviour was responsible for making him the way he was. He lived in terror, like we all did. *But how much of our father's temperament had he inherited?*

Chris came back with my water, topped up his whisky, sat down again and rubbed his bloodshot eyes.

'Tell me what's going on. Why are you camping out here?'

He dropped his head into his hands and without looking at me told me the business was going under and he was having to lay people off. He said he hadn't paid the mortgage for the last few months. He felt trapped by the house, by his marriage. He'd already sold his car. He'd asked the bank for a loan and it had been refused. And the other woman? He'd made her up. All those fancy meals out and drinks on his credit card bill were Chris desperately trying and failing to woo clients to his business, losing more and more money in the process.

'I thought Ella would leave straight away. She's very into monogamy, always said she couldn't bear it if anyone cheated on her. I wanted her to think it was the other woman playing tricks on her.' Chris told me how he'd kept up the pretence: he got a female friend to make an anonymous call and asked her to go to the party with him. He went off to the bathroom, a little unsteady. The whisky bottle was half-empty. He grabbed it when he came back.

'Don't you think you've had enough?'

'Don't tell me what to do.' Chris paced up and down. 'I can't believe you've done this. Meddling in my plan. I should have listened to Dad. He told me never to let women get the better of me, and look at me now. Living in my fucking office.' He took a swig from the bottle.

'We have to get her out,' he said. 'The bank is threatening me with repossession. I've been using her mortgage payments to live on, instead of paying them in. We're running out of time. I don't *want* to hurt her, I thought she'd see straight away it would be better for her to move out. Things have been bad between us since Mum died. I thought falling in love with Ella would be enough to make me forget what happened in that house, but it was eating me up.'

Chris accused me of stirring up things that should have been left alone, left well in the past. I maintained my cold exterior; I'd never show any emotion in front of him, but my pulse galloped. His voice got louder and my insides began to tremble, muscle memory from a long-ago time when another man with similar features raged and ranted, laying his hands on our mother. I tried to recall whether he'd locked the door behind us when we came in. I thought not, and I glanced behind me when his attention was turned to gauge how quickly I could get out before he caught up with me. *Would his fury make him fast?*

I wanted to shake him, make him tell me where my baby girl was, but he was drunk, and no use to me. Yet his words frightened me.

'I'll get her out if it's the last thing I do.' His parting sentence echoed in my mind as I walked down the stairs. In front of the door a familiar key fob hanging on a hook with some other keys – a spare to Ella's car – caught my attention. I grabbed it, just in case, my breath faster now. I had to get back to the house for both of them: to find my baby, who had been lost for so long, and to warn Ella that Chris was becoming increasingly erratic. *Like his father.* I was afraid of what he might do. Falling for Ella wasn't supposed to happen.

How would he react if he knew how my feelings for Ella had changed? I wanted *him* out, now.

CHAPTER FORTY-ONE
ELLA

Where is Alice? Has she gone to be with Chris?

I must have dozed off after the glass of brandy I drank to stop my arms from shaking like leaves in the rain. Outside it's no longer raining but the wind is battering the house and I've been round making sure all the doors and windows are secure. Mr Whiteley has left a message to say he'll be free to start the roof repairs in two weeks' time. I don't know where the money is going to come from. My mind is so muddled it's as if he's from a different world. My life feels like a pile of leaves thrown up into the wind and scattered in countless directions. *I don't even know who I am any more.* I have to read the diary.

I pull on a sweatshirt and jeans and go to brush my teeth. The toothpaste is empty. Alice's washbag is open on the side, a tube of toothpaste poking out. I grab hold of it and a contact lens case falls out. Through the lid I see two dark rings and I frown. *Aren't contact lenses always transparent? Unless...* I unscrew the lid, my hands trembling. These are tinted, dark brown lenses. If I put these in my eyes would change colour. I sink down onto the side of the bath. *Why would Alice want to change her appearance?* The image that has been lurking at the back of my mind clears and I gasp out loud. I rush into the bedroom and take out Mr Mortimer's photograph album, turning to the photograph of Melissa. I picture Alice's face. Without the brown contact lenses her eyes would be blue; she would look just like the girl in the photo. *It's her. Alice. Melissa. Alice is Melissa.* The thought that has been niggling me becomes clear: Alice must have spiked my drink after the meal. That's why I blacked out. But why? Images flash before me. Nothing makes sense. The diary must hold the answers.

If Alice is Melissa, how can she be having an affair with Chris?

Pain clouds my vision. Even before I begin to work out what she is doing back here – her purpose, her motivation – the realisation that she is back for another reason and not for me causes a searing heat to burn through me. 'Alice' turning up at yoga – that can't have been a coincidence. *Did she go there just to find me?* The hours we've spent together drinking, talking, her consoling me, offering advice. Advising me to sell up, not to sell up. *Is this a game?* A pain shoots behind my eye. I wish I'd remained ignorant. *Alice is Melissa, Melissa is Alice. Is anything she has done real?* My cheeks flush as I remember standing at my dressing table, only last night, making myself look nice for her, admiring the new dress I bought for her. One kiss, and oh, how easily I fell. *A schoolgirl crush, for Christ's sake*.

I put the pieces together. Sleepwalking in the garden, the boxes in the shed. *Chris. Chris must know.* I go over the times when they were almost together and something stopped them from meeting up. The unexpected visit when I made him coffee in the kitchen, Alice going AWOL at the party.

I fetch the baby blanket, which has dried out on the radiator, and take it up to my room. Packed away in my bottom drawer is the identical blanket Nancy made for me. For the baby Chris and I will never have. A sob bursts from my throat. I place the blankets with the embroidery and take out Nancy's diary. *The answer must lie in this book.* I skip the pages and turn to the date in question: 30 July 1997. I read fast, gasping as I take in the last sentence.

*

30 JULY 1997

Melissa fell back on the bed, tears rolling down her face, and Edward snatched the baby from my arms, his mouth curled upwards in a smile. I hadn't the energy to stop him.

I read on, eyes blurred with tears, through the next day until I get to the entry for the first of August.

1 AUGUST 1997

She's buried in the garden, I know it. It's the only thing that makes sense.

He found me in the garden this afternoon. The whole place has been raked over and any evidence of him digging holes has gone. Lack of sleep over the past two days makes me wonder if I've been hallucinating, sleepwalking like Melissa used to. Then I pictured her baby's little face with her rosebud lips turned blue before Edward snatched her away. I'm determined to find her.

Doris came out while I was searching and inadvertently prevented a showdown, for the front door had just slammed, signalling Edward's arrival. Doris noticed the tremor in my hands when I slid the envelope into it, hissed at her to keep it safe. '*To be opened in the event of my death*'. The letter is proof that I once had a granddaughter, however briefly, and my Melissa had a daughter. It tells her about the diary and where it's hidden.

I stayed out too long in the garden, no longer seeing the once carefully cultivated flower beds, the beauty that used to give me joy, but looking for my granddaughter's grave. I shivered as the wind picked up and dark clouds landed overhead. Too afraid to go indoors.

I needn't have worried. Edward was dozing on the sofa when I went inside – the drink had obviously knocked him out. My head was burning. The letter is delivered, my children have gone. There is only one thing left to live for—

*

A hammering sound draws my attention from Nancy's diary. I go to the top of the stairs and look down to see who it is. I hear her voice calling my name: Alice. *No. Melissa.* The horror of what she has been through, what she was looking for in the garden, all that digging, hits me. Doris, she played a part too. I sit down at the top of the stairs and sob. Melissa shouts and bangs on the door, just like her brother did earlier. I can't let her in either. Despite what she's been through, I can't forgive her for how she has taunted me. *I no longer know who to trust.*

CHAPTER FORTY-TWO

MELISSA

'Ella, please let me in.'

She didn't respond. The hall light shone through the side window and I was sure she was inside. But the house felt still. It was still when I crept out all those years ago, mourning the loss of my baby, guilt scratching at me for leaving Mum. I'd taken the money from Dad's wallet, a little at a time, planning my escape. He was too pissed to notice. I'd chosen Spain at random, taken the earliest flight I could before he discovered I'd left and came after me. I knew I'd never get away a second time. Not after what he'd done.

Thunder roared and lightning split the sky in two. The trench coat I was wearing had no hood, and the heavy rain poured down my neck. I ran across the road to where Ella's car was parked, took the spare key from my pocket and opened the door. I sat in the back seat, water dripping from my hair, and tried to dry my neck with my hands. Seeing Chris drunk was like a flashback of my father and I was scared of what he might do. Scared he'd take it out on Ella.

A screeching sound made me jump as a van rounded the corner and shuddered to a halt. Windscreen wipers moved fast across the screen and headlights blazed at me. The door opened and a figure climbed out, slowly, too slowly. *Chris*. He lurched towards the house and I was about to go after him when someone rapped on the window. A woman was holding an umbrella, wiping rain off the window, squinting at me. I'd seen her before. I glanced towards the house, but Chris had reached the front door. Ella hadn't let me in; I doubted she'd let Chris in either.

'Are you alright in there?' the woman asked. It was Sadie, from the party. 'Only this is Ella's car... oh, it's you, Alice, isn't it? Only one can't be too careful, you know. What are you doing?'

I got out of the car and Sadie held her umbrella over me.

'It's OK, I'm soaked already. I forgot my key. I'm worried about Ella. I just saw Chris arrive. He's been drinking. I'd better see if she's alright.'

We turned to look at the house and saw Chris getting back into his van and slamming the door. He drove off and I sighed with relief.

'What's that?' Sadie asked, her voice filled with fear.

I looked at what she was pointing to but I couldn't work out what I was seeing. An orange light flickered behind the front door.

Sadie broke into a run. 'Call the fire brigade,' she said. 'The house is on fire.'

CHAPTER FORTY-THREE

ELLA

Chris is here. Hammering at the door. *Why won't anybody leave me alone?* Leave me alone in the house with Nancy and the baby. *Mustn't forget the baby. Nobody wanted me when I was a baby. I won't be like them.*

The air is thick with an unfamiliar smell. My head feels woozy, my thoughts are muddled. Downstairs it's bright, too bright. A voice is calling my name, her voice, Alice. *Melissa.* I mustn't let her in.

More voices outside. Another voice joins in. A vaguely familiar one. I stand up but I feel so light-headed and I falter at the top of the stairs. A searing heat rushes towards me and smoke fills my throat, making me splutter, and I pull my shirt up over my face. Orange flames curl along the carpet towards the stairs and I hear the sound of a siren.

Coughing overtakes me. A thought comes from somewhere: *get down on the ground, crawl.* I crawl towards the bathroom. Like a baby. Thinking about babies hurts, my head hurts, my stomach hurts and my heart hurts so much it could burst. Everything hurts. My eyes are stinging and streaming, and it's so hard to see.

'Ella, Ella!' The voices won't stop. My head is cloudy. *Maybe my mother has changed her mind, come back for me at last.* Everything goes black for a moment. I'm in the bathroom now and the smoke isn't as bad. I crawl to the bath and grab a towel, stick it under the tap, hold it over my face.

I hear a distant voice, a male voice. 'You have to get out, Ella.'

I crawl back to the top of the stairs; I inhale thick, black smoke and cough and cough.

Chris? He's come to rescue me from her, Melissa. He loves me.

The staircase is blocked. The black fog turns orange and yellow, it's crackling now. Fire is eating its way through the house. *Please, not this house. Not my home.* I push my face into the red carpet, red and orange. *Warm colours. Too warm.* I can't get any lower down, and my lungs are burning. I hear the sound of glass shattering from far away.

She'll never find her baby now.

That's the last thought I remember.

CHAPTER FORTY-FOUR

ELLA

I'm getting used to my room at the hospital. I've asked the nurses to keep the door open so that I feel less like a caged animal and I can hear the goings-on outside on the corridor leading down to the other wards and rooms. First thing in the morning I welcome the jangle of a trolley, not so much for the lukewarm, tasteless porridge but for the smile of the woman who pushes it along and gives me an extra cup of tea when she returns to clear the plates. Once she's gone I'm left with my thoughts, which revolve around Alice. *Why did she want to harm me? Did she want the house, too?* My head aches with questions. I've told the nurse not to let Alice in. *Melissa*, I correct myself.

I don't understand any of it and there's nobody to ask. The answer may have been in the diary, but I'll never know. I assume everything was lost in the fire.

A burn makes my side hurt every time I move, but it's not that that makes me cry. Chris hasn't bothered to visit me: that's something else I don't understand. *Did he know Melissa was back?* I thought he'd come to rescue me. I can't imagine him wanting to destroy the house, to destroy everything. It doesn't make sense.

My first visitor is a police officer. I've been aware of her standing at the end of my bed for a while now. I open my eyes slightly and close them again when I see her uniform, thick-soled shoes on firmly planted feet. My chest heaves with relief that it's not

Melissa. But I have to open my eyes eventually, face up to what has happened.

'Good morning, Ella, I'm PC Metcalfe. How are you feeling?'

Her radio crackles, a welcome distraction, but she silences it and pulls up a chair, holding her hat with slender brown fingers.

'I've been better.' My voice sounds croaky; I swallowed so much smoke. The burning smell lingers in my memory as if I'm still trapped in that room. My whole body shudders.

'It's OK.' She takes my cold hand in her warm grip. 'The nurses say you're making a good recovery.'

She drops my hand, takes out her notebook and pencil. 'I have a few questions.'

I nod. *Might as well get this over with.* Her pencil is poised and her determined face tells me she won't be fobbed off.

'How much do you remember?'

I close my eyes and I'm back on the smoke-filled landing, a swelling balloon of panic surging inside me at the sight of my beloved house burning, orange flames licking up the carpet towards me. Thick smoke filling my lungs as I press my shirt to my mouth, getting down to the floor. Lying there, thinking about Melissa. Giving in to the choking fumes.

'I heard Melissa's voice, then someone break the glass, a fireman I suppose. I managed to get to the bathroom… then there's nothing until I woke up here.' *Should I tell the policewoman that Melissa's trying to hurt me? But she kissed me. Was that all part of it?* My head swirls like the smoke from the fire.

'It's bound to be confusing for you, but take your time.'

I squeeze my eyes shut. I have questions of my own. 'Did the fire brigade get there in time? Is the house OK?'

'Downstairs is badly damaged, nothing could be salvaged. But upstairs is mostly OK.'

'The cellar?'

'Gutted.'

The diary was in my bedroom. Did Melissa read it before she left?

'Was there anything valuable down there?'

'Nothing that mattered.' *But the house matters.*

'I'm assuming you have contents insurance? I'm sure it can be put back to how it was. It will take a little time, that's all.'

'Yes, the house is insured. How did the fire start?' I squeeze my eyes shut, scared to hear her answer.

'I'm afraid I'm not at liberty to say as it's an ongoing investigation. Try to forget about it, focus on your recovery.'

The door opens and a nurse comes in. 'Time for your vitals, Mrs Rutherford. I'm afraid I'll need a moment with the patient, Officer.' The name Mrs Rutherford burns more than my tender skin. Tears fill my eyes.

'We're all done here. I've just been asking Mrs Rutherford a few questions and reassuring her that she's in capable hands.'

I turn my head away from the nurse.

'She certainly is.' The nurse pulls the curtain around the bed and PC Metcalfe puts her hat on and disappears from view.

The nurse attaches a band to my arm and runs various checks while a storm swirls in my head. Doubt rumbles somewhere deep down. *Melissa lied about her name, and about everything. Why would she lie about Chris? Was she behind everything? Is she jealous, because of her feelings for me, or are her feelings a lie, too? Was our whole relationship a pretence?* But I know the answer. The kiss was just another ploy to get me under her spell, so she could find whatever she was looking for, something to do with her baby. She wanted to get me out of the house and get him in. The woman at the party must have been the other woman. It wasn't *her* I should have been afraid of, but Melissa, right there in front of me, the whole time. Neither of them will be coming to see me. Deep inside, I know why. *She's in custody. With him. They were in it together.*

*

Mr Mortimer comes to see me. The kindly expression on his face moves me to tears and I am unable to speak. He sits with my bandaged hands in his and talks in his soft voice about his Doris and the things she survived; he says I remind him of her and his face crinkles as he says this and I have to look away. I feel as if I knew her, now I've read the diary. *I'm not worthy of her, of his love.* I'm unable to put into words the questions I want to ask. But he isn't the one who has the answers.

I'm not expecting any more visitors. But Melissa comes in the evening, when it's dark outside, the fluorescent light that gives me a headache is turned off and the night shift is on duty. Keeping me safe, but not safe enough. When I see her in the doorway my heart knocks at my chest and I can't swallow. *Has she escaped?*

I pull myself up to sitting and I see the red cord that hangs behind me swinging into the edges of my vision. If I pull the cord a nurse will come, *but will she be quick enough?* I'm scared to make any sudden movements. Melissa crosses the room in soft, silent brogues. *Did she plan to creep up on me, hold a pillow over my face? Finish off what she started after the fire failed to burn me into silence?*

'Ella.' She's whispering, although there's no one to hear her. 'It's me.'

I nod. I'm sure she can hear my heart beating: the sound is roaring in my ears, filling my head. Light spills in from the corridor and falls on her cheekbones, illuminating her familiar features as she leans over me.

'You're shaking.' Melissa frowns and reaches her hand up to my face. I flinch, letting out a cry.

She recoils. 'Why are you scared? It's me, Ella. I was just going to do this.' I hold my breath as she reaches out again and brushes my hair from my eyes.

I grab her hand. 'Have you come to hurt me?'

Pain surges into her eyes. 'I would never hurt you. The fire, I tried to save you, have you forgotten?'

'Of course not…' I can't let her see that I know she's double-bluffing, pretending she tried to rescue me when all the time… 'I don't know who you are any more. Alice doesn't exist. Melissa: I know that's who you really are.' The name feels strange on my tongue as I use it to refer to Alice for the first time, the double 's' a hiss on the tongue of a snake curling towards her. Accusatory.

'Have you escaped?'

'Escaped?' She frowns, looks at me with concern. 'Escaped from where, Ella?'

'You and Chris… I thought…'

'That policewoman wouldn't let anyone past her. I came as soon as I could. Once the police gave you the all-clear the nurse said it was too late, past visiting hours. Fuck visiting hours. Why do you think I snuck in after dark? I had to know you were alright.'

I study her face for clues. *Does she really mean it?* Hope stirs deep inside me.

'Tell me what happened, back then.' I grip the side of the bed so hard the metal digs into my skin. 'I need to hear it from you.'

'I got pregnant. It was the worst shame I could possibly bring on my family according to my father, Edward. I hated him, hated myself for not defending my mother when he hit her and kicked her, which he did for any tiny misdemeanour. Kit, *Chris* – I never imagined he'd turn out the same way.' Melissa makes an exasperated sound. 'Kit is long gone. Dad stopped me going out when he found out I had a boyfriend. Imagine his reaction when he found out about the pregnancy. Chris had always said he'd leave home, and I stupidly thought he'd take me with him.' Melissa sniffs, trying not to cry. 'But he ran off and left me.' She rubs an angry fist into her eye. 'Mum did her best, begged Dad to let me go to hospital, or at least get a midwife, but he refused.'

She stands and moves to the window, looking out into the night, away from me. 'Mum helped me deliver her, my baby girl. She was perfect, just for a few minutes, then…' She wraps her arms around herself. 'Dad took her, I don't know what he did with her, but he'd been digging a lot in the garden, so I guessed…' Melissa shrugs, sits back down.

'The fire was Chris, he'd been drinking whisky all afternoon. I saw what it did to Dad. He became a different person. Chris was at the end of his tether, he'd almost lost everything: the business, his livelihood, but he couldn't let the house go. He'd have loved to get rid of it. The estate agent was just a ploy to get you out – he would never have sold it, he was afraid that a new owner might dig up the garden. Find what was there. Edward told him he was an accessory to manslaughter by gross negligence, you see, and he believed him. Dad had got complete control of us.'

'Have you been back to the house?'

'Don't worry. The house will be fine. We'll manage, whatever it takes.'

'What makes you say that?' *But I know why.*

She breathes out, a long sigh, and then wilts like a deflated balloon.

'I have to find my baby. My little girl: Alice.'

I gasp.

She nods. 'Yes, that was the name I chose for her. She only lived for a few minutes. As soon as he appeared in the doorway she stopped breathing. It was as if she knew what he would do to her. But we loved her, me and Mum, in those few minutes. I hope Mum could feel that. She tried so hard to stop him, but he'd worn her down over the years. I didn't get it at the time. I hated her. Hated Chris, for leaving without taking me with him, but he wouldn't have been able to pull that off. We've been talking, me and Chris. Dad beat Mum up so badly she could hardly walk and he feared ending up like him. So what did he do? He ran away.'

Melissa laughs to herself. 'When he met you, he thought he could change, but he couldn't bear to be in the house. He hates the house, really, he only came back because he had to after he lost his job and Mum persuaded him to come home, but he and Mum never talked about what happened. Chris suffered from the strain of knowing that Alice was in the house or garden somewhere. Just being in the house meant he could never forget his failure to stop what happened to Alice and me. It got to him. He thought you'd make it better. I'm not sure your relationship would ever have worked.

'It's the reason I came back. Knowing she was in Heath Street, alone, without me. I wanted to find her and let her rest in peace. It destroyed my life, too.' Another wry smile forms on Melissa's face. 'You were always asking who the woman in the photo was – Olivia. She was the love of my life, not my cousin. A letter came from England, from the family solicitor, telling me Nancy had died and left me the house. It was Mum's revenge against Dad, leaving it to me. I resealed the letter and returned it, knowing they'd give up and the house would go to Chris.

'I wanted to stay with Olivia, put it all behind me. But I fell apart, regretted turning down the house and wrote Chris a threatening letter when I was deranged with grief. Knowing Mum was finally gone, the lure was too strong, I had to come back. It eats into you, you see, a secret like that. It was my last chance to find my baby girl. I got in touch with Chris and we formulated our plan to get the house back. He told me his marriage wasn't working but we'd need to get you out first. I didn't say a word about it to Olivia. I unravelled after that – feelings I'd suppressed for years came flooding back. In the end, I couldn't forget. I made enquiries, and when I found out you were part owner with Chris, I went mad. I thought I'd move in, never mind mine and Chris's plan. I planned to try and force you out, so I could be with Alice again. I didn't expect to like you. My obsession with the house destroyed me and Olivia. I had a meaningless affair, to drive her away. I can never forgive myself for hurting her like that. She didn't understand.'

'You can explain it to her now.'

Melissa's face crumples and tears cover her cheeks. 'If I can find her. She told me she never wanted to see me again.' She wipes her hand angrily across her face. 'Chris was the same – he wanted to drive you out. He wrote that letter, you know, the one about the affair. There was never any girlfriend. The credit card bill was him squandering money on clients, desperate for new business. I didn't even know about that, just like he didn't know about me moving in – we didn't trust each other. He had to get you out, so he could deal with the secrets buried in the house.'

'But that woman at the party—'

'She meant nothing to him. It was all a set-up.'

Images flash through my mind: a curvaceous woman in a red dress and spiky stiletto heels. The images fade and tears roll down my face too. *I don't want the house.* Everything I thought I had was blackened with fire. But one thing remained for me to do.

'I'll help you look for Alice.'

CHAPTER FORTY-FIVE

ELLA

30 JULY 2018

Puffy clouds dot the sky and the bright golden sun is reflected in the faces of the marigolds that line the fence. I knew the sun would be out today: it had to be, to give us closure. The white walls of the freshly painted house gleam as if the fire had never happened. From the window of Nancy's room – my room now – I see Melissa wearing a long white dress, sitting in the garden, which has been completely cleared of weeds. We have a lawn and a bench, where she often sits. I give her a moment alone before I go down to join her, wearing my work suit and heels – the occasion demands respect.

Melissa is finally opening up and she's in touch with Olivia again; they're taking it slowly. We've talked about the kiss; we laughed about it in the end. I had to get that conversation out of the way, make sure all our secrets had been shared. Now the divorce is under way I've been seeing a therapist and she's helped me understand how loneliness and grief drove me to Melissa. She was grieving, too, in her own way, but it came from genuine emotion. She hadn't expected to like me, and I know that's the truth. Truth is important to both of us.

It made sense for Melissa and I to swap rooms. The house is hers, rightfully, and I wanted her to have the master bedroom.

It's also right that she bought Chris out; he never wanted this place with all its memories, and he hated growing up here. Melissa wants to forgive him; she's working on it. He went to court for arson and got a custodial sentence. His barrister pleaded mitigating circumstances and he'll be out in a few months. My first visiting order came today – I'm going to go and see him. It's time we had an honest talk. And I need to get used to being single, being alone.

We'll never know exactly where Alice was buried – the blanket was the only clue, so we choose the place we found it for the spot. Melissa never located her, despite all her digging, but she is happy with the way we've chosen to lay her to rest. Our garden is no longer a jungle, but Alice's resting place, which we'll always look after.

Right on time the doorbell rings and I go downstairs to let Fiona in. Nancy's friend from church is a sprightly woman in her fifties. She's agreed to lead a blessing, which Melissa has written. Mr Mortimer is also heading this way, in his 'Sunday best', as he calls it. It's the first time I've seen him without his flat cap.

We stand in a row; Melissa is in the middle. I take her hand in mine and squeeze it. Her arm is rodlike and I shake it gently but she doesn't relax. She needs time, too. A breeze blows and Mr Mortimer's sparse hair trembles. Fiona reads from the script she has prepared:

'Baby Alice was born on this day twenty-one years ago. Her life was all too brief, but she has never been forgotten. Today we lay her to rest, and we will continue to watch over her.'

As Fiona says a prayer Melissa's arm relaxes and she drops my hand. Once Fiona has finished, Melissa lays the white roses she holds in her other hand on the small rockery she has built at the edge of the neat lawn; it can be seen from any window at the back of the house. Water trickles from a fountain next to Nancy's tree. A ray of sun picks out the engraved stone that Melissa has placed at the front. *In memory of baby Alice, who was born and died at 46 Heath Street.*

CHAPTER FORTY-SIX
NANCY'S LETTER

My dearest Doris,

As you are reading this, I will have passed on. Thank you, my oldest friend, for all the kindness you have shown me, enabling me to entrust you with this letter. Firstly, I must apologise for abandoning you. It was not by choice: my husband was a wicked man who wanted me all to himself. He saw my friendship with you as a threat and he put a stop to it. I was afraid of him, too afraid to go against his wishes. I hope you can forgive me.

I want to be able to unburden myself, and for the truth to be known, for the sake of my granddaughter. Yes, this will no doubt surprise you, this child unknown to you, for she had but a fleeting life.

Melissa became pregnant, and once Edward found out he kept her a prisoner in the house. I helped her with the birth; she was a little girl, Alice. She only lived for a few minutes, and I believe Edward buried her remains in the garden.

I am poisoning Edward. Slowly, over a long period of time, but painfully, and eventually fatally. He will have no access to medical care, for he is a helpless man, utterly dependent on his wife to cater to his every need. Alas, I will not tend to him this time. He has driven his son away, he has terrified his daughter away, which only leaves me, his dutiful wife, to care

for him as I see fit – and this is how I choose to repay him.
Mushrooms, picked from the heath. My conscience is clear.
As you sow, so shall you reap.

Your loving friend,

Nancy

A LETTER FROM LESLEY

Thank you so much for reading *The Woman at 46 Heath Street*. I hope you enjoyed reading it as much as I enjoyed writing it. If you did, and you'd like to keep up to date with the latest news on my new releases, just click on the link below to sign up for a newsletter. I promise never to share your email with anyone else.

www.bookouture.com/lesley-sanderson

As with my first book *The Orchid Girls*, in *The Woman at 46 Heath Street* I hoped to create an evocative novel about obsession, secrets and the blurred lines between love and lies. Once again female relationships lie at the heart of my novel, enhanced by the suppression of secrets. The Heath Street in the story is fictitious, and not to be confused with the real Heath Street in NW3.

If you enjoyed *The Woman at 46 Heath Street*, I would love it if you could write a short review. Getting reviews from readers who have enjoyed my writing is my favourite way to persuade other readers to pick up one of my books for the first time.

I'd also love to hear from you via social media: see the links below.

Thanks so much,
Lesley

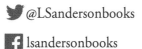

@LSandersonbooks

lsandersonbooks

ACKNOWLEDGEMENTS

So many people have helped me along the way with *The Woman at 46 Heath Street.*

To everyone at Curtis Brown Creative and my fellow writers in the 2015 cohort, for continued support.

To Erin Kelly, whose summer school of 2017 showed me how to be the writer I hope one day to become – you're a true inspiration.

Thanks to the judges of the Lucy Cavendish Fiction Prize for shortlisting me for the 2017 prize, for the kindness of everyone involved with the event and their continued support.

I can't say a big enough thank you to my lovely agent Hayley Steed, and to everyone else at the fabulous Madeleine Milburn agency. Hayley, I'm so proud to be your first 'official client'.

To the Next Chapter Girls, Louise Beere, Cler Lewis and Katie Godman – you know how much you and this writing group mean to me – I couldn't have done it without your belief in me and my writing.

To my lovely editor, Christina Demosthenous – working with you is a joy, and from the very first email, 'Best News Ever…', I knew it was going to be a dream partnership. Kim Nash – thanks for your amazing energy and enthusiasm promoting my book. To everyone at Bookouture – you all work tirelessly and with infectious enthusiasm for your authors, and I'm so proud to be one of them.

And to everyone else – all the other writers I've met along the way, too many to name but nonetheless important – I'm so happy to be one of such a friendly group of people.

Printed in Great Britain
by Amazon